Demon Kissed

by

Karilyn Bentley

A Demon Huntress Novel

Demon Kissed

Cover Art by *Diana Carlile*

The Wild Rose Press, Inc.
PO Box 708
Adams Basin, NY 14410-0708
Visit us at www.thewildrosepress.com

Publishing History
First Black Rose Edition, 2016
Print ISBN 978-1-5092-0561-5
Digital ISBN 978-1-5092-0562-2

A Demon Huntress Novel
Published in the United States of America

The scent of sulfur hangs in the air

like a demonic stink bomb. I want to slap a hand over my nose, but no one else seems affected by the stench.

Must be a demon huntress thing.

"*Justitian,*" Smythe mutters. "Not demon huntress."

"If you don't like my new title, then stay out of my mind."

He glares. I swallow. Cross my arms. Refuse to take a step back. I'm learning not to be intimidated by his anger. Go me.

My *justitia* vibrates, throwing me out of my internal battle, pulling me back to the land of death and minions. The blob of colors pulsates, a glowing reminder of a moment of terror.

The moment the demon appeared to the grad student.

Granted, I'm still taking Demons 101, but I thought demons formed minions in private. Usually after the human committed a crime, not before. A tryout, so to speak. And maybe that happened, but it sure seems to me like the black blob of demon force appeared to the grad student smack in the middle of the hallway.

Or maybe that always happens, and I just now noticed it.

The *justitia's* vibration grows stronger, trembling my arm, my veins. Not its normal excited tremor upon seeing a minion or demon. A rush of images spikes through my mind, scenes of terror coupled with blood and death, memories of the *justitia's* former wearers captured in time by the entity in the bracelet.

I'm not the only one freaked out by the colored blob. How bad was this demon to scare a *justitia*?

Dedication

To my husband:
Thank you for believing in me
and not minding (much)
when I disturb your video games.
I love you!

Acknowledgments

I'd like to thank my wonderful beta readers J.C. McKenzie and Carrie Hamlin for your excellent advice. You ladies are awesome!

I'd also like to thank Phyllis Middleton and Bob Williams for all things police.

As usual, all mistakes are mine.

Chapter One

The other woman never gets invited to her lover's funeral. That's why I'm wearing large sunglasses and a floppy black hat.

And super strong antiperspirant for summer in Texas.

Sweat beads on my chest, pools in my bra. Despite an application of an antiperspirant promising to "never let you down," I feel as though someone shoved me into a damp armpit and then spitted me over an open flame.

Some days it's hard to tell the difference between Texas and hell.

Blake Calder's family sits on a row of padded chairs under a green awning, directly in front of his closed casket. I stand on the periphery of the crowd, tears staining my cheeks, listening as the pastor intones the virtues of heaven while seeming oblivious to the sun tap-dancing on his scalp. My heels sink into the dirt and make little popping noises when I shuffle to a different spot.

I pull a tissue from my purse and rub under my eyes. Blake and I met eleven years ago in college and were off and on lovers ever since. I never expected to find myself standing by his grave, waiting for his coffin to be lowered into the packed clay that passes as earth here in Dallas. Then again, I never expected to be a demon huntress, a *Justitian*, the wearer of a bracelet that turns into a sword. A killer of demons and their minions.

Or for a demon to kill my lover.

Life is full of twists and turns. What happened to staying on the straight and narrow?

It's my fault. If I hadn't put on the bracelet, the *justitia*, which bound the entity in the silver links to my nervous system, then none of this would have happened. Blake would still be alive. I'd only have my empath abilities to deal with, not the demon-slaying powers.

But noooo. I had to fasten the shiny silver bauble around my wrist.

Not that I'd take it off. I've only worn it for a week and a half, but that's enough to know it's mine until death do us part.

Literally.

Jordan sobs over the droning voice of the pastor, snapping my attention from my thoughts and back to the graveside service. Jordan. Blake's girlfriend. Blake's nose-candy using, tanning-bed-blonde bitch of a girlfriend.

Unfortunately, Blake's mother Cecily preferred Jordan's anorexic-looking self over my white trash heritage. Something about Jordan being a better match for her precious son. Something he and I were about to set straight. Something that no longer matters.

Cecily might have stopped Blake from officially tagging me his girlfriend, but her attempt to bar me from his funeral failed. Thank goodness for online obits.

A shadow draws my attention to the other side of

the graveyard where a stand of trees drapes the ground in shade. My mentor, Aidan Smythe, leans against a tree, arms crossed, his black t-shirt pulling across muscles seen despite the distance.

Smythe is my guardian. A mage who pulled the short stick and ended up being my mentor. He's been following me around for the last week, ever since Blake's death, staying in the shadows, spooking little old ladies'—along with some not-so-old ladies'—hormones out of hiding.

I'd trade his sexiness to see Blake's athletic physique one more time.

I dash my tissue under my leaking eyes. Grief dulls with time, but Blake's death is recent enough my chest still aches at his memory. If only he'd lived long enough to see me attempt to avenge him. To know I came for him. Fought for him.

Grieved for him.

I squeeze my eyes shut. Draw in a ragged breath. I can deal with his loss. Really. I can.

Liar, liar.

"Amen."

Blake's family stands, accepts condolences from the guests while the pastor steps out of view. I glance to where Smythe stood, but he's gone.

I pull my heels out of the dirt, square my shoulders and stand in line for condolences. Not what I want to do, but for Blake's sake, I need to apologize to his mother.

She doesn't need to know the demon Jezebeth killed Blake as revenge for me killing her minions or that the Agency, my new demon-slaying employer, cleaned the scene to make it look like he'd died in a mugging. But she does need to know how much he meant to me. That I was more than a booty call.

Cecily stiffens when I draw near, years of inbred good manners forcing her to accept my presence. White lines bracket her mouth. Grief or annoyance?

"I'm so sorry. Blake meant so much to me. I can't believe he's gone."

She nods, her gaze lingering on my hat. "He enjoyed your friendship." Her lips purse in disagreement with her son, and in polite dismissal, she turns to the next in line, reaching out a hand to the person.

I turn, intending to bypass Blake's father who is talking to another middle-aged man. But his dad notices me and grabs my bare upper arm. With his touch, blue overlaid with red slam into my mind, a mix of grief and anger. I jerk back, and he releases me. The thought colors dissipate in the humidity. Mr. Calder raises a brow as I rub my hand where he touched my arm.

Maybe he should try being an empath. See how he feels when someone grabs his arm.

"Gin. Thank you for coming. Blake thought a lot of you."

I stop rubbing my arm and force a smile. "And I him. I'm so sorry for your loss."

"Thank you, my dear. Have you met my neighbor, Professor Dan Sheevers?" He nods toward the man he was talking to. "Dan, this is Gin Crawford, a friend of Blake's."

Dan Sheevers sticks out his hand. "*Dr.* Sheevers. Nice to meet you."

I suck in a breath, releasing it on a hack that I cover with my hand. The good doc drops his palm like I carry a disease. Mission accomplished.

"I'm sorry." Fake cough. "Don't want to give you my cold." What does it say about me that lying is second nature? "It's nice to meet you." Now what do I say? I cough again to fill in the silence. Unfortunately, the professor takes the fake cough for a real one and pats me on the shoulder.

And his hand slips to my bare upper arm, red and black flash into my head, circling him as he lies on beige carpet, black blood surrounding his head, eyes staring the blank gaze of death.

I jerk, dislodging his hand, my stomach a ball of ice. Note to self. No matter how hot it gets, never wear a sleeveless dress again.

"My dear, are you okay?"

I blink. Swallow. "I'm okay. It's just the heat. Not good for a head cold, you know. Better get going. I'm so sorry about Blake." In more ways than Mr. Calder will ever know.

Dr. Sheevers' eyes narrow as if he knows what I saw. But how could he? I try to swallow the lump in my throat.

"I do hope you feel better. That West Nile virus is going around."

I make a noncommittal noise, offer a smile, and hightail it out of line. Since when did my empath abilities become prophetic? I've never seen future events, only the past a person thinks of the moment I touch them. So what did I see?

Where's Smythe? Maybe he knows what's wrong with me. A quick glance toward the trees only proves he no longer stands there. I turn toward the one lane road winding through the cemetery and freeze.

Talk about the day from hell.

Two obviously plainclothes detectives stand in front of a brown sedan, talking to each other while they watch the crowd as if they don't notice who leans against the car, close enough to them to touch.

The detectives aren't the cause of a chill snaking its way down my spine. No, that privilege belongs to the demon next to them. The tall, black haired, olive skinned demon leaning against the sedan's side as if modeling his tight fitting white t-shirt and jeans. A demon masquerading as a man. With any other demon, my bracelet, my *justitia*, would be going nuts, forming a sword, forcing me to fight the walking evil.

But not this demon. For some reason my *justitia* is happy to see Zagan. As if they're long lost friends.

Apparently I have a defective *justitia*.

My hand slaps against my neck, to the mark behind my ear. The mark he gave me. Makeup coats my fingers, the cover-up sticky in the humid summer air. Zagan waggles his fingers, touches one to his eye, and points it at me as if to say *I'm watching you*. I swallow.

I haven't seen him since the day I found Blake's body. Since the day he marked me as his servant.

The servant thing was an accident. How was I supposed to know giving a demon a snack and some blood bound me to him? In my defense, I believed handing him a snack would save my life. Better he nibble on crackers than me. The blood was an accident. His tongue sliced mine when he spelled me into kissing him. Luckily, the *justitia* broke whatever bond he tried to create, so Zagan has no control over me.

I hope.

For a demon, he's not all bad. He saved me right

before Jezebeth dealt me a death blow then let me kill her. On the downside, he captured me, which led to the aforementioned snack and attempted conversion of me into his servant. On the plus side, he healed my injuries from the fight with Jezebeth, probably saving my life.

In a way, that makes me indebted to him.

But not indebted enough to want him following me.

He smiles, gives another finger wave, and vanishes, no one the wiser to his presence. The detectives continue to scan the dispersing crowd as if they never saw Zagan. Great. A demon with cloaking powers.

Shit, shit, shit.

The last thing I need is to be stalked by a demon only I can see.

A hand slaps against my shoulder, startling the ice ball lodged in my stomach up into my throat.

"Sorry." The low chocolaty purr of Smythe's voice chases away the chill. I must be getting used to him. My hormones no longer explode like fireworks when he's near. Thank God. Lusting after my mentor while attending my lover's funeral would be the epitome of bad taste.

"Bad day."

"It's hard to lose a friend." His gaze drifts to the right, memories hidden in the depths of his eyes, creeping out to his face. He also lost a friend with benefits. One of these days he'll explain how. "Must be doubly hard for you to be at a graveside service. I know you don't like cemeteries."

A full second passes before I realize what he's talking about. My only go at tracking a minion took us to a cemetery. Not just any cemetery, but the one guaranteed to freeze my blood even more than a demon on a hot summer day. The one with *The Grave*. That part of my past is better left dead and buried. Literally. But keeping my secrets means lying to Smythe, who now believes I possess a cemetery phobia.

"A girl's got to suck it up sometimes." Part of me wants to come clean with him—it's a small part and easily smothered.

His eyes narrow. Does he realize I'm lying?

"It's not all cemeteries, is it?"

Damn it. He knows. Time for a distraction. "Did you see Zagan standing by the cops?"

Suspicion morphs into surprise as he turns his gaze to the detectives lounging against their unmarked brown sedan. "What?"

"Yeah. He was standing with them right before you walked up."

"Are you sure?"

"What? You don't believe me?"

He raises a brow. "You wouldn't lie about a demon. So why didn't your *justitia* react?"

I shrug. "Maybe it doesn't want to kill him?"

"That's what it was made for. Killing demons."

"Are you sure?"

"Of course I'm sure. The purpose of a *justitia* is to kill demons and their minions. You know this."

"Yeah, but I'm telling you, it doesn't want to kill Zagan. It thinks they're friends."

"*Justitias* don't think. Or have friends."

"Try telling that to it." I hold up my arm with the bracelet and give it a shake.

Smythe grabs my arm. Flesh on flesh but without

the emotional flash. He's the only person besides my twin, T, who can pull off that stunt. I knew there was a reason I liked having him for a mentor.

"This is not the place to have this conversation. Where's your car?"

I point, and he loosens his grip on my arm as he escorts me toward my car. We don't make it far before Dr. Sheevers cuts in front of us, walking fast as if cemeteries creep him out and he can't wait to leave.

He gives me a glance and a nod as he hurries to his car. The vision of him lying in a pool of blood pushes into my mind. Should I tell him to be careful? Mind my own business? Experiencing a vision of things to come is a new one. Maybe the *justitia* gives me new abilities.

What a thought.

"What's wrong?" Smythe's voice draws me back to the present.

"I met him." I point to the good doc's car as he revs the engine. "And saw a vision of him lying in a pool of blood."

"Do you do that often?"

"No. I only feel what others feel or if their feelings are strong, I can see what caused the emotion. I don't see things to come. Maybe something changed?" Please God, don't let anything have changed. Being an empath was bad enough. Being an empath who had a fancy demon-slaying bracelet was worse. Being an empath who sees the future failed to excite me.

"No other *Justitian* can see the future. But you tend to be the exception to all the rules, so maybe something is different with you."

"Thanks for pointing it out." Why am I not surprised none of the other women who wear a *justitia* lack psychic abilities?

"You know what I meant."

Getting mad at a man for speaking the truth makes no sense. The knowledge fails to stop a dose of pissiness.

"Yeah, yeah. The white trash *Justitian* not worthy of the title. Hey, maybe I'll just change it to demon huntress. That has a better sound."

"Except that you don't just hunt demons. You hunt minions more often than not."

"And the minions are infected by a demon. Which this fancy bracelet kills and then prohibits that piece of the demon from returning to its host. Which then hurts the demon. See? A demon huntress. You've gotta admit it sounds better."

Smythe tsks. "Ah, young padiwan. No one cares how it sounds since you can't tell anyone what you do."

Padiwan? My inner geek is falling in love. Which is beyond ridiculous. One should never, and I do mean never, ever fall in love with their boss. It makes the workplace environment uncomfortable.

Not to mention making you look like you're only sleeping with the boss to get a promotion.

Smythe's lips continue to move. Which I assume indicates he continues to talk, and I need to pull my head out of my fantasies and drop back into reality.

Damn it.

"…concerned about your visions."

"What?"

"I'm more concerned about your vision than what you call yourself."

"Right. Maybe we should have told him?"

"A bit late for that now."

I look in the direction he's staring. The only thing left of the professor is the exhaust from his tailpipe and the fading purr of his car's engine. So much for letting him in on his impending death.

Learning about new abilities I don't want, sucks.

"Besides," Smythe continues, "Maybe you got a wrong reading."

"Yeah, because that happens so often." I roll my eyes and shake my head.

"And telling people about your abilities gets you a one way ticket to Blue Shores."

I shudder. Been there. Done that when I was a teenager. Not at Blue Shores, the psychiatric unit attached to the hospital where I work, but one stay in a psych ward was one stay too many for me. As much as it pains me to admit, Smythe is right. The less people know about my talents, the better.

Even if it results in losing a life.

Smythe's phone buzzes, a loud vibration heard over the hushed distant voices of the funeral attendees. He pulls it from his front pocket and slams it against his ear hard enough to give a normal person a headache.

"What?"

Normal people say 'hello.' Smythe seems to take someone reaching out and touching him as a personal insult.

A tinny voice escapes the earpiece, words indecipherable. I reach into my purse, pull out the key fob, and unlock my car. I'm halfway to the cool bliss of air conditioning when Smythe drops the f-bomb. I start the car and crank up the A/C while he walks around the hood to the passenger side door. By the time he slides into the seat, the phone's back in his pocket.

"There's been a shooting at the medical school. In the graduate department, not in the area where they treat patients, thank God. You need to determine if it's a minion attack."

"What makes you think it is?"

"The Agency IT picked up a demon blip on the radar minutes before calls to 911 began. The demon didn't stay long, but its appearance, along with the calls, are worrisome. It could be nothing."

"I thought you said demons didn't like to come to earth." I should know "not like to" didn't translate into "never ever." But I feel compelled to check. Just in case something changed from the last time we discussed this topic.

"They don't." So much for a change. "But as you know, that doesn't mean they won't. Especially if they can commit a crime or perpetrate evil."

"A blip doesn't sound like he stayed here long."

"Right. That's why it's probably nothing, but we'll check it out anyway."

The bracelet vibrates, a thrill of joy escaping into my nerves, fueling a rush of adrenaline. Which makes part of me excited, purpose-filled. The other part wants nothing more than to let the mascara run down my cheeks in the privacy of my home.

Who knew a funeral could be the day's high point?

Chapter Two

After a thirty minute drive, various spicy language and a close encounter with a driver who mistook the Dallas North Tollway for the Texas Motor Speedway racetrack, we pull into the visitor parking garage at Dallas Medical School.

Driving in Dallas, even during the middle of the day, resembles an adult version of dodge ball. Or, more accurately, dodge car.

I take a deep relaxing breath and step out of the car. Only to pause at Smythe's growl.

So much for relaxing.

"Ditch the hat." He uses the slam of the car door as punctuation, end of sentence.

As if he's never heard of hat hair.

Men.

Without waiting for me to comply, he strides toward the walkway into the medical school, his long legs carrying him farther away from me with each step.

I engage the lock and try to catch him, but heels and I have never been best friends. "Hey! Slow down. I can't walk fast in these shoes."

His shoulders rise, fall, but he stops, his eyes widening as he turns to look over his shoulder. "I told you to ditch the hat."

"Ever heard of hat hair?" I yank the hat off to demonstrate and point at my head. "Not to mention the ugly line on my forehead. Unless you have some magic spell to wipe that away?"

"Magic should not be used so trivially."

"Well, then. The hat stays. Besides, it matches the outfit." I shoot him an I-win grin as I adjust the hat to cover my sweaty hair.

He shakes his head. "Detectives don't appear in hats."

"They don't appear in a black t-shirt and jeans either." I gesture at his outfit. "Tell them I'm a consultant for the department."

One side of his mouth twitches as he checks out his clothes. "I forgot I had this on."

"Smythe, Smythe, Smythe. You always have that on. Whatcha talking about?"

"I do not always wear this outfit."

"Smythe. You have an entire closet full of black shirts, jeans, and shitkickers."

"And a suit." The lip twitch spreads into a grin. "Don't forget the suit."

Smythe's smile sends a shot of arousal straight to my core. What's wrong with me? I just attended my lover's funeral. Am I some sick freak or what?

If he notices my red cheeks, he pretends nothing's wrong. He starts walking, slower this time, and I fall into step beside him, a companionable distance apart.

"Don't speak," his footsteps emphasize the warning. "Let me do the talking. Your job is to locate minion trails. If there are any."

"And you'll work your magic and make the cops think we're detectives. Like you did when Will was shot." Dr. Will Wunderliech, an acquaintance since high school, who now works with me in the ER at Blue

Forest, was shot by a minion during our shift at the hospital. Luckily he lived. I discovered his bleeding body in one of the exam rooms and the *justitia* in my scrub pocket. When I touched him as he lay bleeding out, I saw into his memories and knew his mother gave him the bracelet, tasking him to keep it safe, before a minion killed her.

Which fails to explain how it mysteriously appeared in my pocket and remains the mystery of the month. Will's excuse: he wanted me to have it.

I want plenty of things too. Like winning the lottery.

So much for wishes coming true.

"Always." Smythe gestures at the crowd gathered in the hall. "We're at the crime scene. Look smart."

"Right. Because I made it through nursing school by failing all the classes."

He closes his eyes. Draws in a breath. Releases it, opens his eyes, and gives me The Look.

What? If he doesn't like my attitude, he shouldn't have signed up for the mentoring job.

Although in all fairness, I don't think he had any more choice in the matter than I did.

Ain't life grand?

Smythe ducks under yellow crime scene tape strung across the hallway, and I follow. People huddle in small groups on both ends of the hall, eyes facing the crime scene. Cops with CSI jackets form a barrier around a person I assume to be the victim. Make that victims. All I can see are shoe-clad feet. I'm hoping all those feet are attached to bodies. I swallow. A potent aromatic mix of blood and fear saturates the hallway. Blood spatter arcs across beige walls like a macabre

Jackson Pollock painting.

Seeing patients in the ER has not prepared me for visiting a crime scene. Stabilizing a patient focuses on compartmentalizing the injury, treating the life threatening problems first before moving to the minor cuts and bruises. Being present at a crime scene is too close to the event. Fear, a palpable tremor in the air, roots my feet to the floor. The coppery scent of blood hangs in the air, thick enough to taste.

I swallow.

It's my job to determine if a minion created this scene.

I focus on my *justitia*, on how to see minion trails and ask it to allow me to see those trails.

Nothing happens.

Smythe pulls an ID out of his back pocket and flips it open to the nearest cop. "Special Agent Smythe, and this is the department's consultant." He touches my back and a thrill of power slips beneath my skin.

Has he spelled the cop or me?

Probably the cop since the man nods his head and gives us a rundown of what happened. A grad student walked down the hall, yelling about demon infestations, pulled out a knife and started stabbing people, then turned the knife on himself. Two dead, three wounded.

And the *justitia* refuses to show me minion trails.

Why am I not surprised?

While Smythe chats with the cop, I get busy focusing on my troublesome *justitia*. How did I do this before?

Sex and riding a bike might fall into the category of things one never forgets how to do, but clearly seeing minion trails is not part of that listing.

C'mon, c'mon, come on. Time is of the essence.

I take a deep breath. Close my eyes. Shake my arms. Release my pent-up air on a whoosh. With my eyes closed, I can see the entity in the *justitia* attached to my nervous system. Tamping down the natural reaction to run screaming, I offer the thing a chance to help kill a minion.

When I open my eyes, the tactical grid otherwise known as minion trails appears across my vision. Deep red mingled with black appears like a bomb at the opposite end of the hall from where I stand. Tendrils snake outward from the tangles of color, red and pulsing, slithering into the room closest to the burst, then out toward one of the victims. Presumably the grad student.

Or should I say minion.

Red streaks bounce around the hall, punctuated by bloodstains. I'm both fascinated and sickened. Or maybe that's the *justitia*. The bracelet vibrates like a pulsing homing beacon headed straight for the explosion of deep red that started this crime.

Unfortunately, the CSI unit frowns at my walking through a crime scene. At least I assume they don't want my dirt and grass covered heels stepping into congealing pools of blood.

Okay, I don't want that either.

I give Smythe's shirt a tug. Offer a smile when his eyes narrow on me.

"Excuse me." The cop nods at Smythe's words, turns and tries to act like he's not listening in.

Telepathy time.

Smythe let on a few days ago he was able to read my mind. Unlike my twin brother T, whom I can converse with telepathically and then form a barrier to kick him out of my mind, Smythe smashes through my wall like it's formed from pebbles cobbled together with mud. Rather scary.

Which meant I need a way to block him without him discovering my motive. No problem. My mentor wants to help me learn to keep those pesky demons out of my head. So what if I place him in the pesky demon category of mind readers? Little white lies never hurt anyone.

And I learn how to strengthen my defenses.

I need to get to the other end of the hall.

Did you want a better look at that odd burst? Any idea what it is?

For a brief moment, I'm stunned. He sees the red explosion. Then I remember. Mages see minion trails too.

Which begs the question of why they even need *Justitians* if they can see trails left by the walking evil.

I've explained that to you before. Smythe crosses his arms.

So much for learning mind barriers.

But I remember the lesson. A mage can only kill the minion, allowing the life force to return to the demon. A *justitia* destroys the demon's life force that animates a minion, which weakens the demon.

We are needed.

I think.

You need to stop reading my mind.

Say what? Both of his brows try to touch his hairline. *You're the one who invited me in.*

To carry on a conversation, not read random thoughts.

Keep the random thoughts behind a barrier. Like I taught you.

Yeah, yeah, yeah. You gonna help me get to the other end of the hall or keep chewing my ass out?

First off, I'm not chewing your ass out. I'm clarifying a lesson. Learn the difference. One last punctuating glare and he turns to the cop. "Officer, my colleague and I need to get to the other end of the hall. What's the best way? We don't want to disturb the scene."

The cop gives detailed directions to walk down a different hall, hang two lefts, and presto, the end of this hall. A minute later we stand by the red and black burst, the colors hanging in the air, drops of acid rain on a pristine lake.

A full body shiver shimmies down my spine, spreading chill bumps across my flesh. The scent of sulfur hangs in the air like a demonic stink bomb. I want to slap a hand over my nose, but no one else seems affected by the stench.

Must be a demon huntress thing.

"*Justitian*," Smythe mutters. "Not demon huntress."

"If you don't like my new title, then stay out of my mind."

He glares. I swallow. Cross my arms. Refuse to take a step back. I'm learning not to be intimidated by his anger. Go me.

My *justitia* vibrates, throwing me out of my internal battle, pulling me back to the land of death and minions. The blob of colors pulsates, a glowing reminder of a moment of terror.

The moment the demon appeared to the grad

student.

Granted, I'm still taking Demons 101, but I thought demons formed minions in private. Usually after the human committed a crime, not before. A tryout, so to speak. And maybe that happened, but it sure seems to me like the black blob of demon force appeared to the grad student smack in the middle of the hallway.

Or maybe that always happens and I just now noticed it.

The *justitia's* vibration grows stronger, trembling my arm, my veins. Not its normal excited tremor upon seeing a minion or demon. A rush of images spikes through my mind, scenes of terror coupled with blood and death, memories of the *justitia's* former wearers captured in time by the entity in the bracelet.

I'm not the only one freaked out by the colored blob. How bad was this demon to scare a *justitia*?

Chapter Three

Smythe lets loose a low whistle. "Haven't seen that before."

Words to give a girl heart palpitations. "Does it look to you like the demon just appeared to the grad student? Or am I imagining things?"

"No, you're not. That's the way it looks to me. I've never seen that before. Making a minion is usually done in private."

Nice to know I retained my lesson. Not so nice to know this demon doesn't fit the normal profile.

"What does it mean?"

"Hell broke loose."

If I'm not mistaken, Smythe made a joke. His weak attempt at humor makes me groan.

"Be serious."

"I am serious. If I'm not mistaken, and I rarely am, that demon made a minion of an unwilling human. That's just not done."

"Clearly it is done, or we wouldn't be looking at it."

He shoots me a get-real look. "It's so rare as to be not done. A footnote in a textbook, not an occurrence in real life. Demons prefer to choose those with threads of evil. Giving a part of themselves to an unwilling victim in hopes of creating a lasting minion is stupid. Demons are many things, but stupid isn't one of them."

"Then explain what we're seeing."

"I can't. There must be something we're missing."

I take another glance at the pulsing blob and shiver. Or maybe that shiver is from the *justitia*. The bracelet vibrates to the tune of escape.

A little more insight into this badass demon would be nice. Something besides the *justitia's* faded memories of past emotions and crimes. Something like a name.

The *justitia* remains silent, choosing to tremble instead of speak.

Figures.

"Maybe we need to look at the other victim." I gesture to team CSI cataloguing evidence on the dead student the minion killed.

"I need my laptop."

Right. The magical laptop. Never get between a guardian mage and his computer. "What does your laptop have to do with the dead guy?"

"How do you know it's a guy?"

I raise a brow. "I don't. But most women don't wear shoes that size."

He ignores my comment. "Best guess is the grad student went crazy when the demon placed a part of itself in his body. The victim has nothing to do with it. He was in the wrong place at the wrong time."

"What if you're wrong?"

"I suspect we'll learn soon enough. Is there anything else you need from the scene?"

"This is my first active crime scene. You tell me."

He stares at the hall, at team CSI circled around the victims like vultures picking at a carcass. "We've seen enough. I need my laptop to continue the investigation."

"You mean hack the Dallas Police Department's server."

"Same thing. Come on, let's go."

After a last glimpse at the colored blob, which I swear has grown and now mocks me, I follow Smythe back the way we came. He nods and does some silent male ritual with the cop and then we're on our way to the car.

After a harrowing journey avoiding distracted drivers and road construction, we arrive at my house. T's truck sits at the curb in the spot Blake always parked.

Pain constricts my chest. Heat blooms behind my eyes, and I blink away the moisture clouding my vision. Once. Twice. At least I saved the break down until I pulled into the driveway.

Which is one thing going my way today.

Smythe pats my thigh, his palm warmer than the hot Texas air and more soothing than a relaxing bath at the end of a hard day. The pain in my eyes eases, tears no longer blossoming like weeds. Some gestures mean more than words.

I squeeze his hand as I drive the car into the garage. A quick hit on the clicker and the door slides shut, sealing us in. Smythe pulls his hand back, the loss of his warmth leaving a cool spot on my thigh.

Damn, I'm all emotional today. No more funerals for me.

Smythe follows me up the garage steps, through the door onto my back porch, then into my kitchen where I pitch my hat on the table.

Did he cast a spell on me? Tears no longer block my vision, but grief lodges in my chest, a writhing ball of expanding pain.

Maybe it was a half-assed spell.

T leans against the doorframe from the kitchen to the living room, arms crossed in that classic she's-my-twin-and-you're-not-good-enough-for-her position he takes whenever Smythe is around. You'd think he'd have gotten used to my mentor's presence, especially since Smythe has saved my ass a couple of times. But apparently ass-saving only stops an ass-whooping and does nothing for male posturing.

Great. I now have two alpha males standing in my kitchen trying to prove who has the bigger biceps.

T breaks the tension by walking to me and gathering me in his arms. I lay my cheek against his chest, and a muted sense of peace creeps around me like a shawl. Touching each other brings a calmness normally missing in our lives. A little odd, but then neither of us could ever be called the poster child for normality.

Our alcoholic parents took pains to ensure we never fit in that category.

Grief leaches from my soul, comforted by the touch of my twin. Until a high-pitched squeal breaks the moment.

"T! You didn't tell me your sister was coming home so soon." Jackie, T's double-D, blonde-bimbo of a girlfriend, sashays into the kitchen and places her hand on his shoulder, breaking our connection.

No more moment of serenity.

"When did you think I was coming home?" I step away from T, and catch a glimpse of what she's wearing.

Or not wearing.

Her sheer teddy barely covers her privates and gives me an unwanted view of her assets. Parading around like a ho on display doesn't seem to bother her.

I'm a fine one to be talking. The first time I met the Agency, the esteemed group of mages running the minion-finding show, I was dressed in a pair of hooker-short shorts with a tank top and sporting a bedhead 'do. Blame it on Smythe, he kidnapped me without allowing me to change clothes.

At least I had the decency to be embarrassed.

Jackie merely offers me a dim-witted smile and a shrug. Clearly intelligence is not on T's list of womanly attributes.

My brother turns, eyes flaring as he glimpses Jackie's choice of outfit. "Babe, go get dressed."

Her brows knit, gaze drifted down. A hint of red smacks her cheeks. "Oh. I forgot."

Right. Because air hitting all your parts isn't a subtle hint about your lack of clothing. Idiot.

"What?" T glares at Smythe as Jackie wanders back to the bedroom.

Smythe raises a brow, a response I'm learning translates to *what's your problem?* T, though, takes it as a form of aggression and points a finger at my mentor.

"Don't ogle my girlfriend."

"It's not ogling if the goods are set out on the counter for full display."

"Okay, okay." I step between the men, palms held out toward each one. "Jackie can't help her lack of brains."

"She's not stupid," T growls.

I ignore him. Men blindsided by double-D's tend to not see the truth.

He takes a step toward Smythe and freezes, a pale cast slipping beneath the tan of his skin. Sweat beads at top of his forehead as his eyes widen.

Both Smythe and I turn to where T stares. Nothing except the counter and table. Which I cleaned before leaving for the funeral. No dirty dishes to cause his what-the-hell reaction. No visible reason at all. Which left the not so visible reasons.

Ever since That Day long ago, T freaks when he sees a ghost.

And he sees a lot of dead spirits.

According to him, they are all around us.

I grab his arm. "What—" but the sentence dies on my lips as a presence takes shape, the outline filling in with transparent colors, forming features as recognizable to me as my own face.

Blake.

Chapter Four

"Fuck." T swallows. "I knew I should've come back with iron filings."

"What?" Smythe looks at the empty table, back to us, back to Blake.

I point. "Blake?"

The ghost nods.

"Fuck," T wipes a hand across his forehead. "You're supposed to stay in the grave."

Blake shrugs and his lips move, but I can't hear him. My heart jumps, a quick-step stealing my breath. Blake returned to me. A shot of joy bounces through my veins, only to come to a stop at the realization he was not alive.

Still dead. Dead, dead, dead.

So why can I see him? The only time I've ever seen a ghost was when I first put on the *justitia* at the hospital, after the bracelet appeared in my pocket. If memory serves, I touched T then, too.

I drop my hand, and Blake vanishes. Touch T. Blake reappears.

What the hell?

"Careful?" T's eyes narrow, color returning to his face. "Yeah, you better be careful, buddy. Or I'll put iron filings and salt around the house. See if you get in then."

Blake shoots T the double bird. Something he

never would have done while alive. Very few people choose to mess with T. But then, what can my brother do to a spirit besides talk to it? Guess Blake feels more secure as a ghost.

Gah. What the hell am I thinking? You know you live a screwed up life when you see a ghost and wonder about its confidence issues instead of run screaming from the room.

"Careful?" Smythe narrows his eyes, gazing to where Blake stands, searching for the ghost. "Why?"

"Fuck. I'm not gonna talk to him anymore than I have to." T crosses his arms, knocking my grip loose.

I place my hand on his shoulder. Less chance of him knocking it off. No way am I going to miss seeing Blake. Even if he is transparent.

"I'm going to ask. You're going to oblige." Smythe's tone brooks no argument. "Deal?"

After a few seconds of staring, T nods. For the first time in a long time, he's not opposed to speaking to a ghost. Probably because he knows the ghost.

"Fine. But you owe me one." T stares at Blake. "Did you hear the question, or do you need me to state it?"

Since T doesn't repeat Smythe's question, I assume Blake heard it. Blake's lips move in reply.

Blake closes his mouth and glances my way. *Please.* This time I see the word on his lips.

"Please, what, T?" I shake T's shoulder. "What did he say?"

"Geez, Gin, give me a chance to answer. He says he can't cross over until he knows you are safe. He wants us to make sure you stay safe. Begged Smythe and me. Something bad is going down, but he's not sure where or when. Or who."

"That's a shitload of help." Smythe leans against the counter and perfects his glare on T. "Why does he think something's about to happen if he doesn't know anything about it?"

T shrugs, faces Blake. "You heard him."

Blake's lips move with sound only T hears. Again, he looks at me, mouths the word, *Please.*

"He reiterates for us to protect Gin." T clears his throat. "As far as what's going to happen. His spirit was on its way to the next plane when he heard voices talking about evil in Dallas and how the new demon-slayer was going to get her ass whooped. So he requested to return and warn us."

"And they let him?" Smythe raises a brow.

"Why wouldn't they? Ghosts often walk this plane to assist the living. Even if most people don't see them."

"Who spoke?"

"He doesn't know."

"T, tell him I'm sorry." Three sets of eyes focus on me. "Tell him"—I swallow the lump breaking my voice, clear my throat—"Tell him I came but was too late. I'm so sorry."

A hot press of tears clouds my vision, pressure knots a tight band around my chest. Blake looks at me, and his lips turn into a sad smile. *I know,* he mouths. *I saw. Stay safe, Gin.*

Then he vanishes as if someone hit the off button on his remote control.

My tears disappear on a shot of adrenaline as I give T's shoulder a shake. "Where did he go?"

"I don't know." T's brows slam over his eyes.

"He vanished?" Smythe squints as if that will help him find a disappearing ghost.

"Said, *Stay safe, Gin,* and poofed away." I swipe a hand across my damp cheeks. "What do you think happened? Is he okay?"

"Is who okay?" Jackie walks into the room, teddy off, clothes in place. Thank God.

"Nothing," Smythe and I say together. No sense causing Jackie to think about ghosts. It might blow what little mind she has.

"Honey, what's wrong? You don't look good." She wraps an arm around T as I take a step back.

She might be a blonde bimbo, but at least she cares about my brother. Or pretends to. Nah, deceit would require intelligence. She definitely cares.

"Nothing, babe. Don't worry about it."

His brushing off her concern scratches like fingernails down the chalkboard of my spine. Do men actually think women are too stupid to deal with things?

Oh, wait. I forgot who he's talking to. Jackie probably doesn't understand the subtleties of being patronized. She smiles at T like he's the best thing in her life.

Maybe he is. Scary thought.

Almost as scary as the demon at the medical school.

Or a disappearing Blake.

"I need my laptop." Smythe brushes past Jackie into the living room.

I follow him. Hacking into the DPD beats watching my twin and his double-D wonder make googly eyes at each other. Yuck.

Smythe grabs his laptop off the coffee table, flops

30

on the couch and pops open the lid. His fingers dance across the keys. I ease into the spot beside him, my attention drawn not by the screen, but the clash of pots and pans coming from the kitchen.

Holy crap. Jackie is placing cookware on the stove like she intends to poison, I mean, cook us dinner. Or burn the house down. Does she even know how to operate a stove? I'm halfway off the couch before I see T standing beside her.

I'm fairly certain he won't burn the house down. At least not by fixing dinner.

"What?" Smythe's fingers stop their flight of the bumblebee parody, his gaze drawn to mine.

"Jackie's cooking dinner."

He glances toward the kitchen, eyes wide. "Should we stop her?"

"T's in there with her. Who knows, maybe she understands operating a stove."

He snorts. Turns back to the laptop. "Don't get your hopes up." A couple of taps, and he points at the screen. "Ah-ha. Here we go. The case file's already been opened. The grad student, Mason Tinkle, works in a lab operated by Professor Dan Sheevers. No mention of what the good professor works on."

"Wonder if that's the same Dr. Dan Sheevers I met at Blake's funeral."

"The one you saw dying?"

"Yep."

"Says here Dr. Sheevers wasn't at the school when the crime occurred."

"Yeah, 'cuz he was at the funeral. A little hard to be in two places at the same time."

"Provided it was the same guy. Maybe we need to

go talk to this professor."

Just what I want to do. "You mean return to the med school?"

"You think he's there or at home?"

"Probably back at the school. Most professors spend more time in their labs than their houses. Especially if one of their students was killed."

"Right." He glances at the kitchen. "Should we sample the cooking or leave now?"

"Let me change, and we can leave. These heels are killing me."

I slip the shoes off and stand. Ah. Freedom. Why do cute shoes always hurt my feet?

Carrying the shoes, I slip into my bedroom and close the door.

"Blake?" My whisper echoes in the afternoon shadows, a plea for another glimpse, another chance.

Nothing answers except for the whine of the overtaxed air conditioner.

I drop the shoes on the floor and fall onto the bed, not bothering to conceal the warm rush of tears falling down my cheeks. No one here to care if my mascara trails off my chin.

Why did Blake disappear? Was he in trouble? Do ghosts even get in trouble?

Why does no one but me seem to care where he went?

A knock on the door startles me from my thoughts. I swipe a hand across my face. So much for no one seeing my mascara run. "Come in."

Smythe shoves the door open. "What's taking…oh." The slight tint on his cheeks speaks his embarrassment louder than words. He takes a step into my room, closing the door behind him. One heartbeat later, his warm palm lands on my shoulder. "I'm sure he's fine."

I sniff. Dash my mascara stained hands on my dress. Yet another use for a little black dress.

"You have no idea, do you?"

He clears his throat. "Ghosts aren't my specialty."

"Find anything on your computer about Blake?"

"Not about Blake."

"Did you even try?" I shoot him my best glare. Which works better without red-rimmed eyes and watered down makeup.

The quick pat on my shoulder is a Smythe gesture for *let's calm down*. Knowing I can now read his mind from his actions fails to bring comfort.

"As far as I know incorporeal beings cannot be destroyed. Corporeal ones can. Focusing on Mason Tinkle and the student he killed are our best bet to stop what's happening. You heard Blake. He has no idea who spoke or what's going to happen."

He's not very helpful floated through my mind. At least Smythe had the decency not to speak it aloud. Common sense dictates I shouldn't be upset by his thoughts.

Not unless I want him to be upset with me for mine.

Scary idea.

"What if you're wrong about ghosts being destroyed? What if Blake is hurt?"

His brow drops, his jaw tensing. Right. Male mentors are never wrong. Silly me for forgetting.

A second later, his expression softens, sympathizes.

He pats my shoulder twice as if the action gives him patience. His sigh drifts on a gentle brush of air. "We're not going anywhere, are we, until you get your questions answered."

Amazing. Someone besides T who understands me. Even Blake took months before he learned to read me.

"No one seems to care."

Another shoulder pat and he steps away, flopping onto my bed, hands resting on his knees. "His concern is admirable, but his information is sketchy. And despite what your brother says, ghosts might be plentiful, but they aren't so direct."

"How would you know, 'Mr. Ghosts Aren't My Specialty'? You couldn't even see him, let alone talk with him."

"How often does T talk with the spirit world?"

My fingers twist in the folds of my dress. Used to be all the time. Until one ghost helped by offering advice. "Not too much lately."

"So how would he know? The Agency had a ghost talker who wrote manuals on the subject. It would do your brother good to learn instead of fearing."

"Don't let T hear you say he fears anything."

"If it walks like a duck…"

I shake my head. Smythe has a point, but I can't change T's mind when I understand where he's coming from. "If you get out I'll change into something more comfortable."

"Don't make it too comfortable. We're going back to the med school as detectives. Try to look professional."

"Always."

His raised brows and quick sweep of my body

sparks the memory of me appearing before the Agency for the first time wearing sexy sleep shorts and a barely there tank.

"Hey, that was your fault." I point a finger at him. "You kidnapped me without giving me a chance to change clothes."

He smiles, lips twitching as if he fights not to laugh. "Get dressed. Just dump the hat this time."

With that parting shot, he's off the bed and out the door, leaving behind a mixed scent of spice and man. Yum. Too bad he's my boss.

And my boyfriend's funeral was today. What kind of a horrible person am I to lust after one man while crying over another?

But it's always been like that with Smythe. Instead of reading his emotions when I touch him, I usually get a shot of do-me-now. Not sure which is worse.

At the moment, it's embarrassment over wanting him tied to the bed instead of leaving the room.

Embarrassment I can live with. Him seeing the fantasy of us in my mind, not so much.

Time for another practice session of keeping my mind-reading mentor out of my mind.

****

A few minutes later, I walk into the living room dressed in tan pants and a white short-sleeved dress top, my hair pulled back in a bun. Which is the only acceptable way to wear hair after subjecting it to a tight hat on a hot day. A fresh application of cover-up on my neck hides Zagan's mark.

Item number one on the list of things to hide from my mentor.

Speaking of mentors…mine relaxes on the couch,

shit-kickers propped on the coffee table, laptop across his thighs, a fine sheen of sweat on his forehead.

Due to the barely-there A/C or fear of Jackie's kitchen skills?

Taking a deep breath, I face the kitchen. Whew. No evidence of a fire. "Hey, T."

T steps away from the counter, a knife balanced in his palm. "Why you got on that getup?"

"We have to go out, but we'll be back."

"Dinner'll be ready in an hour or so."

"Okay." So far, the house was intact, and the kitchen remained smoke free. Perhaps I could be polite and sample the Double-D Wonder's cooking. It wouldn't kill me.

Being polite, that is. I'm not so sure about the meal.

A metallic click sounds from behind me, followed by a heavy thud of shoes. Smythe's palm rests against my shoulder.

"We'll be back." He sounds ominous. As if it's a threat instead of a promise.

T narrows his eyes, points the knife at Smythe. "One hour." The 'or else' goes without saying.

Smythe lifts his chin to Jackie, and T points at something on the counter. "Hey, babe, what's that?" Jackie turns her back to us.

Smythe opens a portal while she's not looking.

Warm air billows out of the portal, luring me to believe the in-between is as comfy as a beach, but I know better than to fall for the deception. Smythe grabs my hand and yanks me into the ice-cold, color-swirling depths. Breath freezes in my lungs, locked there by the chill of the portal.

Good thing I'm hot going into the thing. Travel by portal might be the fastest way to get around, but the chill prohibits me from liking it. Beads of sweat freeze around my hairline like miniature hailstones by the time the portal spits us out in a dark corner of a parking garage.

The splash of heat melts the ice, leaving me with a damp forehead and nape. I run the back of my hand across my forehead as I stride to catch Smythe who is already halfway to the staircase.

"Hey!" My voice echoes off parked cars, "You know my legs aren't as long as yours, right?"

Smythe pauses, shoulders raising, lowering. He turns, his gaze running over my legs. "I'm not walking that fast."

"The portal froze me. Took awhile to be able to move."

He shakes his head. "It's not that cold." When I draw even with him, he starts down the stairs. "We'll see what the good professor knows about his grad student. Let me do the talking."

"You do realize I'm somewhat intelligent, don't you?"

"You do realize there's a difference between being intelligent and knowing how to conduct an investigation, don't you?" A hint of a grin turns his lips.

"Okay, so I'm a newbie. That doesn't mean I'm going to say something stupid."

He raises a brow as an answer. I'm not mad at Smythe for his lack of confidence in my investigative interviewer role, but the devil in me likes teasing him.

A bit too much, judging from his tense jaw.

Or maybe that's his normal expression before

conducting an interview.

Smythe shoves open the door leading into the med school. A blast of cold air greets us as we walk into a white linoleum-covered hallway. Goosebumps prickle my skin, and I rub my hands up and down my arms as we stride down the hall. A few moments later, we arrive at the crime scene.

The bodies are gone as are most of the bystanders, but CSI still crawls around the hallway like fleas on a dog. Smythe walks up to the same cop he spoke with earlier.

"You're back." The cop narrows his eyes as he takes in my change of clothes.

"Yep. We need to talk to Dr. Sheevers. Do you know where his office is?"

"Already have personnel on it."

"Good. Where's his office?"

Prickles cross my skin as Smythe works a spell on the cop. The cop's brows relax, his eyes giving a glimpse into a calm mind.

"Up a floor, almost directly above us." One finger points upward.

"Thanks, man." Smythe claps him on the shoulder before grabbing my arm and walking to the nearest staircase.

Guess he's never heard of an elevator.

"Do you always cast spells on cops?" I whisper once we hit the stairs.

"Only when they get too curious."

"Remind me not to get too curious around you."

"It doesn't apply to you. You aren't a cop." He shoots me a half-grin that triggers an unwanted set of fantasy-producing tingles.

Geez Louise.

I snap barriers around that errant reaction before the man reads my mind. No sense adding fuel to his overconfident self.

He pushes open the door to the hall and the first thing I see is a couple of cops spilling out of a doorway. Bingo. Office found.

Smythe walks up to the cops and flashes his fake badge. "Special Agent Smythe and my consultant. If you're finished interviewing Dr. Sheevers, we have a few questions to ask."

The cops look at him. One starts to speak, but his eyes glaze over as prickles cross my skin. Yep, no wonder Smythe wanted me to remain quiet. My talents don't include spelling cops into submission.

Although maybe I should learn. Imagine all the speeding tickets I could get out of.

"Yeah, we were just finishing up. Come on in."

The cop steps to the side, allowing Smythe and me to crowd into an office filled to overflowing with African artwork, a thick Persian rug probably worth more money than I make in a year, and the requisite bookshelves stuffed with paper journals and leather-bound books. Oo-la-la. Standing room only for the cops and us.

The same man from Blake's funeral leans against a fancy wooden desk stacked with papers, gaze bouncing between Smythe and the cops, a thin sheen of sweat plastered across his brow. His eyes widen as he sees me. One hand runs through his graying hair, causing it to stick out like he stuck his finger in an electrical outlet.

"Why are you here?" He takes a step toward us,

thinks better of it, and returns to his leaning position.

"I'm a consultant."

One of the cops looks at me as if noticing me for the first time. Smythe snaps his fingers, a quiet sound against his leg, and the man's attention once again focuses on the professor.

"Dr. Sheevers," Smythe speaks before the professor can comment on my consultant status. "Please tell us about your grad student, Mason. We understand he worked in your lab."

Dr. Sheevers runs both hands through his hair, not improving his crazy professor look. "I already told them, he was a good student, helpful to my work, but I didn't know anything else about his life. We're busy in the lab."

Yeah, and I'm busy in the ER but still manage to learn some things about each of my co-workers. Maybe it's different for a lab full of men.

"What're you working on?" Smythe asks.

The professor drops his hands and spins around. "I can't discuss it. It's government work. Classified. If you want to know, you'll need a warrant."

Smythe stiffens, as do the cops. Who needs a warrant when they have an empath. One touch and it's all mine. Bwahahaha.

Or, instead of chortling evilly while touching the distraught prof, we can march to the nearest computer terminal and look up his specialty.

Technology to the rescue.

"You do realize we don't need a warrant to know what your specialty is, right?" a cop asks.

"Look," Dr. Sheevers raises his hand halfway to his head, then drops it, gripping the desk until his fingers blanch. "I'm really sorry he died, but I have work to do. Unless you plan on arresting me, I need to get to my lab. It's a timed project and time is almost up."

"Don't go far," the other cop warns. "We might have more questions for you."

"Fine, fine. I won't leave town. I need to get to my lab." He shoves off his desk, barreling toward the door like an alcoholic toward whiskey, fast, and without a thought to anyone else.

Smythe steps out of his way, but I stick my hand out, stopping the man in his distraught tracks.

"Thank you for letting us talk to you." Steeling myself for his thoughts, I wait for him to grasp my hand.

After a brief second as he stares at my palm like he's never seen one before, he grips my hand, giving a quick squeeze. This time I don't see his impending death. Beakers and powder-filled vials along with other lab supplies slam into my mind, chased by panic and a case of nerves strong enough to race my heart.

His gaze never meets mine as he releases my hand and scurries down the hall, the fast click of his loafers a testament to his rush. Wonder what kind of timed lab project gave that kind of reading? At least my "gift" worked correctly. No visions of the future this time.

A different clip of heavy shoes on linoleum snaps my attention in the opposite direction. Smythe strides away from the cops, his quick departure generating puzzled looks as he leaves without a word. I shoot the two detectives an apologetic smile and a shrug before speed-walking after my mentor.

He turns down a hallway and stops so fast I run

into him.

"Oomph. What the hell? You should've said something to them before buzzing out of there."

He turns halfway through my speech, crossing his arms in his classic about to ask a question stance. And he fails to disappoint. "What did you see?"

"Not up to reading my mind?"

"You appear to have learned a lesson."

Score! Nice to know I can finally form a mental barrier strong enough to keep out a nosy mage. I offer him a half-smile coupled with a wink. "I must've had a good teacher."

"It's a fluke." He grins, the expression creating an unwanted flutter in my chest. "What did you see?"

"His lab. He was telling the truth about being upset and needing to get to it."

"Why?"

"No clue. Laptop time."

He pokes his head around the corner, looking back the way we came. "Looks clear. The cops are gone. Let's check out his office."

"Why, Smythe. That's illegal without a warrant."

"We're not cops."

Several strides later, he shuts the door to Dr. Sheevers' office behind us. Good thing we're not the police. I'm pretty sure being in this office is against several rules.

Although it's not really breaking and entering if the door was already open.

I hope.

The only light in the room comes from the bright florescent bulbs crossing the ceiling. Smythe ruffles through papers pitched across the desk. A sign of a disorganized mind or too busy to straighten out the mess?

I walk around so I stand beside Smythe. A computer monitor rests in the middle of the desk, picture frames huddle on one side while a stack of professional journals keep its other side warm. Since Smythe's fingers are dancing a jig across the keyboard, I check out the pictures.

One of them is of Dr. Sheevers standing on a hiking trail in front of a brownish-pink hill which pokes above a straggly ring of trees. A site I recognize. Enchanted Rock outside of Fredericksburg, Texas. A hiker and collector of art. Multi-tasking.

The other picture is older, a wedding shot of a much younger doctor and his wife. The happy couple smiles for the camera, arms intertwined to share champagne. How sweet. A vague tension strokes deep inside. At one time, I wanted that harmony. Back when I played with dolls. Before my parents' dysfunctional marriage ravaged my reality. Before I realized being an empath, a freak of nature, eradicated any chance of a happily ever after fairytale.

"Did you find something?" Smythe's voice snaps my attention away from memory lane to the present.

"Pictures. You?"

Smythe shakes his head as he shuts down the computer. "Can't get through the password."

Seriously? Mister I-Can-Hack-Anything stuck on a password? Day-um. "Does that happen often?"

"Never. I suppose he'd notice if I took the hard-drive."

I snort a laugh at the serious look on his face. "Probably."

"It's not funny."

"Sorry." I glance toward the door. "We should leave before he returns."

"We have time. Did you see the way he tore out of here?" But he stands and shoves the chair under the desk. "I want to know what he's hiding."

"Maybe he's not hiding anything. Maybe he really had an important lab project to finish."

"Do you believe what you're saying?"

I recalled the professor brushing off the officers' questions, hauling ass out of his office, remembered the weak grip of his hand as he paused to shake mine. Fear and panic were intertwined in his thoughts. Sure he was thinking of his lab, of beakers and potions, and whatever else goes on in a working laboratory, but was he really thinking of his experiment?

I look at Smythe, shake my head. "Not in the least."

"So what's he hiding?"

"No idea. Why don't we go home, and you can Google him or whatever it is you do."

"As you wish." He mutters words under his breath, hand outstretched to a corner of the office. A portal forms and he grabs my arm as we step into its depths. "Maybe Jackie can cook."

Crap. I forgot all about her kitchen experiment. Do I even have a house left?

Chapter Five

"Thanks for dinner, Jackie. It was good." Amazingly so, as a matter of fact. And the house remained standing, no fire in sight.

Who would've guessed?

Maybe there's more to Jackie than her double-D's.

Nah. No sense in getting overly optimistic.

Jackie smiles and pats T's arm. "I had some help."

T gives her a one-armed hug and a kiss on the cheek. Gah. I shove back my chair and grab my plate. Watching the lovebirds smooch at the table makes me want to puke.

Juvenile, yes. But we can't help the way we feel.

Smythe grabs his plate, sticks it in the sink, and joins me in the kitchen exodus. I should be polite and offer to clean the dishes but that would require me to watch the lovefest.

Not happening. Not tonight.

Smythe pops open his laptop and pulls up a browser before his butt hits the couch cushion. Fingers tap a mad race across the keyboard. He squints at a link then taps enter. I lean over the back of the couch, reading text over his shoulder.

The medical school's webpage offers a glimpse into Dr. Dan Sheevers' work. Professor of Microbiology and Immunology. No mention of experiments or his specialty.

"That's it? You're better than that, Smythe."

His brows furrow a question as he points at the screen. "It mentions his home address."

"That's helpful for a pissed off, vengeful student, but not so much with us. I guess it doesn't really matter what he works on. We need to focus on the grad student and try to figure out why the demon targeted him."

"True. But, like how you got that bracelet, it's a missing thread. Those bother me."

"I told you." I poke his shoulder with my finger. "Will thinks he slipped it into my pocket after he'd been shot."

"And did he?"

"That's not the way I remember it."

"Yeah. As I thought. We need more research on that. Speaking of research." His fingers smack the keys, changing the screen view. "I looked into your genealogy since we still don't know why you can wear the *justitia* when you aren't listed in our *Justitian* bloodline records." He points at the screen. "Look what I found on your mom. She was adopted."

"Gee, I never knew." I have one memory of my grandmother, and it wasn't warm cookies and hugs. No wonder Mom drank herself to death. Maybe if she'd known her birth mother things would have been different.

As far as I know, she never tried looking.

His glare frosts my skin. "As I was saying. She was adopted, and there is no record of her birth mother."

"Because they hid those types of things back then."

He rolls right over my reasoning as if my lips never opened. "We didn't realize anyone was left of your *justitia's* ancestral line after its last *Justitian* died during

World War II. That's why we held the bracelet at the Agency."

"I remember you saying that." Genealogy never interested me. Who wants to discover your entire family tree was full of alcoholics and wife-beaters? Even knowing Mom was adopted failed to cause me excitement over the prospect of knowing my ancestors.

Genealogy might not intrigue me, but my *justitia* does. Will knew next to nothing about the bracelet. Of course, interviewing him right after he came out of a coma might not have helped.

"You aren't excited." Smythe pats the sofa next to him, and I talk while walking around to sit.

"Yippee. Tell me more about why my bracelet was taken in by the Agency."

"I already did."

"Give me a refresher. I've slept since then."

Smythe shakes his head and sighs. "Your line died out. Or we thought it did. Clearly we were wrong, since you can wear the *justitia*. It would help to learn more about your mother's past."

"If you know my line died, then why don't you know who was my direct relative?"

His lips flatten. "Apparently records were not kept as well as they should be. We don't know which *Justitian* gave birth to your ancestor or even when. Your mother was adopted, but she was born after we recorded your line died out."

"So what you're saying is I could be a direct descendant of a number of *Justitians*?"

A grin twists his lips. "Technically you can only be descended from one."

"Duh, Smythe. Duh. I know that." I shake my

head.

"Sorry. Couldn't resist." His eyes twinkle as he continues his explanation. "Each bracelet can only be worn by the descendants of the original wearer. You can be a *Justitian,* but you can only wear the *justitia* of your line. Therefore, we know which line you came from, but our records show it no longer exists."

"And you think Mom is the key to knowing?"

"I hope."

What I really want to know is why the Agency has no record of my direct line. If they take such good records, then what happened to my history? Clearly Smythe didn't know, so asking was out of the question. Looks like a discovery to save for another day. On to more answerable questions.

"Okay, how did Will get it? He said his father had it and told his mother to keep it safe. I'm assuming that meant if anything happened to him. How did his dad get it?"

"I have a theory. But it needs some more work. I haven't found Will's birth certificate."

Birth certificate? "What does that have to do with anything?"

"This is all theory, mind you."

I nod. Theory? Right. In Smythe's world, theory equals fact.

"I suspect his father worked at the Agency and stole the bracelet. There's no other explanation for how it disappeared. The average Joe can't get through the doors, and even if he managed, the vault is high security. Magical security. No getting through that without the code."

"Magical security?" Never heard of that one.

"You know. Spells." He grins, waggles his fingers.

"Hey! We're going outside to have a beer. In case you need us." T's voice snaps me out the conversation, a reminder my brother and Jackie are still hanging out in the house, overhearing our conversation.

"Thanks." I give him a little finger wave. "Have fun. And thanks again for dinner. It was good." The fact Jackie knows how to operate a stove and oven is a little shocking, but I decide against saying that thought. T already knows I think Jackie's a couple of sandwiches short of a picnic.

After shooting Smythe a glare, T walks out the back door with Jackie, who carries a six-pack. Specifically the one I bought to relax at the end of the evening. After the day I had, I deserve a couple of bottles.

Looks like my needs were going unfulfilled.

I rise to go reclaim my beer, but Smythe grabs my wrist, fingers clasping over the silver links of my bracelet, and the beer craving vanishes.

Wish that little trick could be pocketed.

"Ever thought of going to AA?"

"I don't have a problem." Liar, liar.

Yeah, right appears on his face as if stroked by a pen. I don't need to read his mind to know he's all over my lie.

Time for a topic change, otherwise known as the key to distraction.

"So, my bracelet was in a magically secure vault when it vanished?"

Smythe narrows his eyes. Blinks twice for good measure and sighs. Distraction complete. "Yep. The why it vanished is a mystery. But I believe Will's father was the one who took it. Why else warn his wife—"

"Girlfriend."

"As I was saying," he nails me with a frosty glare, "why else warn his girlfriend to keep the bracelet safe."

"She was killed by a minion searching for the bracelet." The same minion who shot Will and later that day tried to kill me. Good thing my *justitia* turned into a sword and stabbed the sucker. "Why wouldn't she just give the minion the bracelet? Why keep the secret?"

A thought slams into my mind. "Oh, I have it. Maybe she was a mage too. Or a *Justitian* in training. Or a sister of a *Justitian*. Because if someone is trying to kill you over a bracelet, wouldn't you just tell 'em where the thing was in an effort to save your life?"

He shrugs. "Good theory. But it still doesn't explain how the *justitia* ended up in your pocket."

Now it's my turn to shrug. I too have my suspicions about the how. I think the bracelet answers when you make a plea three times. Since I've used that ability to escape Smythe—albeit unknowingly, and before he became my mentor—I'm hesitant to tell him.

Who knows when that ability might come in handy?

As the song says, know when to hold 'em. Or redirect 'em.

"Maybe Will's recollection of putting it in my pocket is correct. That's not how I remember it, but seeing him shot freaked me out. I could've forgotten something."

He raises a brow. I don't need to read his thoughts to know my story makes it onto his not-fucking-likely list. So much for the redirection.

"We've been over this."

I wave a hand. "Yeah, yeah, yeah."

"We're working on the assumption Will's father is the culprit. Any thoughts as to why he took it?"

"To sell it? To hide it? Why would you steal a *justitia*?"

"I wouldn't. It doesn't kill demons without a woman of a certain lineage to wear it. Why would I want it?"

Good point. "Money makes the world go round."

"Okay. Let's say he wanted to make a profit. Why give it to his girlfriend and tell her to keep it safe?"

"No clue. Do you see *detective* tattooed on my forehead?" I point to my head.

He gives me a get-real stare. "Think, Gin. You have a brain."

"So do you. Why do I have to come up with the answer?"

"I need another viewpoint."

"I don't know." I shrug. "And I've had a crappy day. And I work a long shift tomorrow. More discoveries aren't looking promising right now." The only thing looking promising is me letting T keep my six-pack. Who knew a spell could nix my cravings?

Smythe taps one finger in an impatient rhythm against the laptop. "I'm sorry about Blake. But we need to focus on solving this."

"Which this? My ancestors? My missing and suddenly found *justitia*? Or why the hell a demon appeared at the med school and made a failed attempt at creating a minion?"

"Yes. And it wasn't a failed attempt. It made a minion. It just chose its minion poorly."

"Whatever. That's the real mystery."

"You are, too."

Just what I wanted to hear. After all the effort I've been spending on distraction and redirection, the least he could do was stop thinking of me as a mystery. Some things should be left to rest.

"Mysterious? Me? I'm an open book." Liar, liar.

His eyes narrow, his mouth opening as if to speak, until another idea crosses his mind, strong enough to morph his expression into excitement.

Oh, great. Something tells me I'm not going to like what he's about to say. And it gives me no pleasure to realize I'm right.

"Why don't we go talk to Will?"

"I told you, he doesn't know where his father got the bracelet."

"I can get him to remember."

"I'm sure you can, but he just got out of the hospital yesterday and needs his rest. It's a medical miracle he's even alive, let alone out so soon." After being shot in the abdomen a week and a half ago, then falling into a coma, then recovering quicker than anybody believed possible—hell, even his treating doctors thought him a goner—Will deserves a little rest. And time to grieve.

"That medical miracle as you call it is a red flag for him being a mage."

Will? A mage? "Why do you think that?"

"First off, if my theory is correct about his father being a mage, it's probable Will is one too, since the ability runs in families. Secondly, mages heal as fast as *Justitians,* even from potentially fatal wounds. Remember?"

Not really. But what he doesn't know won't hurt.

"Oh, right. As fast as *Justitians*, eh?" He thinks Will's a mage?

"I see we need to review some lessons."

I fail to stop the eye roll. "If mages heal so fast, why did you need to rest after you rescued me from Zagan's?"

"I burned through too much magic. That's completely different than tissue damage and requires a longer time to heal."

The intricacies of being a mage. "And here I thought Will's quick healing was a miracle."

Smythe shrugs. "Call it what you like. Magic. Miracle. Mage. If he is a mage, he should learn how to harness his powers. I can help him with that." He sets the laptop on the coffee table and stands. "Come on. At least we can solve one mystery."

I want to protest, if only for the well-being of the shot, yet healing faster than normal, patient. But discovering the secret of my *justitia* fills me with excitement. While giving me glimpses into its past, the damn thing refuses to show me how Will came to have it.

A little bit of detective work never hurt anyone. And Will might be happy to have visitors.

Especially if they bring him something to eat.

"Let me make a plate of leftovers."

One plate, two minutes, and a chilly portal later, we appear on the side of Will's humongous home. If only I hadn't been the high school freak when we first met, this might all have been mine.

Yeah, right. Not even in my dreams. By the time we met again in the ER, Will wore a wedding ring, and I have higher standards than to rest my boots under a married man's bed.

Unfortunately for him, his wife was killed the same day he was shot. When the minion failed to get the *justitia* from Will, it came to this house and killed Will's wife.

And now we come with a plate full of food, as if that will comfort a grieving husband and soften the questions we need to ask.

Steam wafts off the now-cold plate, the condensation of water droplets covering the plastic wrap. I'm not the only thing freezing from the portal. At least the August air chases away the chill bumps covering my limbs.

Smythe leads me to the front door and rings the doorbell. A few seconds later the door swings open. A private nurse wearing scrubs and sneakers looks us over like we're trying to convert her to our religion.

"May I help you?" Her pinched tone of voice indicates her lack of enthusiasm at the prospect.

Sticking on a fake smile, I hold out the plate. "We're bringing Will dinner. May we come in?"

"Let me take that. He's resting."

Mid-reach, Smythe clears his throat, snapping her attention to him. Her arm drops, eyes losing focus.

"Are you sure we can't come in and speak with him?"

She blinks at his question, then nods, a vapid smile turning her lips.

Nifty trick he has there. As long as it's not me he's spelling into doing his bidding.

"Come on in. He's in the living room." She steps back, gesturing toward a room the size of my house.

Open wooden beams support a two-storied roof.

Stone walls and a slate floor lend a coolness to the room not even the outside temperature can obliterate. I'm so busy ogling the display of money I almost miss Will sitting in a recliner, watching what has to be a seventy-inch flat screen TV.

Will raises his brows as we walk into the room, obviously confused as to why his nurse let us in.

Always nice to know I'm wanted. I plaster a smile on my face and offer him Jackie's leftover dinner. "We brought you something. Thought you might want a home-cooked meal."

"Thanks." He points the remote at the TV, lowering the volume. When he looks at me, his eyes widen.

At the same time, a brush of air strokes the back of my neck, raising prickles along my skin. Smythe. No one else causes that otherworldly sensation coupled with an annoying vision of sex-tangled sheets.

"Will, meet Smythe. Smythe, this is Dr. Wunderliech."

Smythe nods. After a two-beat pause, Will returns the gesture, eyes narrowed on my mentor as if he can see into his soul.

The nurse grabs the plate out of my hands, no doubt ensorcelled to leave us alone. Her tennis shoes make soft squelching noises as she heads toward the kitchen.

Will waves at a modern sofa that reminds me of a medieval torture device, blood red and curved. "Have a seat." Despite the words and gesture, his tone indicates he'd rather us exit stage left instead of getting comfortable, if comfort is even possible on that couch.

Normally I'd pick up on the silent cues and leave,

not needing empathic abilities to know when I'm not wanted. But I'm outvoted by my mentor who perches on the edge of the couch like it might give him a disease.

Oh, well. I pull out the rudeness card and sit beside Smythe, grin plastered on my face, an uncomfortable tension holding my spine straight.

With any luck, Will won't notice that my smile covers a dose of embarrassment.

"I need to ask you a couple of questions about Gin's bracelet." Smythe touches my wrist, eliciting an unwanted jolt of over-active hormones.

Will's eyes widen as he licks his lips. "Like I told Gin, I don't know much."

Smythe catches Will's gaze.

"Why do you want…?" Will's words fade away as his mouth slackens, eyes glaze. But only for a couple of seconds. Smythe doesn't even have time to ask a question before Will shakes his head, fingers rubbing his brow as he closes his eyes.

Anger flashes across his face as he raises his gaze, nailing Smythe with a glare that frosts my skin like a portal. "What the hell do you think you're doing? You're one of those people my dad warned me about. Get out." He points to the door. "Get out now."

I'm halfway up, apologetic grin turning my lips, when a strong hand clamps my wrist, tugging me back down.

"Not bad." Smythe nods in time to his words. "With some training, you'll make a good mage."

Will blinks, arm stretched out, finger pointing at the door. "I said…" he pauses, brow scrunched, "…what do you mean mage?"

"I assume your father worked for the Agency. An organization that is comprised of mages who guard the *Justitians*, the women who wear bracelets like Gin's. Like the bracelet you gave her. Mage abilities run in families. Judging by your reaction to my test a minute ago, you possess those abilities. That's why we're here."

Only part of why we're here, but hey, little white lies never hurt.

Will's arm drops, the angry expression giving way to curiosity.

Embarrassment still rages in my soul. But like Will, curiosity wins out. What he has to say involves me. And my *justitia*.

Who knows? I might learn how Will's father got the bracelet. Peppering the recovering doctor with questions makes Smythe happy and gives me a sense of accomplishment. It's a twofer, a win-win for all involved. I hope.

"Then why mess around in my head?"

"As a test. To make sure you were what I hoped. It's not often a mage doesn't realize their powers. Tell me how you knew I was in there."

"Dad trained me to recognize if someone was messing with my mind. But that was a long time ago."

"I'm sorry for your loss."

"Yeah." Will stares at his balled fist for several seconds. "So you came to test me? Or to ask questions about my bracelet?"

"Both. Keep in mind that's not your bracelet."

Will's eyes flash. "It was Dad's."

"How did he get it?"

"I don't know, okay? It was his. He gave it to

Mom, and she gave it to me—" His voice cuts out as if he meant to say more. His face whitens. His gaze drops. Neither of us prompts him to continue as we both know what happened next. His mother gave him the bracelet right before she died, the night he hid under his bed, listening to a minion beat his mother to death, fearing the man would come after him next.

I want to comfort him, to soothe away the grief enveloping him even after all these years. But I don't. I already glimpsed into his mind the day he was shot and the thought of another jump into his past sends a shiver across my limbs. My fingers clasp each other as if to keep his memories at bay.

"And the bracelet helped you, didn't it?" Smythe's calm tone soothes the grief lines zigzagging across Will's brow.

"I guess. The man never saw me. Looked right at me and passed by." Will shudders, arms crossing in an unconscious gesture of protection.

"Why did you give it to Gin?"

"Like I told her, I don't remember much of that day."

"May I look and see?"

Will's arms drop, eyes narrowing on my mentor like he's a misbehaving child. "More mind stuff?"

"Perhaps I can unlock your memories of that day."

"And why would I want you to? What would that help? I had the bracelet that morning and obviously gave it to Gin. Why do the in-between parts matter?"

Smythe's fingers tighten against my wrist, the only indication he dislikes Will's answer. Did he really expect Will to jump on the invade-my-mind bandwagon? Especially after the good doc tried to make us leave?

"You carried it to work?"

"Yeah. I usually wore it. As I said, I don't remember much of that day, but I do remember wanting Gin to have it for some reason." He glances at the wall, back to Smythe, his voice dropping to a whisper. "Almost more than I wanted to live. Like an obsession, this little voice inside telling me to give it to Gin."

"You didn't tell me that." When I visited him in the hospital, he only said he'd wanted me to have it. Not that a voice told him.

"Yeah, well. Telling people a little voice told you to do it never goes over well." He offers me a half-smile.

"I know what you mean." Telling people you see inside their minds, read their emotions, and sometimes their thoughts, doesn't go over so well either. Hence my stay many years ago at a Blue Shores equivalent.

"You said weird things have happened to you since you've had the bracelet." Will clearly remembers our conversation from his hospital room when he came out of the coma. "What did you mean?"

Before I can explain, Smythe answers for me. Note to self: remind mentor that in this day and age, women can answer for themselves.

"You'll have to agree to mage training before I can tell you."

Seriously? He didn't seem to have a problem with Blake or T knowing about minions, demons, and *Justitians*. What changed? Yet another question for my mentor once we leave.

"Or what? You'll have to kill me?"

"Don't be dramatic. Mages don't kill mages."

Only *Justitians*. And only if the mage's name is Samantha, aka the bitch who hired a regiment of minions to try to kill me. Not that anyone except Smythe believes she did it. But hey, what Will doesn't know won't hurt him, right?

The grip on my wrist tightens as if he heard me. Damn. My mental barriers aren't as good as I thought.

"And if I agree? What then? What does this training involve? Why train?"

"Mages are the protectors against evil."

Can he get any more dramatic?

"You fight evil? Like comic book characters?"

"We don't have capes."

One side of Will's lips turn up, as if he thinks Smythe jokes. "I'm too sick to train. You'll have to come back."

"You'll heal fast. All mages do."

"Is that why I'm here despite being told my only ticket out of the hospital would be a celestial discharge?"

"Yep. I'll come back in a week. Train you. Explain things. Deal?"

"Okay." He draws out the word with all the speed of a turtle running a race. "You have a deal, Smythe." Will holds out his hand.

Smythe crosses the room to shake it.

Looks like I have a new training partner.

So why am I not more excited?

Chapter Six

We arrive via portal in my kitchen. A soft peel of feminine laughter lets me know Jackie and my twin continue to drink my beer in the backyard.

"So why wouldn't you tell Will about the demon and minion fighting when you didn't mind Blake and T knowing?" I ask as we walk into my living room.

Smythe takes his usual seat on the couch, pulling on his laptop like most people pull on shoes. "I wanted to make sure he'd let me train him."

"You lied?"

"No. I plan on telling him next time we talk."

"You lied."

He scratches the back of his head. "An omission. Not an outright lie."

"Uh-huh. Call it whatever makes you feel better."

He shakes his head, gives me one of those half-grins that means he thinks I'm funny. Annoying. But funny.

I'm learning to read him too.

"I'll let him heal up, then next week go over there and explain the new world to him. We could use him as a healer at the Agency."

"Thinking ahead, eh? You do realize he not only got shot and almost died, but his wife was killed in that house?" I shudder. I don't blame Will for not wanting to return home. Sure, a minion was killed in my house, but he definitely wasn't someone I cared for. If T, Blake, or even Smythe had been killed in this house, I'm not sure I could live here anymore.

"Even more incentive to leave."

"His tragedy shouldn't be seen as an incentive."

"I didn't mean for it to come across callous." He sets his laptop on the coffee table and turns his full attention to my rigid, fists-balled posture. "It would be hard to lose your spouse the way he did."

I suck in a gulp of air, release my irritation on the exhale. Smythe might kill minions with the expediency of an exterminator facing a roach, but he's not cruel. And he doesn't laugh at others' misfortunes. I know better than to accuse him of cashing in on Will's tragedy.

"I'm sorry. I know you didn't mean it like that. I'm just…" I wave a hand, letting the motion encompass my day.

"You've had a bad day too. You and Will have a lot in common. Not only do you work together, but you've both suffered a recent loss." His jaw locks, lips flattening.

A shot of joy-joy dances through my system. I refuse to examine why his jealousy puts me in my happy place.

"I guess we do." Knowing Will and I have something in common wipes the joy over Smythe's jealousy right out of my system, leaving my chest aching like a boulder sits on my ribcage. "I'm going to bed now. Have fun surfing the web."

"It's not even dark." Master of the obvious Smythe is.

"I have to get up early. Tomorrow's a twelve hour

shift day."

"We need to do something about that."

"Talk to management." I head toward the hall.

"You know what I mean."

"As I've said before, give me a paycheck equal to what I make at the ER, and I'll demon hunt full time for you. Until then…" I turn and wave my fingers. "Good night. Oh, and you might need earplugs if you plan on sleeping on the couch."

"Earplugs?" A ridge furrows between his brows. "What for?"

I point to the wall separating the living room from T's room. T's old room. He's supposed to be living with Jackie but since I've become a *Justitian* they've spent most nights here. Loudly.

Smythe's gaze bounces between the wall and me. "The wall doesn't make noises."

"Okay, then. See you tomorrow."

He's spent the night here plenty of times. You'd think he would start packing the earplugs. Or maybe he's such a sound sleeper he doesn't notice T's extra-curricular activities.

Stranger things have happened.

"Good night, Gin." A dull click of the keyboard follows his words, as he pulls up a browser to research whatever we talked about before visiting Will.

I pause halfway in my room, remembering our topics of discussion. Demon. Will. Mom's adoption.

Crap. Mom's birth has nothing to do with my secrets. So why can't I shake the feeling Smythe will discover what T and I want to remain buried?

****

Streaks of waning light flicker across my walls and

ceiling as I lie in bed, staring at nothing. Low laughter trickles past the curtains from Jackie and T's outdoor conversation. Much better than other noises the two can make.

Semi-cool air blows across my skin as the air conditioner whines a pitiful cry. Do I have enough saved to fix the damn thing? How much do half-dead A/C units cost?

Will Blake visit me tonight?

Maybe he's already here. I sit straight and glance around the room. Shadows gather in the corners, around the furniture, but no ghost. At least no ghost I see. Which isn't saying much. Unless I touch T, I can't see the spirits.

Another new gift, courtesy of my *justitia*.

I flip onto my side, one hand reaching for the knob on my nightstand for the girl's-best-friend. Halfway there I stop. At one time in my life, opening that drawer brought relief. Smythe's spell stopped the beer craving but did nothing for the emptiness creeping through my soul.

Bottom line, I don't know if Blake will stop by for another visit. Even if he did, what kind of relationship would we have?

Better to lie on top of the covers with my battery operated, feel-good-now toy.

Closing my eyes, I picture Blake as I last saw him, alive, happy, leaving for work. Feel the touch of his lips against my skin. Tears form a hot press against my lids. My attempt at calm fails, allowing the wave of sadness, of self-pity, of guilt, to break through my soul. I curl onto my side, my cries muffled by the pillow.

A squeak startles me awake, tears crusted to my

face, my heart an erratic pounding rhythm. An eerie quiet bathes the room with a lack of noise only achieved at the nearness of a predator. I stop moving, breath frozen in startled lungs, ears searching for the source of the sound.

The chair. Oh my God, someone is sitting in my chair. I am not alone.

What do I do? Scream? Fight? Run? How long until he notices me?

The intruder curses, a rumbling of an ancient language. The chair squeaks again as he stands, his shadow an elongated black stain on the wall.

A scream rips up my throat but freezes on my tongue when tingles shoot up my arm, stemming from my *justitia*. The damn thing is ecstatic, which only signifies one thing.

Zagan is in my room.

Yeah, I'm supposed to kill demons. But not this one. Even if I wanted to, the *justitia* wouldn't let me.

Smacking sense into the silver links doesn't work. I've tried. The knowledge fails to stop me from trying again. A low chuckle rumbles through the room, double-timing my heart rate.

As if he scents my fear, Zagan walks toward me.

I scoot to the other side of the bed, a mad scramble to escape. Not that escape will help me.

Zagan gestures toward the window. "It was kind of you to let me in."

Two tries later and words squeak past an almost frozen larynx. "The window is closed. And I didn't let you in."

White teeth shine in the darkness, a slash of glee on a torturer's face. "Closed, yes. But the intent was there.

Your blood calls to me, remember?"

His words tug like a lover's caress on my skin, and my mouth turns dry. My stomach churns. Fear? Or anticipation? He shouldn't know my inner thoughts, my wicked desires. My fingers tense on the sheet. As if the flimsy material could prevent a demon from having its way with me.

Do I really want to prevent him?

Gah! Of course I do. Note to self, demons make one insane.

What was he talking about? Right. Blood. "That's only because you took some of mine."

"It called before that day. For many years now. When they gave me the chance to destroy you, to take," the unpronounceable name of my *justitia* rolls off his tongue, "as my own, I could not end your life. You…attract me."

Another spit-less swallow and my stomach flutters a jig. Warmth spreads through tingling limbs. If the *justitia* had lips they'd be smiling. Instead, my whole body reacts to the demon's words like they crawled over my skin. A shiver sinks into my core, firing an unwanted sexual response.

Unwanted, right?

What about this damn demon makes me so conflicted?

"What do you want?"

"You." He takes another step toward my shivering form. "Why do you ask questions you know the answer to?"

In hope the answer has changed? "Why do you continue to stalk me when you know the answer?"

"We've been through this." His arms cross, eyes

narrowed on where my fingers clutch the sheet to my chest. "You should be my servant and yet, you are not. You should obey my every command, and yet, you do not. It is perplexing."

Way to go, Gin. Give a demon something to chew on. Oh, wait. What am I thinking? Anything the demon chews on besides me is preferred.

"Sorry?" I'm not, and he knows it.

His soulless gaze meets mine. "Perhaps in the days ahead, you will value my help."

"I—" *won't*, sits on my tongue but I snap it off. Perhaps it makes me a bad person, but as long as the demon won't eat me, kill me, or fuck me, who's to say he shouldn't help me?

How screwed up is my life that I can think that with a straight face?

And how hella bad is my life going to get to need to call upon said demon's offer of help?

I don't even want to know.

"That's kind of you to offer."

"Perhaps a kiss to seal the deal?" His gaze rakes down my torso, back to my lips, the look as tangible as a feather stroke.

"No chance." Not again. The only time Zagan kissed me, he ensorcelled me first, drew my lust to his, joined the two together like strands of rope. Then his tongue sliced into mine, while his evil thoughts bored deep into my brain, threatening a hemorrhage. If it hadn't been for T's consciousness jumping into my body—a perk of being twins—Zagan would have controlled me. Or killed me.

And yet, part of me—a defective part—craves him.

Luckily the flawed part cedes control to the more

rational one. For now.

The demon chuckles. "You think it will never happen again. You are mistaken. But today is not the day to prove you wrong. That day will come. For now, heed my warning."

You know you're in deep shit if a demon has to warn you.

"There is nothing to fear but fear itself. Do not let fear conquer you."

A deep breath in, a slow release. I blink. Waiting. Waiting. His lips remain closed. "That's it? You quote FDR and tell me not to let fear conquer me?"

"Heed my warning."

"What kind of warning is that? We called that Tuesday when I was a kid." I cross my arms and glare at the demon. Not smart, but hey, a glare is a good response to already known advice.

And it keeps that annoying do-me-now voice squashed.

Zagan shrugs. "It is a fair warning." He stiffens, stares at the bedroom door. "And it's all you'll get. Tonight. Good-bye, little *Justitian*. Until we meet again."

In a quick flash of portal colors, he disappears, taking with him a good deal of the shadows hiding in the room. Or maybe my eyes have finally adjusted to the dark.

A knock sounds on my door. "Gin?" Concern rumbles in the depths of Smythe's voice.

"Yeah?"

To Smythe, *yeah* equals *come on in*. He shoves open the door, eyes narrowing on my upright, sheet clutched to chest position. "What's wrong?"

"Um…" Where to start. With the demon? My *justitia's* reaction? Or why part of me wants a freaking demon?

Not going to that last one.

"Bad dream." I throw up a flimsy mental shield and tack Blake's face on it.

Smythe's tense posture relaxes a fraction. Enough for him to walk into the room. His nose wrinkles as he sniffs the air. "Why does it smell like sulfur in here?"

"I don't smell anything." I don't. While parts of his lair may smell like sulfur, to me Zagan smells, well, nice. Like home after a long, hard day.

Gah. Where's a toilet when I need to puke?

"I smell a demon." Smythe stands in front of the window, arms crossed, nose sniffing like a bloodhound on the trail of a missing person.

Busted. "Zagan might have portalled in. Did you find out anything else about my bracelet or Mom's adoption?"

His eyes flare.

I need to get better at sudden topic changes.

"Gin." The low rumble of his voice vibrates my nerve endings, the deep bass of thunder before a storm. "Why was Zagan here?"

His gaze catches mine in the half-light, reels me in, drowns me with compulsion.

I don't want to tell him. Part of me wants to hold Zagan's visit to myself, keep him hidden. Lie. The other part wants to spill all. Wants to tell Smythe everything.

Guess which part wins? Damn mage compulsion. "He gave me a warning."

One brow rises. "A warning?"

"He quoted FDR. There is nothing to fear but fear itself. Then he told me to not let fear conquer me." I bark a laugh, breaking Smythe's compulsion. "You'd think if he'd wanted to help he would have come up with something less obvious."

"That's it?" Smythe walks to my bed, sits on the end and twists to face me. "He didn't say anything else?"

"That's all." All I'll tell, that is. The rephrasing of *you're mine* I'll keep to myself. Why worry the mentor?

"He portalled into your room and gave you a warning?"

"Pretty much."

"That doesn't sound like a demon. Why give a warning? About fear of all things?"

Good point. "Do I look like I understand demons?"

"Demons don't warn people. He clearly wanted something."

"Yeah. To give me a warning about letting fear conquer me."

"Which makes no sense." He shakes his head. "I wonder why the Agency's computer didn't notify me Zagan was in your house."

"Faulty programming?" Doesn't the esteemed demon-identification computer program catch all appearing demons?

"I'll have to—" A puzzled expression crosses his brow, interrupts his sentence. He draws in a deep breath and leans closer. "Why do you smell like sulfur?"

All thoughts of the defective computer program vanish. He's kidding, right? Humans do not turn into a Hell's scent plug-in after meeting with a demon. I bring my arm up and inhale. A faint whiff of rotten egg wrinkles my nose, which naturally kick-starts my heart into a pounding this-ain't-happening beat. "What the hell?"

"You tell me."

"He didn't even make it to my bed. I mean, he didn't leave the window area. Stayed across the room." I'm babbling, an annoying habit I tend to do when nervous. Or scared shitless.

Zagan had healed me from a potentially fatal brain hemorrhage right before he tried to turn me into his servant. Something had popped deep inside, allowing a part of him, a part of his essence, to lodge deep in my being. But I thought that part had been eradicated when the Agency healer gave me a potion to counteract the poison in my body from where his claws scratched me.

Apparently I thought wrong.

I look at Smythe. "What does this mean?"

"Now that's the question of the day. I have no fucking idea."

And that scared me worse than Zagan's visit.

Chapter Seven

After a long day at work, all I want is an evening of rest. Instead, I find another item on my house in need of repair. The garage door opens halfway, emits a sound reminiscent of a train wreck, and shudders to a stop. Rather like my life in my younger years. Yep, I got my shit together. Eventually. Not so sure I can say the same about the vibrating door. I hit the opener again. And again. And once more for good measure. The gap between the seal and the ground turns into a mocking smile complete with maniacal laughter.

Definitely need a drink if I'm imagining a demon in an empty space.

Seeing how a demon appeared in my bedroom last night, I suppose one under the door isn't that far out of the question.

Talk about a sad commentary on my life.

The door is going nowhere fast. Not up. Not down. *Shit, shit, shit.* Just what I need. Another thing broken. So much for parking my car in the garage.

Where's T when I need him?

Using our mental connection, I pop into his mind. And out again fast enough to make my vision swim. Eww! Could've done without the Double-D porn show. At least he's at Jackie's. No loud noises echoing around the house tonight.

I throw the car into park, turn off the engine and

open the door.

"You okay?" Smythe stands on the porch as if he watched me drive up, his gaze bouncing from my face to the car, tension tightening his shoulders.

I wave toward the garage and step out of the car.

His attention snaps from me to the gaping space. "What happened to the door?"

"It died."

One brow raises, and his voice takes on the tone one uses with a petulant toddler. "Really?"

I shrug. Does he actually expect me to give him the low down on why the door broke? Something tells me he wouldn't believe the obvious "the world ganging up on me" explanation.

His mouth opens, closes, as if he wants to say something, but holds his words. Huh.

I guess wonders really don't cease. After a pause where I can almost see the internal wheels of his mind spinning, he strides toward the misbehaving door. Gives it a shove. Big surprise the thing stays put. "Not good."

"No shit, Sherlock."

Ignoring me, he ducks under the gap into the garage. The door shakes as he pushes it. Shakes some more. "Try pushing the button."

I lean into my car and do as he asks. A metallic *thud, thud, thud*, rips through the evening. Smythe grunts. The door starts to rise.

Hallelujah! "You fixed it!"

"Nope." The door clears his torso, his black t-shirt straining against flexed pecs, his biceps bulging as his arms stretch over his head, a nice muscle show to wrap up my day. "I found the release hook. The motor is fried. But you can manually open and close it. Do you want to park in the garage?"

"Yes. Thanks. You rock." A few seconds later, my car sits in its usual place. Every girl should have a handy mentor around. Now if he would give me the money to pay for the motor.

Chance of that happening? Zippo.

He pulls the door shut, snapping the locking bar in place. When he turns around, he does another open and close of his mouth, making me wonder what he's hiding, what he's refusing to say.

My stomach uses that moment to whine about its lack of lunch. I slap a hand over my abdomen and shut the door.

"Sorry." I walk up the stairs onto my back porch, talking over my shoulder. "I'm hungry. And tired. Long day."

"Right. I made you dinner."

"You what?" Was dinner the reason he looked like he was hiding something?

Smythe waves a hand at the back door. Is that aroma of baked bread coming from my kitchen?

I yank open the door and step inside. Yep. Definitely coming from my kitchen. The place looks like pots and pans exploded out of cabinets and into the sink, complete with caked on food, but I'm not complaining.

Smythe cooked me dinner. And made bread.

The man can dirty my kitchen anytime he wants.

I spin around to tell him thanks and slam against a muscular chest. How does he move so quietly?

Who cares? He. Made. Me. Dinner.

"You made me dinner. I think I'm falling in love."

A smile twitches his lips. "Glad to be of service." The chocolate timbre of his voice strokes low, lodging deep inside.

I step away from him before I do something stupid. Like run my hands under his shirt and rub against his skin. End my bad day with a bit of fun.

Like I used to do with Blake.

Sorrow sucker punches me in the solar plexus and I turn to the stove. Don't let Smythe notice, don't let Smythe notice, don't let Smythe notice.

"Gin?" A tinge of panic laces his tone.

I rub a hand over my sternum. Inhale a deep breath. "What?"

"What did you just do?"

I turn and face him.

His brows slash over narrowed eyes, his hands fisted at his sides as if about to throw a punch.

I force myself to remain still, sorrow yielding to my stupid ingrained reaction to his anger.

He won't hurt me. Really. We've been through this before. *Get a grip, Gin.*

"Turned to get a glass?" Thought of Blake and wanted to cry?

"For a split second, you disappeared."

Was my theory correct on making a wish three times to the *justitia*? Did my words cause me to vanish from his view? Or did Smythe smoke crack while I wasn't looking?

"I'm not a mage."

"How did you disappear?"

"It was really nice of you to cook my dinner. I really appreciate it." I turn and grab a glass out of the cabinet.

One large palm encircles my wrist, while his other hand removes the glass from my grip.

My breath hitches, a flood of adrenaline hitting my system like a snort of cocaine. Try as I might I can't stop the fine tremor jerking the muscles in my limbs.

Smythe releases my wrist like I'm contagious. Then he wraps his hand around my bracelet, and a soothing wave of peace rocks through my body, lowering my heartbeat, calming my breathing. Yeah, I'm controlled by an entity living in my nervous system.

At the moment, I don't care.

"The disappearing?" Remorse carves a path in the muscles of his face, fading into determination as he speaks. So much for redirecting him.

Looks like I have to tell the truth. Or some semblance thereof.

"I thought of Blake and didn't want you to see the reaction. So I turned away. Since I didn't leave the kitchen, I'm not sure why you think I disappeared."

"You vanished, and I had to concentrate to see you. What did you think right after you turned?"

I don't want to give away my newfound secret. I might need to use it one day. But as I look into his eyes, I'm sucked into their depths, a gentle wave of wanting to come clean washing over me. I want to tell him exactly what happened. No hiding. No lying.

The next thing I know my lips form the words. "I repeated 'don't let him notice' three times. I didn't know that would make me vanish."

Damn it. Did he just use his magic compulsion mojo to make me admit what should be kept secret? One of these days I'm going to learn how to resist his allure. And his spill-all spell.

Good luck with that one. His thought or mine?

"Has that happened before?"

"How should I know? I can't tell if I vanish. Can I eat dinner now, or are you going to quiz me all night?"

Indecision flashes through his eyes, but he steps back and gestures toward the oven. "I put your plate in the oven to keep warm."

"That was really nice of you." What a shame he spelled me into telling the truth.

I pull open the oven door and blink a couple of times. Smythe really made me dinner. Steak, a baked potato, and string beans with cut almond slices along with a thick slab of fresh baked bread decorate a stoneware plate.

He. Made. Me. Dinner.

Holding the plate like the precious thing it is, I straighten and head for the table, swallowing what feels like a ball of molten lava. Sure, T's fixed me dinner. Blake's brought something over. But neither of their dinners caused tears to form behind my lids.

Must be PMS'ing.

I'm no longer mad at Smythe. He's my new BFF. If being spelled to tell the truth results in a free dinner, hey, spell away.

With the first bite, I swear I've died and gone to heaven. "This is really good. Where'd you learn to cook?"

"Taught myself. You've never had that reaction before?"

I swallow. Stab a green bean with my fork. "Nope. It's nice to have dinner on the table when I get home."

"Thank you, but that's not what I meant."

"You're like a dog with a bone."

"No other *Justitian* can disappear on command."

"How do you know? Maybe they all can and just keep it a secret."

"If that was true, after several millennia, the secret would've come out. Yet another enigma about you."

Dinner suddenly tastes like dried ash. The bond formed between the *justitia* and me is different, but so are other things having nothing to do with my shiny new bauble and everything to do with a past better left alone. How far will Smythe pry before realizing my life is a glossed over mess?

I plaster a cheap smile on my lips and hope he thinks a full mouth causes the expression. "Can't say I'm not unique."

Smythe sits across from me. "No one ever said I'd have an easy job."

"Thanks a lot. Love you too."

"Something needs to be done about your job situation."

"You know how I feel." Pay me equal to my job and I'm theirs full time. Until then…

"You're too tired when you get home. If you were called to a minion attack, you wouldn't be in prime condition."

"A girl's gotta make money somehow. Preferably legally."

His lips twitch as he rubs the bridge of his nose. "How bad was it today?"

"Why Smythe. First dinner and then concern. I'm beginning to think you want something tonight." I waggle my brows.

He knows I'm teasing.

I think.

For a brief second the air tingles with tension as his gaze meets mine. A jumble of thoughts dance through my mind. Smythe and me in bed. Sweat beading on our skin. The scent of sex heavy in the air. And then the moment vanishes, snapped out of my mind like a door slamming shut.

Smythe swallows.

I stab another green bean and stuff it into my mouth. Definitely not acting on that thought. The eleventh commandment of Gin states: thou shalt not sleep with thy boss. Or mentor. No matter how sexy buff he is. Nope. Not happening.

"I know you had a bad day, but something happened." His raspy voice clues me in I'm not going to like what he's going to tell me.

I should've known dinner wasn't out of the kindness of his heart. Whatever news he's about to share must be bad. Really damn bad if it required a steak dinner and homemade bread to smooth over.

"Blake's father was shot and is in a coma. They aren't sure he's going to make it."

Chapter Eight

My fork pauses halfway to my mouth. Someone shot Mr. Calder? No wonder Smythe looked like he wanted to tell me something when the garage door broke. "What happened?"

"He went to visit his neighbor. Our good friend Dr. Sheevers. Police suspect Blake's dad walked in on a robbery since he was shot in the entryway, but no one's sure what exactly happened because Dr. Sheevers is dead. Said he died from blunt force trauma to the head. Found his body in the living room. Blake's dad is in surgery at Dallas County Hospital."

A cold ball of ice slams into my middle, spreading to my limbs, confusion turning my mind to mush. Mr. Calder shot and Dr. Sheevers dead? Who would do that? Why?

"Okay. I see why you cooked me dinner." I shove the last green bean around the plate, no longer interested in eating. If I didn't know better I'd think the shooting was related to Blake's death.

"I had planned on dinner. But I thought the bread might help."

"Smart man."

One side of his mouth kicks up, pride written in the crinkles around his eyes. "We probably should check it out. Since a demon paid Dr. Sheevers's grad student a visit."

"Are you kidding? Not tonight."

His expression goes from proud to you-did-not-just-say-that in under a millisecond. Must be some sort of record. "We need to check it out before the trail goes cold."

"You're assuming there is a trail. And minion trails can last for more than a day. As you said yourself, I'm not in top performance shape since I worked all day. We can go first thing tomorrow. Do you really want to share space with the police?"

"The police don't bother me."

"You don't think they're going to connect big hunky guy with false credentials with a string of recent murders and attempted murders?"

"They don't know my badge is false. They see it as real."

"You're missing the point."

"No, I'm not. And no, they won't connect the dots." He points to his chest. "Mage." Waggles his fingers on either side of his head. "Spell. No connecting the dots."

Okay then. "Look. Lying to the police aside. You just told me Blake's father was shot and Dr. Sheevers is dead. And since I saw his dead body in a vision, that means I have a new freakin' unwanted talent." Damn it to hell. "I need some time to process this. I thought my new job description involved hunting minions and the occasional demon. Not horning in on a police investigation. Do I look like a frigging cop?" I point my fingers to either side of my head.

"You know a good percentage of crimes are committed by minions. The sooner we check it out, the sooner we can continue to hunt the med school demon."

When put like that… "Sorry. But I'm not going anywhere tonight. Are you sure it was Mr. Calder?"

His eyes close, a sigh leaving his lips, deflating his shoulders. "Yep. Positive. It was on the news and a police report. We'll go first thing tomorrow. You look tired."

About time he noticed. "Yeah." Grabbing my plate, I stand. "Thank you again for dinner. That was a nice surprise."

"Here." He takes the plate from my hand. "I'll clean up."

"Seriously? You don't want help?"

"You're swaying on your feet."

Considering the room tilts back and forth and no liquor passed my lips today, he might have a point. "Guess so. Bright and early tomorrow then."

"Sleep well."

A tingling jolt of electricity passes into my palm as I squeeze his bare arm while walking past. Both of us freeze. No emotional reading despite my skin touching his, yet I know his desires. They echo mine. I drop my hand, severing the connection. He swallows.

"Good night Smythe."

"Night."

My bedroom looms dark, twilight shadows chased away by me turning on the light. I shut the door, lean against it and try to recover from Smythe's info bomb.

Mr. Calder was always nice to me, something that couldn't be said for his wife. And even though I didn't know him well—Cecily hated me to come over—the knowledge he hung by a thin thread of life twisted my innards into a rock hard ball.

He couldn't be shot.

And yet Smythe wouldn't lie about something like that.

I run a hand through my hair and release a pent up breath. I can't let this affect me. Other things need more of my attention.

Like will Zagan visit me tonight. I check the corners for moving shadows. No Zagan. The Big Guy upstairs must have my back.

For once.

No Blake in my room either. Which doesn't surprise me. The surprise would be if he sat on the bed and I could see him without T's help.

Will Blake return? Weren't ghosts supposed to follow the bright light and move on to another plane?

You'd think I'd know the answer to that, seeing how T sees ghosts like the average person sees cars. But ever since what happened happened, he no longer likes to discuss ghosts.

And I no longer ask him questions about the spirit world.

Chillbumps pop across my skin, and I rub my arms. Nope. Not remembering the past. I have better things to do. Like sleep.

Or work on finding Mr. Calder's shooter and Dr. Sheevers' murderer.

As if I'm a cop. Never saw that one coming. The idea of Gin Crawford as a member of law enforcement falls into the ludicrous category.

But I do make a good minion slayer.

Provided a minion shot Blake's father and killed the professor.

I should feel sorry for the dead professor, instead my thoughts turn to Mr. Calder. Poor Mr. Calder. A better person would call Cecily and offer condolences. First her son dies, and now her husband might not make it through the night.

I'm not a better person. And she wouldn't believe I called to be considerate. I know her well enough to know she'd peg my concern as sarcasm.

Maybe she's right.

Now look what I've done. Introspected myself into a funk.

I lock the door—as if that will keep out a pissed off portal-forming mentor or a demon spouting advice—and head for the bathroom. A few minutes later, I'm ready for bed.

The nice thing about working in the ER is rarely having to report for duty two days in a row. The downside is more time to hunt minions.

A jolt of joy pings through my system. Definitely not my joy. The *justitia* enjoys hunting minions. And most demons. Sometimes it can convince me to enjoy it too.

Tonight is not one of those times.

I turn off the lights, crawl under the covers and am asleep two breathes after my head lands on the pillow.

Only to awaken as an eerie scream echoes through my room. The sound raises the fine hairs on my arms. I sit straight, covers clutched to my chest as if the action keeps me safe. Upright I realize the source of the noise.

My mouth.

I stop screaming and gulp down enough air to give a horse bloat. A dream. No, not a dream. A memory. The memory. The event that changed my life and T's forever.

How long has it been since the memory invaded

my dreams? Since I relived the memory in vivid flashback?

That night stays with me, with T, but not until I was set up by the mage Samantha and attacked by minions in a park in San Antonio did the memory become a constant reminder.

Footsteps slap a fast rhythm against the wood floor—Smythe to the rescue—at the same time T pops into my head. The perk of being telepathic twins, we know when the other is disturbed even when we're miles apart.

Are you okay?

Bad dream.

Bam! Bam! Bam! "Gin!" Smythe stops pounding the hell out of my door and rattles the knob. "Are you okay?"

I paste a picture of Blake on the front of my mind, shove T to the back and face the door. "Yeah. Just a bad dream."

A pause. "Want me to come in?"

"It's okay. I'm okay now. Sorry about that."

"Nothing to apologize for. I'll be in the other room if you need me."

"Thanks, Smythe."

Heavy steps tread away from my door, fading as he returns to the living room. T pops out of his hiding place.

Was it Blake or The Dream?

The Dream. Same one.

His sigh drifts around my mind. *I'm sorry.*

Not your fault.

I could've…

We've been through this before. I shake my head

for emphasis. *What happened, happened. It's not your fault. It was me, not you.*

A real man doesn't let a woman do his dirty work.

You almost did the dirty work. Just drop it. We have to move forward.

Does Smythe suspect? Fear laces his angry words.

I draw my knees to my chest and lower my head. Does Smythe know what happened all those years ago? What would he do if he discovered our secret? *I don't know.*

He's more curious than a cat.

He wouldn't hurt me. He's saved me too many times to want me dead.

Saving you is his fucking job. That doesn't mean, given the chance, he won't turn you in.

He won't. I hope.

Don't stake our lives on it, Gin.

You know me better than that.

Long after T leaves my mind, returning to his, I sit with my knees drawn to my chest, my thoughts whirling a macabre dance. Closer and closer my memories creep to that day years ago, passing by before landing, much like a moth circles around a light. And like that moth I'm drawn in, fooled by the brightness, mistaking death for peace.

The memory spits me out in the past, fifteen years ago, in high school, from when terror filled my evenings, when I wore pancake makeup to cover bruises. Another ghost inhabits my mind, one with spittle on the sides of his mouth, his breath a fetid mixture of unbrushed teeth and too much whiskey, his right hook like unyielding steel capable of dropping me unconscious on a filthy shag carpet.

I shove at the memory, but it shoves harder and I'm back in that house, my father screaming his vile words—"You're nothing but a split-tailed whore, you little bitch"—his fist knocking me to the ground, pain a dull throb along my jaw.

I hang onto consciousness by will alone. T can't help me. Not this time. He's crumpled on the floor, a knot the size of Alaska on his head from where he hit the nightstand.

Carpet fibers dig into the skin of my back as my father pounces. My father's fists smack in time to the words tumbling off his tongue. Black spots rush across my vision. Unconsciousness beckons, the peace of death calling my name. *I need to end this. It's up to me. I will finish this.*

My fingers scramble across the grimy carpet, seeking, searching for what I'd hidden, anticipating this moment. Cold metal meets my skin, rolls as my blood-slick fingers search for purchase. Blood, thick and coppery fills my mouth. My fingers finally clasp the tire iron.

A swing. A whoosh of air. A meaty thunk.

Silence.

My father's body lands on mine in a twisted mimicry of love.

My breath fills my ears, a rush of adrenaline fueling my movements. A shove, a roll, and I'm free. I crawl to T's side.

He's moving, arms and legs flexing. He takes one glance at our father's body. His eyes flare. "You did it."

I collapse beside him on the worn gray carpet, my blood a rush of cheering in my ears. We lived. We beat the old man. Never again will he hurt us, bruise us, make us watch as he hurt the ones we love. Just like we vowed. Never again.

T grabs my hand, his face tightening as he trails a finger through the air above my swollen jaw. Anger and guilt fire his thoughts, torpedo them through my mind. He wanted to kill the old man. His hands. Not mine. But he taps down the emotions, buries them under quick planning. Seals our fate. "Don't worry, Gin. I know what to do. We won't get caught."

Only because a ghost told him what to do. The dead serial killer walked us through disposing the body. Helped us lie to the police.

I really don't blame T for never wanting to speak to a spirit again. Talking to them until their thoughts permeated your waking moments was halfway to being possessed. And cozying up to evil stained your soul.

What does that make me?

The old man had sworn he'd never hurt any of us again. We'd all heard his weak promise. The fact I hid the tire iron obliterates any self-defense plea. Might even put his murder into the realm of pre-meditated.

Hell, yeah, it was planned. Maybe not that particular night, but we wanted him gone. Having a dead killer giving T advice just helped matters along.

Not that we could explain that one to the cops.

Yes, officer. That ghost in the corner gave us an idea.

Yeah, right. Yet another trip to a psych ward, this time minus the get-out-of-jail card.

No, we took care of the problem. All the way around. The police never suspected. Mom only cared that the beatings stopped and the liquor continued to flow. Sure, his drinking buddies came around but not for long.

But Smythe wanted to know my past. Smythe was able to read my mind. Smythe would find out one way or another.

And then what would happen?

Chapter Nine

The morning struck hard and fast, light popping around the blinds and smacking my face like grease on bacon. Mmm. Bacon. I smell bacon. Am I dreaming?

My eyes open with all the speed of an ice-cold engine, in starts and fits. Definitely morning. And the aroma of frying bacon leads to one conclusion.

Smythe woke early and wants to get the seek-a-minion party rolling. Good for him. I want to avoid contact with the man who might use a mind trick to discover my secret.

But that man is currently in the kitchen with a skillet of bacon. Not to mention coffee. I can't hide under the covers all day.

Time to put all those mind-blocking sessions to good use. Provided I can remember the lessons.

I scrub a hand down my face and roll out of bed. Worrying about things outside my control never helped nothing. I didn't get this far in life by spending my time worrying. It wouldn't do to start now.

Pep talk finished, I dress and walk into the kitchen. Smythe stands at the stove, flipping bacon and scrambling eggs. Yum. Nothing like seeing a man cooking for you first thing in the morning.

Especially after he cooked for you the night before.

Yep, I could get used to this set-up. Clearly having him staying here wasn't as bad as I feared.

"Hey." I head toward the full coffee pot, the dark liquid a beacon call for the sleep deprived.

"No more bad dreams?"

Does he know? My hand pauses on the handle of my mug before I pull it out of the cabinet. "Nope. You?"

"Slept fine once I got back to sleep. Do you have those often?"

"Mmm." Non-committal noises worked best. Hopefully he'll think I'm not functioning well since I haven't downed a cup of wake-me-up.

"Want to talk about it?"

"Not really." I take a sip of the hot brew. Perfect.

Now it's his turn for the non-committal noise. Would he try to read my mind? At the start of our mind-reading lessons, he had emphasized how reading minds without permission was an invasion of privacy. You could send and receive thoughts, but to pry deeper was off limits.

Unless in the middle of a lesson.

Even then, to pry deeply, to forge past the surface thoughts into the dark recesses where memories lie like fragile filaments of gold, was dangerous. If you didn't know what you were doing you could damage the person. Permanently. Unless I brought my secrets to the surface, unless I rehashed the memories, Smythe wouldn't discover that which should remain buried. Time to think on something else.

"Gin? You okay?"

"What? Oh. Sorry. Still sleepy." Was there such a thing as a gold star sticker for best liar?

"You looked lost in thought. Still remembering the dream?"

"Something like that." I swallowed a gulp of coffee and let the heat burn away my thoughts. "So, what's on the agenda today?"

"Slight change in plans. We'll still drop by Dr. Sheevers' house but won't stay long. You'll have to get a quick reading on whether or not it was a minion."

"You'll help, right?" Mages saw the minion trails as well as *Justitians*, if not better. But for whatever reason, they let us lead the minion hunting parties. From what I gather, the only reason mages need *Justitians* is for our shiny demon-killing bracelets. Despite Smythe's assurances we are needed, it makes me wonder. How hard was it to devise a spell for activating the bracelet into a sword?

A topic for a different day.

He grins and flips a piece of bacon onto a paper towel. "As always. You'll need to eat quickly though because we're due in an hour at the Agency."

The coffee goes down wrong, and I choke. "The Agency?"

"Yep. Samantha's called an emergency meeting."

"She can do that?"

"She's one of the higher ranking mage guardians. So yes."

"Shit."

Samantha tried to kill me shortly after I became a *Justitian*. Portalled me into the middle of a horde of minions in a park in San Antonio and gave them orders to off me. Before I could stop her, she opened a portal and disappeared, leaving me to my fate. Luckily for me, Smythe came to my rescue, but no one at the Agency believed Samantha capable of such a dastardly deed so she went unpunished.

On the other hand, she came with Smythe to rescue me from Zagan's lair so I had to forgive her for the attempted murder. Somewhat forgive her. Okay, not really. She's still on my hit list. I'm still on hers. She thinks I'm white trash and shouldn't be allowed to wear the *justitia*. What do I have to say to that? *Get over it, bitch.*

Something tells me she won't.

I need to be the bigger person here, need to suck it up and play nice with despised co-workers. Really. I can do it.

"She can't hurt you at the Agency. And she's smart enough not to try it again. She knows I'm watching you."

"You were watching me before. She still tried to off me."

"You're better watched now. Want some bacon?"

Better watched? I know he can track my *justitia* somehow—that's how he found me when Samantha took me and when Zagan captured me—but his words imply another meaning. What kind of metaphysical camera spies on my life?

Did I actually use the words metaphysical camera? Talk about living a screwed up life if I can pull those words out of my back pocket without blinking.

I grab a plate and shove it toward him. "What do you mean better watched?"

"I beefed up the spell on your *justitia*." He plops two pieces of bacon on my plate and a scoop of eggs.

Some women get weak-kneed when a man gives them jewelry or flowers. Me? Tell me you can prevent my future capture by a blonde bitch mage, and I'll love you for life.

"Aw, Smythe," I grab the plate in one hand and my coffee mug in the other and head for the table. "You really know how to turn a girl on."

He snorts. "Glad to be of service. Eat up."

I don't eat so fast as gulp coffee. Past experience with Smythe and minion hunting parties left me with little coffee and a bad attitude. I'm halfway through the first cup and have two more to go before we can leave.

"You can take the coffee. Just hurry it up."

"Yes, captain." Thank goodness for small miracles.

Ten minutes later I've finished eating, brushing my teeth and changing out of workout shorts into a button down shirt and khaki capris complete with white and gold sandals. At least I look better than the first time I appeared at the Agency, the time Smythe kidnapped me.

Embarrassing.

This time I look relaxed professional.

Smythe forms a portal in my kitchen, grabs my hand, and whisks me into the passage between space and time. We land along the side of a house in an upscale neighborhood, the landscape full of manicured grass and impeccable flowerbeds. Damn them all.

The scent of roses clings to the air, guaranteed to put a grin on your face, and a stab of jealousy everywhere else. Why can't my yard look like this one?

Oh, yeah. My bootstraps didn't yank me this far up the social chain.

"Gin? What are you doing?" Smythe stands at the corner of the house, hands on his hips, one brow raised.

"Checking out the view. Pretty, eh? I can't even afford to fix the garage door."

"Don't worry about that. I took care of it."

I blink. And again. "You did?" A swallow of coffee clears the lump in my throat connected to my tear glands.

"You didn't think I'd leave it broken, did you? Come on. We need to get a quick glimpse of the murder scene. Time's running out."

He cooked me breakfast and fixed my garage door. The man needs a permanent spot in my house.

Or my bedroom.

Gah. What am I thinking? What the hell is wrong with me? I cannot make a pass at my mentor.

Taking a sip of coffee in hopes the hot liquid will pull my mind back into the action, I sweep those errant fantasies into a dark hole and follow Smythe to the front yard.

Yellow police tape strings around large oak trees two houses from where we appeared. I recognize Blake's family's home next to the crime scene. I've only been there once, but the stone mansion was hard to forget. Dr. Sheevers' house was smaller, not as ostentatious, but expensive nonetheless. The man must've been pulling down some large grants to afford a home in this neighborhood. Or maybe professors made more money than I thought.

"Do you see anything?"

I close my eyes, reach deep inside where the entity in the *justitia* joins to my nerves and ask it to show me the minion trails. The bracelet responds with a subtle vibration, its answer to my request. Had it always answered this way, and I'd never noticed?

Probably. Focusing on learning a new skill meant overlooking small clues while understanding the larger picture. Now that I have the larger picture, I can focus on the small changes and hints the bracelet gives me.

When I open my eyes, nothing but yellow tape and landscaped yard greet my vision. No minion trails. And yet I know the *justitia* responded to my request.

Guess the person who shot Mr. Calder and killed Dr. Sheevers was a garden variety criminal.

"I don't see minion trails."

"Neither do I. But there's a demon energy field leaking from the side of the house."

"Say what?"

He points, and I draw in a sharp breath. My *justitia* trembles like a tail-tucked dog. If the thing could hop off my wrist and sprint down the street, it would. I don't blame it either. What I see gives me the same reaction. Saliva freezes in my mouth as my limbs root to the ground.

A black blob of energy pulses, the twin to the demon appearance at the medical school. Judging from the reaction of my *justitia*, the same demon. The demon the bracelet fears. Yet no minion tracks dot the premises. Maybe the demon appeared too late. Maybe the thing wanted the perpetrator but arrived late for the party.

Who knows. If the *justitia* fears the demon, I sure as hell don't want to run into the beast.

"That's the same demon that appeared at the medical school."

"Looks that way to me, too." Smythe's eyes narrow as he stares at the black blob of demon energy.

"Why? What's it after? I thought you said demons didn't like to appear on earth." Although in my experience that wasn't true. Take Zagan for instance. Earthly appearances seem like his daily pastime.

"They don't normally. Looks to me like it's after Dr. Sheevers."

"Yeah, but why? Dr. Sheevers died. Doesn't look like the demon went into the house. Wasn't he found in his living room and Mr. Calder right inside the door?"

"Good point. We need to find out what Dr. Sheevers' work involves. This demon seems to be targeting him."

"It can't target him anymore. He's dead."

"Whatever he worked on still exists."

"Okay. So who killed him and tried to kill Mr. Calder?"

"It's no longer our problem. It wasn't a minion. The demon, though, we need to work on. But not now. We're about to be late for our meeting at the Agency."

Great. Just what I wanted to do. Show up at the Agency.

I get I'm supposed to kill demons and minions in this new gig. Ridding the world of evil makes me feel like a superhero. Most of the time. But the thought of meeting with Samantha and Smythe's father, David, an Agency bigwig, tenses a muscle between my brows.

I'd rather face the bill for my A/C repair.

Smythe grabs my hand and pulls me to the side of the nearest house. No windows by where we stand, only manicured bushes, no one to watch as we jump into a portal. The last thing I see are the demon strands pulsing with a vile energy. I shiver, either from the nearness of evil or the Antarctic temperatures of the portal.

We arrive in the white landing room of the Agency, the only entrance into the building I've seen. Smythe strides to the door at the other end of the room, giving a brief nod to the row of teenagers manning the computer terminals. According to him, those teenagers are mages in training and can stop a demon from invading the Agency. I'm not convinced they can manage anything other than popping a zit on the arriving creature. But seeing as wards protect the Agency from demons and minions, my theory won't be tested anytime soon.

"Coming, Gin?" Smythe holds open the door.

Time to get with the program and move. In theory movement warms a body. In this case, movement brings me closer to a meeting I want to avoid.

Decisions, decisions.

Smythe waves his fingers, hurry-it-up written across his face. I walk toward him, but stop halfway there as I pass by the row of computer terminals. The first time I came to this white room, a demon appearance in Austin occurred, catching the attention of the teenagers who initiated a call to action. Maybe they know which demon appeared at Dr. Sheevers'.

"Hey, did you guys note a demon appearance yesterday evening in Dallas?"

The nearest geek stops staring at the screen and meets my gaze. "Let me look." He drops his gaze to the screen, fingers tapping a dance against the keyboard. "Huh. Looks like there was a blip but nothing substantial. Must've been a flock of birds."

Right. Because flying birds resemble demons. Uh-huh.

"How long does a demon have to be on earth in order for your computer to pick it up as an appearance?"

Hot breath falls on my neck, Smythe's nearness

sending tingles down my spine. I glance over my shoulder.

My mentor stands beside me, clearly annoyed at getting nowhere with holding the door.

Geek boy replies, "I'm not sure."

"Thirty seconds is the answer you're looking for." Annoyance seeds Smythe's voice with a low growl.

The computer geek pales. Swallows. "Yes, sir. I'll read up on it."

"You do that."

"So," I poke Smythe in the ribs, forcing him to look at me instead of glaring a warning at the geek. "The demon didn't stay long. Your computers need to get better at locating demons. Maybe they pop onto our plane more often than you thought."

He places a hand on my lower back and propels me to the door. "Maybe. Good idea to ask if they saw it."

"Thanks."

Smythe opens the door with one hand and gives me a little push with the other.

Yeah, yeah, yeah. I get the silent message sent by the guiding hand. Move it, move it, move it.

"The demon didn't stay long enough. And you're right. We need to get better at reading the signals. I'll mention that to Dad."

I nod, my attention caught on the opulence of the hallway. Gold and crystal chandeliers line the ceiling while plush carpeting swaths the floor in a style not seen outside of Trump's apartment. How rich is The Agency? And if they have money to burn on chandeliers in an office hallway, why can't they pony up and pay my salary so I can hunt the baddies full time?

Do I even want them to pay my way? Getting my degree in nursing and my RN license took a lot of hard work, both in school and in my personal life. Do I really want to throw the hard work away for a free ride?

Did I seriously ask myself that question?

The free ride wouldn't be so free if I had to hunt and kill minions in exchange for a paycheck. And I like my job in the ER.

But still. These folks in their gilded offices had money to burn. The least they could do was to stop complaining about me working and do something to fix what they considered to be a problem.

"Gin? What are you doing?" Smythe stands by a door, hand on the handle, his tone a perfect mix of curiosity and impatience. No wonder. He's at the end of the hall.

I'm still gawking by the door to the white room, or as he calls it, the landing room. I offer a half-smile of apology while hurrying to his side. Then he opens the door to a conference room, and I'm back to gawking. A row of windows slices a wall, the scenery overlooking the Boston harbor. A table the size of my living room sits in the middle, facing a screen. A projector hangs from the ceiling. Enough chairs squeeze around the table to fit half the city.

No way in hell they can't pay my salary.

Why are they being so stubborn? The amount of money in this place guarantees that to them my yearly salary is what they earn in a day. Just goes to show the rich hold their money closer to their chests than us poor folk do.

"You're late." David, Smythe's dad, gestures to the clock hanging on the wall across from the bank of windows. Sure enough we're one minute late for the meeting.

Big whoop.

"Sorry. Had to stop by and check out a murder scene."

"Stop giving excuses, and sit your asses down."

Smythe stiffens, a fine tremor tensing his jaw. Pissed off barely scratches the surface of the emotional wave that rolls off him and smacks into me.

Family Feud 101: How to belittle your offspring in less than ten words. A game I'm familiar with.

After an uncomfortable few seconds of a glaring contest between father and son, Smythe yanks out a chair and gestures for me to sit. I sit. No sense in antagonizing an already angry mage. No telling what magical spell he might zap my way.

Once Smythe lands in the chair next to me, David clears his throat, the start to all meetings everywhere.

"Samantha has a proposition to make, so I'll turn it over to her."

As she stands, leather creaks, either the chair or her skin-tight black pants. How she shoves her ass into those things and manages to walk is over my head. My girlie parts would throw a hissy if I tried on her outfit.

Not that I would. I'm pretty sure I'd have cellulite showing in places highlighted by those pants. Doesn't look like she has that problem.

Damn her to hell.

"As you know," Samantha's glare coats my skin in ice, "My ward Micah is still in a coma from the fight with Zagan. In order to rescue Gin," yet another frosty glare glides my direction, as if I'm to blame for Zagan capturing me and injuring the *Justitian* Micah, "we traveled to his lair and mapped the way. We've never been able to do that—"

David clears his throat, raises a brow.

"Excuse me. We've not been able to do that in centuries."

David nods as she corrects her statement.

"So, I suggest we use this opportunity to wreak havoc on the demon and send him back to Hell where he belongs. Who's with me?"

The room explodes into a cacophony of voices for and against her idea, all vying for attention. My *justitia* reacts with a violent shaking, and I slap my hand on the vibrating links then drop my wrist in my lap before someone notices the malfunction. Why does my bracelet react so oddly to Zagan?

Damn thing is supposed to kill demons. Not cozy up to the creatures.

When I was captured, it was happy to see him. Now it refuses to hurt him. *No, no, no, no, no,* echoes through my head.

Not my thought. I'm down with killing the demon who tried to turn me into his servant. If only to ensure I never become his servant. A shudder worms its way through my body. How can I think of killing him? I don't want to kill Zagan. I don't want him to come to harm.

What am I thinking? Am I conflicted? Or going crazy? I'm no longer sure which one.

As long as no one here notices. Knowing Samantha, she'd convince everyone to kill me instead and take the *justitia*.

Won't let them. Can't kill Zagan.

Samantha continues to talk, answering questions,

but my hearing fades as the *justitia's* voice screeches through my head. *Can't kill, can't kill, can't kill, can't kill.* It's never spoken to me before. Given me images and feelings, yes, but nothing like this. An unhappy *justitia* is not a thing to take lightly.

The chant echoes in my mind, circling round like water flowing through a narrow channel, the rush an overwhelming flood. I slap both hands over my ears. I want to scream its words, its agony, its dilemma, but I refrain.

Smythe places a hand on my arm, his breath a hot whisper in my ear. "Are you okay?"

His touch should comfort, instead warning signals fire. What if he gets into my mind? What if he reads my thoughts and realizes I'm closer to Zagan than I should be? What if he decides the *justitia* is better off without me?

I gather all the mental barriers I can find and lock them around my thoughts. And pray that will keep Smythe from invading.

"Bad headache." Not a lie. A state of conflict tends to give a person a migraine.

"Is something the matter?" David's angry tone cuts through Smythe's concern.

"Headache. She needs to go home."

"Bullshit, son. She's going on this mission, headache or not."

Is he crazy? What if I was really sick and not using a headache as a cover-up for my still vibrating *justitia*? Of course, if you are the leader of a group of mages whose job it is to kill demons and you've been awarded the ticket to a demon lair, you're going to jump on that express train, sick employees be damned.

Can't blame him for wanting a dead demon.

But what can I do to stay behind?

"Get another *Justitian*." In any other conversation the finality in Smythe's voice would end the discussion. Unfortunately, David fails to pick up on the ultimatum.

"There's not another available."

Seriously? Are the other eleven engaged at this very moment in minion fighting?

Smythe's face mirrors my thoughts. "Gin is the only available *Justitian*?"

"We thought this mission would work best if the mages took it on. We can kill the minions. Might not permanently damage the demon, but it would hinder his ability to create chaos on earth if we take out his force."

"Might work better with a couple of *Justitians*."

"Don't want to risk the loss of lives."

"But my life is okay to lose?" What the fuck?

"I didn't say that." David leans forward, hands slamming against the table. "You've been there before. You know what to expect. And that's the most powerful *justitia*."

Yeah, but as it's doing the shimmy on my wrist, most powerful is not the thought that comes to mind.

"She's…" Smythe pauses, his sentence continuing in my mind, *not ready*. But as completing the sentence would reflect poorly on him as a mentor, he swallows instead. Nice to know my own mentor considers me amateurish. I am, but still. A little support would be nice.

"Yes, son?"

"She's not well experienced in combat."

"Nonsense, son. She killed a minion the first night she wore the bracelet. She's experienced enough.

Besides, we're sending in a team that can protect her. She's going. Understand?"

Smythe glares but jerks his head into a nod.

"Good. The vote shows we'll leave in an hour. Samantha, give us the run down on the attack."

Samantha's speech blows by me, her words a hum of background noise. How am I going to get out of this?

While I don't mind killing Zagan's minions, the thought of going up against him sends a jolt of anxiety through my system. My *justitia* refuses to fight the demon—okay, who am I kidding, I refuse to fight him, too. Can't blame all my anxiety on the pesky bracelet. After all, he saved my life. Rescued me from a demon about to annihilate my ass. Sure, he tried to make me his servant, appeared in my bedroom, and in general creeps me out, but a part of me relates to him.

It's a defective part and usually smothered. As long as I don't have to go on a mission to kill him.

Smythe leans over, his lips brushing my ear. Tingles dance a tango across my skin, chasing away my case of nerves.

"It's not really a headache, is it?"

When I face him, his lips are only inches from mine, but he doesn't move. A jolt of awareness slams through my system, a do or die reaction having nothing to do with swords, and everything to do with a little horizontal action.

Yeah, right. We're in a boardroom. About to fight a demon. Sex should not be on my mind.

And since he asked a question, I focus on speech and not a million other things I could be doing with my lips. "Not really."

"Cramps?"

"Smythe!"

Oops, I said his name a bit too loudly judging from the cessation of attack plans and the curious stares thrown our way. I wave a hand.

"Sorry."

Samantha gives me a final glare and continues the battle plans.

I turn back to Smythe. My mentor wears a grin the size of Alaska. The little devil. "Shouldn't you be paying attention to the plans?" I whisper.

"Shouldn't you be telling me the truth?"

I blink. No, really, I don't think I should. But I'm saved from a response by David clapping his hands twice.

"Grab your stuff and meet in the landing room. We leave in forty-five minutes."

The room empties faster than a keg at a frat party, leaving Smythe and I parked in our chairs.

David stops by his son on his way out the door, a wrinkle creasing his brow. Worried about the mission? Or some other aspect of his job? "Stay safe, son." One hand clamps on Smythe's shoulder and releases, the male way of showing silent support.

"Thanks. See you on the other side."

Tension rolls off David, and my fingers itch to touch his skin and get a look into his emotions. His eyes narrow on me as he pats Smythe's shoulder twice. Does he know what I'm thinking? I wouldn't put it past him. Smythe has an uncanny tendency to read my mind without me knowing he's inside, so why wouldn't his dad have the same scary ability?

I drop my gaze to the table before he spells me into telling the truth.

After two more pats on Smythe's shoulder, David marches out the door, ramrod straight, taking with him the roiling mass of tension.

I shove the chair back and stand. No sense in staying in here. "Did you catch anything they said?"

"No," he shrugs. "But the game plan rarely changes. I'm more concerned about you. If not a headache, then what?"

Why couldn't I have been assigned a mentor who forgot easily? Instead I get the human equivalent of a bulldog gnawing a bone. I've only been with Smythe a week and a half, but I know once he gets a hold of something he won't let go until I spill.

Talk about annoying.

"I'd rather not say."

"Are you going to have a problem fighting?"

"I'm good to kill minions. No worries." As long as Zagan wasn't there.

"Is your *justitia* moving?"

Great. He noticed.

"Maybe."

"Why?"

"It's happy? Come on, let's go. Tell me how this works."

"You know, you have a habit of changing the topic when you're hiding info. What is it this time?"

Busted. Shit. "Really. I'd rather not say."

"Don't make me use magic to pry it out of you."

I shove the chair under the table and hope my glare gives him pause. He crosses his arms and raises a brow, silent speak for *spill it*.

Do I dare? He knows Zagan tried to make me into a servant, but does he realize the extent I feel for the demon? How my *justitia* refuses to harm him?

"It's complicated."

"We have forty minutes."

"My *justitia* is friends with Zagan."

"Excuse me?"

"Friends. Pals."

"I know the meaning of the word, Gin." Apparently Frosty Glares 101 is a required class for guardians, judging by how Smythe excels at it. "Why do you say they're friends?"

"It's screaming in my head not to kill Zagan. That it can't kill Zagan."

"That doesn't make them friends."

Should I tell him how happy the bracelet was to see the demon? How the demon called it his old friend?

In for a penny, in for a pound.

"When he captured me, my *justitia* was happy. Happy, Smythe. Like one of those videos of a dog greeting its master whom it hasn't seen for months." The *justitia* jumps, silver links pinching my skin. I shake my hand until the sting dissipates.

The bracelet is not happy I told Smythe. What did it expect? For me to lie? If it wanted that outcome, it should've tried a little harder not to be so conspicuous and stopped dancing a jitterbug on my wrist.

Lying might be second nature to me, but there was only so much spin I could put on the obvious.

I expect f-bombs to rain like hailstones, instead Smythe throws a couple of blinks and a what-the-hell expression at me.

Then his eyes narrow on my *justitia*, a teacher's stare to a disobedient student. "After your capture you mentioned they knew each other, but this is not what I imagined."

"It's not something I wanted to share."

"No kidding. Why does your *justitia* feel that way?"

"I don't know. I think there's a lot about the *justitias* the Agency failed to mention."

"You're new so there's a lot you don't understand yet. I've been here my whole life, and I can pretty much promise you talk of *justitias* and demons being friends has never happened."

"Neither did talk of what the runes mean. It took a demon to explain those to me." Three sets of runes encircle my bracelet. According to Zagan one set is his name, one set is the name of my *justitia,* and the last set is the name of the first woman to wear the bracelet. The fact the runes meant something surprised the Agency.

"Zagan is a liar. Good God, Gin, he's the demon of deceit. How do you know he spoke the truth about the runes?"

Oh, let's see. I have his symbol tattooed on my neck courtesy of his claw. The same rune is on my bracelet. Doesn't take an idiot to know Zagan tells the truth.

He might be the demon of lies and deceit, but he's telling the truth about the *justitia.*

I might be spilling the proverbial beans on the clandestine friendship of my *justitia* and Zagan, but I'm not talking about my unwanted tattoo. At least not until I figure out why it's on my neck. .

No sense in worrying the mentor more than he already was.

"The *justitia* confirmed it. Not everything he says is lies. He says someone at the Agency wants me dead and hired him to do it."

"As I said before, you can't hire a demon. You bind it to you and it's a stupid thing to do. Not to mention dangerous. Your spell could backfire and leave you a servant of the demon. Forever."

Yeah, bad idea. Don't have to tell me twice on that one.

"But Samantha hired minions to try to kill me."

"Minions are still humans. No magic mojo involved. Money would hire a minion." His eyes widen. "Why didn't I think of that earlier? Where's my laptop? I need—"

"Hold on there, buddy. While I'm down with you finding evidence to put that bitch in her place, it's about time for us to meet up with everyone else. And we have no supplies. What do we need?"

Smythe blinks twice in rapid succession. "Oh. Right. Supplies. I need my sword. Leather pants. You need something more geared toward fighting. Business clothes won't get you far in a demon fight."

I follow him to his apartment and into his bedroom, too lost in thought to pay much attention. I snap out of it when the door clicks shut behind him, leaving me staring at a pile of clothes on the bed. The lack of remembering my trip to here bothers me less than the upcoming fight.

How the hell do I avoid meeting Zagan? Has Smythe done the math and concluded I'm in agreement with my *justitia* over the plan to not attack the demon? What will happen if someone on the team notices my indecision?

Maybe they'll think it's because I'm a newbie. It could happen.

More likely they'll try to kill me. Which they might try to accomplish anyway.

I do not have a good feeling about this mission. Not at all.

But there's not much I can do to stop it.

Chapter Ten

A dominatrix minus the whip and heels stares back at me from the mirror. Skintight leather pants encase my ass and just as I thought, the ole booty doesn't look half as good as Samantha's. Damn it. A long-sleeved black t-shirt and a pair of thick-soled black ankle boots round out my new look. I don't even want to know who left these clothes in Smythe's apartment. Okay, that's a lie. I very much want to know. Clearly he's not telling me something. First thing to do before today's adventure: ask why he has women's fighting clothes in his closet.

Another glance in the mirror proves leather pants are not my friend.

Neither are mirrors.

Time to stop wishing I'd paid more attention to my butt at the gym and get this party started.

I open the bathroom door and step out into the living room of Smythe's apartment.

My mentor stands arms crossed, face bunched into we're-running-late creases. He's dressed in identical black leather pants, but his pair highlights muscular thighs and ass and makes women in a five-mile radius drool. A black tee, shitkickers, and a dangerous aura round out his outfit. Mr. Lethal with a killer bod.

I sure wouldn't mess with him. Fuck him, yeah. Mess with him, not likely.

Since the Agency doesn't pay me to imagine Smythe's muscular body thrusting into mine, I lock those thoughts away for another time.

Like when I'm alone in my bedroom.

"Are you ready?" Irritation slides off his words. "We're almost late."

"Just trying to figure out how to move in these pants. Speaking of, since when do you have women's clothes lying around? Something I should know?" I waggle my brows, trying for teasing to cover the green tinge of jealousy wending around my heart.

Being jealous of Smythe having a potential girlfriend ranks up there with banging one's boss.

Stupid, stupid, stupid.

But I can't help how I feel.

He freezes, color slipping off his face. Crap. Him telling me about a friend with benefits pops into my mind. A former friend. One currently keeping company with Blake in the afterlife.

Damn. And here I had to go remind him of her.

I step closer, give his shoulder a squeeze. "I'm sorry. I forgot."

He waves a hand in a no-big-deal motion as color returns to his cheeks. But the look in his eyes belays his casual tone. "I got rid of all her clothes but the fighting ones. The pants, the shoes, the shirts. Thought another mentee might need them."

Another mentee? His last fuck buddy was his mentee? Clearly Smythe has never heard of the eleventh commandment.

"Smart thinking." Saving the clothes, that is.

He shrugs, holds open the front door, gestures me in front of him. "They look good on you. You should wear them more often."

"That would imply a lot of minions. And I'm not sure my girlie parts can take this for long." I yank on the crotch, wiggle my ass. Ah. Relief.

A chuckle escapes his lips, low and throaty, as his gaze rakes my body. "Better not hurt those things. Now get a move on."

He strides to the elevator and punches the button. Within seconds we're gliding down to the first floor and fast stepping it to the landing room. The clock above the row of computers shows one minute to the hour, but we're the last to arrive.

No one talks. Maybe it's some sort of mage ritual to remain silent before a demon fight. Or maybe they're just as nervous as me.

David speaks as soon as the clock strikes the hour. "May your spells strike true, and may many minions fall. See you when it's over."

Samantha steps forward, hand held toward the wall, palm glowing hellfire red. Her words wrap around my ears like cotton batting, thick and muffled. Latin? Or something older?

A portal opens in the corner, a huge, warm air-belching wormhole big enough for the twenty of us to walk through. I grab Smythe's hand. I don't trust Samantha. For all I know her portal would drop me into the space between time where I'd drift in nothingness forever.

Smythe grips my hand hard, letting me know he won't let anything happen in the portal. En masse we walk into the in-between. The icy chill sinks into my marrow, catches the breath in my lungs. A zinger of panic explodes in my chest. What if I die in this cold space between places? What if…

The stench of sulfur assaults my nose a second before a flash of light illuminates the exit, the combination soothing the burgeoning panic. Unfortunately, it fails to help me breathe. Was the stench of sulfur this overpowering the last time? I don't remember it being this bad.

Trying to survive a head injury, a demon capture, and the grief of losing my lover apparently dampened my sense of smell. Who would've thought?

We step into a small room, walls and floor paved in gray stone. I remember this room. Zagan healed me here, tried to turn me into a servant three paces away from where I stand. Kissed me.

I shudder. Not diving into that embarrassing memory.

Samantha stands by a metal door, the door leading into Zagan's throne room/bedroom/study of bad interior decorating. Her hand raises in a fist, the other grips the knob. One, two, three, her fingers count down. She points at the door while yanking it open. Twenty mages and I storm through the doorway and into the middle of the room before stopping. Where was everything? Even the tacky, clichéd throne was missing.

Nothing stood in the large room except the pillars and white marble. A shimmy of joy shakes my bracelet and reverberates through my system.

Safe, safe, safe, safe, safe, chants through my mind.

My lips tug upward, and I fight to keep the grin off my face.

"Damn it," Samantha slams a palm against the nearest pillar. "He escaped."

The metal door slams shut and we all jump.

Tension saturates the air like humidity before a storm, thick and suffocating. None of us stands near enough to the door to have closed it. Maybe a strong draft no one noticed blew through the room. Better guess: we just walked into a trap. A bead of sweat trickles down my spine.

One of the mages strides to the door and tries the knob. "Locked."

A chorus of expletives echoes against the cold marble. And then the door on the opposite side of the room opens, a contingent of minions spilling into the room, each wearing a shit-eating grin and a sword strapped to their back in a harness.

Back-harnesses-R-Us for evil beings must be making a fortune.

A couple of mages crack their knuckles, while others grab their swords. With a battle cry that would make a Viking proud, Samantha leads the mages, swords clashing as the two sides meet. I press my back to the wall and hold out my wrist.

Come on, come on, form a sword already.

Since when does my *justitia* not go into sword mode when a minion is around? Damn malfunctioning thing.

I close my eyes and imagine the entity attached to my nerves then send it a signal. A loud, start working right signal.

As if it suddenly becomes aware of its surroundings, the links tighten on my wrist then release with a pop, the sword extending outward two feet. Finally. Nice to know the thing has no problems with killing minions, even if the evil humans do belong to Zagan.

Now for a test run of the leather pants.

I dash into the melee and engage the nearest minion. Stab, slash, and his head rolls. Must be a newly made one. Or a lucky strike on my part. Gray mist hovers in the air like smoke in a club, the demon's essence escaping dead minions. I should stick my *justitia* into the middle of the mist, killing the essence, weakening the demon.

But I can't. The gray mist belongs to Zagan.

Clearly I have problems. And they have nothing to do with the minion rushing toward me.

I raise my sword, step back into a defensive posture, waiting for his attack. Before he gets to me, a rush of warm air blows onto my back and a strong-arm bands around my waist, pulling me against a broad chest. Too short for Smythe. My *justitia* shakes a greeting a second before the minion's eyes widen. He pulls his swing, skidding to a halt, a mixture of shock, disbelief, and fear streaking across his face in alternating waves.

Then he bows. Oh shit. My heart jumps as if shocked by a defibrillator, my breath and limbs freeze. My only movement the *justitia* happy dancing along nerves.

Nice to know one of us is thrilled.

"My apologies, master." The minion speaks to the floor, bent over in the middle of a fight. How is everyone missing this scene? A quick glance shows minions and mages engaged in a battle, not a one paying me a lick of attention.

"Never," Zagan speaks, his accented words rumbling from his chest into my back, "harm this one."

"Yes, master."

"Go."

The minion rises from his bow, his eyes locking on mine, his gaze searing my soul. A tingling starts in my feet, and the minion vanishes, left behind as a kaleidoscope of colors and Arctic temperatures swallows me into its depths. A portal. The damn demon snagged me in a portal. Again.

This time I'm uninjured and not frightened. Relatively speaking. Aw, hell, I really need to stop lying to myself. Despite the *justitia's* happy vibration, I'm scared. Maybe not as scared as the last time but scared nonetheless.

I will not pee my pants. I am an adult. Pulling these pants off will be enough of a challenge dry.

We land in another marble hall complete with Zagan's things. Antique wardrobes and four-poster beds mixed with modern furniture gives an eclectic feeling. Those were the nice parts. The rest looks like a cross between a BDSM trade show and a blast into the 70s. A green and yellow plaid couch sits on red shag carpet overshadowed by a table containing chains and shackles. The table looks familiar. Kind of like the one Samantha blasted my ass into the last time we paid the demon a visit.

Almost the exact same furniture arrangement as the last time I was here. Including the throne. Twisted in the shape of writhing humans, the iron monstrosity sits on a dais at the end of the room.

Remind me not to hire his decorator.

"Mmm," Zagan's lips brush behind my ear, over the rune of his name, and an unwanted shot of lust drives into my core. "I like my mark on you. It smells good."

I shove against his strong arm, wanting to be free, wanting to be wrapped in his arms. Conflicted is not a state I enjoy. He chuckles and drops his arm from my waist.

As soon as he releases me, I step forward, putting as much distance between us as possible without running to the opposite side of the room. When I turn to face him, I'm greeted by a wall of glass overlooking the fight.

As if we stand in the same room as the fight, but out of sight. I run my damp palms along the sides of my hips.

"Where are we?"

One brow raises, his tone that of dealing with a toddler. "My home."

"But there wasn't a wall of windows the last time."

He tsks. "Don't you sense what is happening? Or has your guardian not shown you illusions?"

"Demons can cast illusions?"

His laugh tightens my skin, shivers goosebumps out of hiding. "Some demons. You of all people should know things are not always as they appear."

I swallow. "So we're in the same place but you made it look different."

"I'm good, yes? Do you think they are fooled? Yes? Good, good. I have plans."

I cross my arms. Who's pretending to not be afraid of the big, bad demon? "You always have plans. I'm not going along with them. I refuse to be your servant."

One side of his mouth kicks up. "Ah, yes. I believe you've mentioned that before. This refusal confuses me. But it is what it is. For now."

"For all time."

Demons must take classes in how to give shit-eating grins guaranteed to twist a human's innards into soft spaghetti. "We shall see. For now, you must kill me."

I stiffen, my *justitia* freezing my nerve endings. My head shakes before my mind weighs in on the movement.

"No? I see," the name rolling off his lips belongs to my *justitia*, ancient and unpronounceable by the human tongue, "hates the idea. Do you know why?"

"It considers you a friend. Don't ask me why."

He laughs. "I like your mouth." He eyes my lips as if he remembers the taste of my blood. The taste I accidentally gave him. An experience I hope to never relive. "More lore the esteemed Agency forgot to tell you."

"They don't know half of what you told me the last time. And I'm not going to help you." I lick my lips but manage to straighten my shoulders. Fake it until you make it. I will not be afraid of the hot demon. I will not. "I'm a demon huntress. Demon killing is my specialty."

Dark eyes open and close, his lips twitching. "Demon huntress?" One hand slices through the air. "Another day. Time is short. My plan must be completed. You will kill me."

I shake my head. I can't kill him. I can't.

"Pretend to kill me."

Okay, now that I can do. I no longer question why I can't kill him. I should question many things about him, about us. But standing in this gaudy throne room, next to a demon I don't want near me and yet can't get enough of, I hesitate. Refuse to voice the million questions dancing through my mind. Refuse to wonder why I want to help him. Refuse to tell him no.

How can I be a *Justitian* and work for the Agency if I can't destroy this demon?

Maybe he really does control me.

Help him, help him, help him, my *justitia* chants.

Do I have another choice?

"Pretend to kill you? Why?"

"Curious little human aren't you? I find I like that about you. But I need you to act, not question. Here's what will happen."

When he finishes speaking, my breath catches. Can I do this? Can I lie to the people I work with? Can I deceive Smythe?

It beats the alternative of killing Zagan.

"Okay."

Before I can blink, he's by my side, a portal forming around us, popping us back to the fight. It takes less than a second to realize no one missed me, and two seconds after that for everyone to focus on Zagan. Including the minions.

Do they know his plan?

I find Smythe in the now-still crowd, his eyes narrowing on the demon standing beside me.

"What?" My voice squeaks as I slow turn toward Zagan, as if I'm clueless and don't realize he stands beside me.

Now my eyes widen. He's there, but not there, light fading through and solidifying on snarling features. He looks mad, but I see through the illusion, see Zagan standing feet away, not beside me. The image projected raises a hand, forms a fist. My *justitia* releases a laugh that streaks across my nerves, fuels my strike.

My sword stabs through the illusion's chest, blood streams in a fall of red as the fake Zagan drops to his knees, hands clawing at the sword before face planting on the hard white marble with a meaty thud. Flames explode, the body incinerating into ash. The minions disappear, vanishing as if they never lived.

Shit. Didn't see that one coming. Zagan must have cloaked them in his illusion.

Smythe's eyes remain narrowed, his gaze bouncing from me to the downed fake Zagan. Everyone else claps. Amend that. Everyone else except Samantha. You'd think she'd be happy. As far as she knows her plan worked. Unless she saw through the illusion.

I'm pretty certain Smythe knows a fake when he sees one.

Several things happen at once. I'm surrounded by congratulatory mages patting my shoulders, offering praise for a job well done. Samantha stands to the side, arms crossed, her face a mask of emotions impossible to read from this distance. Smythe stabs his sword to the side as if he sees a minion standing there. As it requires effort for him to yank the thing back, maybe he does.

Above all else, I hear Zagan whisper in my ear.

I spin and, yep, the damn demon stands next to me, invisible to all the mages surrounding me. A shot of joy pounds my heart into a happy-happy rhythm, tempered only by the realization I'm a worse person than I thought. I let a demon live. Helped him create an illusion.

What kind of person does that?

Friend saved, friend saved, friend saved. My stupid *justitia* chants a mantra of my deceit.

"Good job, little *Justitian*. My grateful thanks. I'll see you later." His farewell touch on my arm burns against my skin through my shirt and I shake it off as he forms a portal and disappears.

But I can't shake off the six five mound of muscle elbowing the mages out of his path.

"Smythe. Did you see?" I point to the burning pile of fake Zagan and hope he thinks my shaking hands are due to the fight and not a byproduct of lying.

"We need to talk."

"I'm sure we do, but not now."

Did you think you could get away with this? Did you think I wouldn't see?

Uh-oh. If he resorted to a telepathic accusation, he's madder than he looks. And he looks like a Texas spring storm, a black fury complete with bursts of lightning warning of a potential disaster. On the plus side, he's not yelling. Out loud, that is. So much for Zagan's illusion being foolproof. Time for an attempted redirection. *See what?*

Don't play games with me. The growl in his words vibrates through my mind like a slap.

My gaze drops to my feet as I struggle to stand still and not run. He's not going to hurt me. This is Smythe I'm talking about. Smythe. Not a memory, not a learned response to an angry voice. Smythe. My mentor.

I will not run. I am strong. He's just upset. And can I really blame him?

I clear my throat. Raise my eyes. Pitch my voice to a barely audible level. "Can we do this later? No one else noticed."

His jaw locks, fingers flexing, and once again I freeze. Only to shake it off. Smythe is not a character

123

from my past. He would never hurt me.

I really need to work on my reaction to his anger.

"Let's go." Samantha kicks the pile of smoldering ash, interrupting our silent conversation.

This isn't over. His words leave a sour trail of anger in my head, my stomach echoing the response.

I swallow the urge to puke. I accomplished my goal of getting out of this fight alive and without killing Zagan. But was hiding behind an illusion worth angering Smythe?

Chapter Eleven

We march behind the pack into the stone walled room that smells like sulfur, Smythe's hand like a heavy stone on my shoulder, weighing me down with guilt.

Would he interrupt the exit? Tell the mages I didn't really kill a demon? Or tense his jaw tight enough to grind his molars into dust?

I glace at him. Option three it is.

Samantha forms the portal home and part of me wants to take my chances with her instead of trusting Smythe to get me there safely. He keeps his mouth shut, but anger roils over the edge like a boiling pot with a tight lid.

I want to apologize, to plead for his forgiveness, to ask for his understanding. Would he understand? How can I explain a relationship I both fear and crave? How do I explain the need to protect Zagan?

Protect a demon? It's official. I've lost it.

He's a freakin' demon. He can protect his own damned self.

I'm telling Smythe everything. Everything.

If he'll listen without yelling.

The portal swallows us, spits us out in the landing room, the brightness of the white walled room frying my retinas. I blink but have no time to adjust. Smythe grabs my arm and marches me past excited voices toward the door. Wait, wait, wait. Scratch what I said earlier. Talking to Smythe while he wears his fuck-off expression ranks lower than partying with Samantha.

"Shouldn't we stay?"

"No." He yanks the door open at the same time David spots us.

"Son! Glad you made it back okay. Where you going?"

Smythe pauses, shoves me through the opening into the hall. "Out."

"Heard you killed the bastard."

"I didn't touch him."

"Wasn't talking to you." He nods my way.

"I stuck my sword into him, and he burned into a pile of ash." Gah, that sounded like a line from a bad romance novel.

David grins, for all appearances believing my tale. "Good job, Gin."

"Thanks." I paste on a smile and hope it seems real.

"We're leaving." Smythe takes a step forward, stopping when David puts a hand on his shoulder.

"Why the rush?"

"I need to talk to Gin."

"Can't it wait?"

"No. You know I don't like parties."

David drops his arm, his eyes gleaming blue daggers. "Then enjoy your talk."

Smythe waves and marches me down the hall. I turn, one hand offering David a little wave. But he's gone, the door to the landing room clicking shut, leaving me alone with an angry mage on a mission.

The elevator chimes a welcoming beep and the

doors slide open. Smythe releases my shoulder the minute the doors snap shut. Guess he realizes there's nowhere in this tiny box for me to run.

And I want to run. His anger wraps around me, thick and smothering. I tighten my left hand into a fist until the knuckles blanch. *Stand straight, don't slump, don't act afraid. I am not afraid. This is Smythe. Smythe. Smythe. Smythe. Not a ghost from my past.* The doors ping open and he gestures me out first.

Spine straight, I quick-step past him. No fear. Yeah, right. I vacillate between knowing he won't hurt me and thinking he might. But no brush of air warning of an impending strike tickles my nape. Only the whispering glide of the closing doors. The pounding beat of my heart echoes in my ears, shudders through my veins, a trembling chant of doom.

Smythe strides past me, holding open the door to his apartment as if he's trying to impress me. More like he's trying not to explode where others can hear.

I'm two feet into the apartment when the door clicks shut. Not slams. Clicks. He's madder than I thought.

"Gin," his soft tone creeps along my skin, the low weight of my name on his lips more a warning than a shrill bell.

A full body shiver snakes through me as I turn and step to the side. Out of his reach.

Or so I thought. His hand bands around the *justitia* and a cold spell twists through my veins, rooting me in place. Electricity spirals through my limbs, along nerves, testing the connection between the *justitia* and me, searching for another entity.

Full-blown panic sets in as the spell weaves from

my lower body, across my torso, settling in my neck. Over Zagan's mark.

Shit.

With a pop, the spell releases me, and I sag. For half a second, I think Smythe will let me land on the floor, but he grabs me under the arm and then around my waist, lifting and carrying me the few feet to the recliner.

My mentor, infuriated but still kind. Because he's a gentleman or to mess with my mind?

Why am I so distrustful? This is Smythe I'm talking about. Like certain computer specs: what you see is what you get.

And currently what I get is a man pawing strands of loose hair away from my neck, his finger scrubbing off cover-up. It's too late to yank away. To try and run. Besides, I want to tell him everything.

Don't I?

Smythe curses a string of his favorite f-bombs. Okay, so clearly right now is not the best time for a metaphorical purging of my soul.

He stops pacing by the kitchen counter, back to me, hands on hips, his sword sheath covering his spine. The hilt pokes out a few inches above the leather sheath, black leather covering steel. With a quick grab and twist, he could yank that sucker out and whack off my head.

"It's tempting." My telepathic mentor turns, crosses his arms, and leans against the counter.

I swallow and do my best to move as little as possible. "Glad you are refraining."

"What were you thinking? You lied to me. How am I supposed to trust you if you lie?"

"I know what it looks like, but I didn't lie."

"Then how do you explain that mark on your neck?"

"I don't know how to explain it. So I didn't. That's not a lie."

His jaw stiffens. "That's a fine line, and you know it."

I shrug.

"What else are you hiding from me?"

Plenty. None of which involve Zagan. None of which I'll tell. Stick to the topic of demons.

"The mark appeared a couple of days after he clawed me, but I didn't sense him inside me. I only sensed the *justitia*, not him."

"Why didn't you tell me about it?"

My fingers clench, knuckles whitening. Admitting fear is hard for me. Admitting fear when I want to appear strong even harder.

"I was scared." The words barely pass into the land of audible, but Smythe hears them. Some of the anger wrapping him in tension abates.

"You should have come to me."

"What would you have done? What are you going to do?"

"My spell shows his presence in that mark, but no place else inside. You were right about that. It's not a strong presence, but after that stunt you pulled today—"

"Wasn't a stunt. And I didn't pull it. Only followed along."

"Same difference. What the fuck were you thinking?" His fingers clench until they blanch. "You are supposed to kill demons, not join them in theatrical illusions."

"I can't kill Zagan. My *justitia* won't let me. It knows him. They're friends."

"Friends?" One brow raises in disbelief. "You said that earlier."

"Yep. Friends." I hold up the bracelet and give my wrist a shake. "It won't work right around him. It'll kill the minions, but not their essence. It refuses to hurt Zagan."

"Impossible."

"Yeah? Then how do you explain its wailing in my head at the meeting, refusing to kill? It told me to help him. I can't kill him. Even if the bracelet refuses to do its job. I can't kill Zagan. I don't want to." My voice drops to a whisper, an admittance of a wrong I don't understand.

"So you plotted with him to make it seem like he was dead."

"I did no such thing. I obeyed his request." Yeah, like that sounds a whole hell of a lot better.

"Are you his servant?"

"Of course not! I don't think so. I don't want to be. But I can't kill him. Only him. Other demons"—I point at my chest—"I'm your huntress."

"*Justitian.*" His grin sticks on his lips not affecting the pissed off gleam in his eyes. "Why did he insist on the illusion? Why not fight us? Or just disappear?"

"He wants the Agency to think he's dead."

"Clearly. Why?"

I throw my hands up, the universal sign for no effing idea. "I don't know. Do the others suspect?"

"I'm surprised no one noticed." He shakes his head. "You'd think they would've realized the minions vanished instead of dropping to the ground like they usually do when their host dies."

"You killed one, didn't you?"

His lips twitch. "Yep. Wanted to make sure I saw through the illusion."

"I couldn't see them. Just your motions. And I really don't know why Zagan wants to pretend to be dead."

"You'll understand if I don't believe you."

Trust is a valuable thing. Once it's gone, retrieving it becomes challenging, if not downright impossible. To think Smythe doesn't trust me, to think my actions today damaged the burgeoning respect between us, twists in my chest like a knife.

But I have no one to blame except myself. He sure as hell didn't ask me to cozy up to a demon. No, Smythe asked for nothing but my truth.

And truth for me was hard to give.

"I'm sorry."

"A little late for that now."

"Where do we go from here?"

He sighs. "I don't understand this relationship you have with a demon."

"You and me both."

His eyes narrow, and I close my smart mouth before it gets me in more trouble than I'm already in.

"Tell it to me from the beginning."

I draw in a deep breath and release my entire experience with Zagan like a purge of toxins. The longer I talk, the higher his brows raise, until I come to where Zagan talked me into helping with the illusion, and his brows slam low over his eyes, muscles tensing in his biceps as if he aches to throttle someone.

I stutter and keep on going. Perhaps it's foolish, but

I trust he won't give into the impulse.

When I finish he draws in air through his nose. I expect steam to come out his ears, but instead he stares at me as if I've grown an extra appendage.

Silence settles, a smothering stillness. I want to drop my gaze, to stop staring into his eyes, but I don't. Holding his gaze puts me on equal footing, not collapsing into a trembling heap. I'm stronger than that.

Fake it until you make it.

"Why does a demon want a *Justitian* as a servant? Why does your *justitia* react that way to him? Why does he want the Agency to think him dead?"

"You sound like a petulant toddler, Smythe. Why, why, why."

His eyes tighten then a grin twitches his lips. "They're valid questions. You don't seem to know the answer to any of them."

"You should know the answer to the last one. I'd think all demons would want the Agency to think of them as dead. Then they wouldn't be hunted by my sword sisters."

"Sword sisters? Never mind. All demons want the Agency to stop hunting them. So far none have pretended to be dead."

"How do you know?"

He pauses, blinks, as if the thought never occurred to him. "It's been centuries since we tracked a demon to its lair. Most kills happen when they appear on earth. And once dead, they stay that way."

"Okay, okay, I cede the point. Speaking of demons walking the earth, any idea why one was outside Dr. Sheevers' house?"

Smythe sighs, one hand rubbing over his head in a

gesture reminiscent of T when frustrated. "Maybe it's tracking a killer?"

"Then why appear at the med school? Why kill a grad student?"

"Now you sound like a petulant toddler." His grin spreads to his eyes, and tension releases from my muscles. Our argument might not be forgotten, but he has on his game face, concentration on the problem demon top priority.

Thank God.

For once my sudden topic change works.

"They're still valid questions. Where's your laptop?"

"Your house." His face shutters, as if anything having to do with me makes him remember our argument. Dammit. "Let's go. I'll take you home."

"Shouldn't we at least pop in for the party?"

"No. It's not really a party."

"You said…"

"I know what I said. It's probably over anyway."

"Did you lie to your dad?" I raise a brow.

Red tinges his clenched jaw. "I do not like attending parties. So no, I did not."

"Uh-huh." I point to him, "Kettle," touch my chest, "Pot."

Why am I not surprised he ignores the jab?

"Come on, Gin. I'll take you home."

Chapter Twelve

I drop my clothes into a pile in the bathroom. Surprise, surprise, the leather pants came off. After a few tugs. And what's up with all the red creases marring my backside? Allergic reaction to minion blood? Rash? Too tight pants?

Ding, ding, ding. Answer number three. As if there's any question.

On the plus side, black leather hides bloodstains and spatters, and protects my skin from minion cooties. Guess I'll be wearing those bad boys again.

My shower takes less time than removing the pants. When I walk into the kitchen, Smythe sits at the table, laptop whirring a merry tune of internet hunting. Can he really find info about *justitias* and demons online? Maybe he browses the demon-net.

Demon-net. Ha. Aren't I funny?

He lifts his head as I walk to the cabinet, his gaze full of tension that flails against my skin, a whip of distrust.

I caused this ache between us, my behavior, my fault, my responsibility to heal the break. If only I knew how.

As far as I know, time travel doesn't exist. Of course, up to a couple of weeks ago, I thought demons didn't either, so clearly what I know is questionable.

"Hey, find anything?"

A long pause, as if he debates whether to tell me his findings. Sadness curls behind my heart, leaks into my tight chest. I hate this tension. Knowing I screwed up. And not just me. My *justitia* and its refusal to do what it was designed for and kill Zagan held most of the blame. I'm pretty sure it overrode my impulse to rid the world of a demon and replaced it with cozy feelings for said demon.

That's my story and I'm sticking to it.

For now. Later I'll try to communicate with the damn thing and get it to tell me what its problem is.

I lead a strange life to think communicating with an entity in my bracelet is doable.

Smythe releases a noisy breath. "You won't like it."

"Give it to me anyway."

"Micah died."

My hand pauses halfway to my glass. She died? Samantha's ward died? I expected news about the demon, not what happened to my fellow *Justititan.*

"I thought she was getting better."

"They were unable to bring her out of the coma. At first she got better, but then she took a turn for the worse."

"Is that why Samantha led the attack on Zagan? Because she knew her ward was dying?"

He thumps the laptop screen. "From the records it looks like she was improving when Samantha decided to plan the attack. But while we were in Zagan's lair, Micah took a turn for the worse and passed away."

Head injuries are fickle things. But usually a turn for the worse lingers longer than the time it took for us to attack Zagan's lair. Usually.

Smythe's narrowed eyes make me think he feels the same. I reach for the tentative connection between us, the pathway of our joined minds and run into a metaphorical brick wall. Guess my telepathy lessons have ended.

"I'm really sorry to hear she died. I bet Samantha is freaking out." I even feel a tad bit sorry for the blonde bitch.

But only a tad.

"Does a head injury patient who's recovering die that fast?"

I nod and fill my glass from the fridge. "They can."

"I think someone killed her while a good number of mages were on a mission."

"That's one hell of an accusation."

"I know," he shrugs, "but it's what my gut tells me."

"What does the old gut say about who did it? And how?"

"How's easy. Two spells come to mind. Dark magic, though. The kind Agency mages shouldn't use."

"Then how do you know them?"

He raises a brow. *Nope, not going there* rushes through my mind. Telepathy? Or facial expression?

Either way my curiosity is piqued.

A question for later. Once he trusts me again.

If he trusts me again.

A tendril of sadness unfurls behind my sternum, and I rub at the ache with my free hand.

"Fine. Don't tell me." I take a sip of water as he continues to stare in silence. "Who do you think knows a mysterious spell of dark magic?"

"Do you try to be a smart ass, or does it just come

naturally?"

I offer him a friendly finger gesture as I take another sip.

He shakes his head. "Several mages know those spells. All of whom were at the Agency when she died."

I want to point out that not all who knew the spell were at the Agency, but my lips stay shut. He already thinks me a smartass.

"I can't believe any of them would want her dead. Why go to the trouble?"

"Maybe she knew something they didn't want told."

"Micah?" He gives a double brow raise. "She was by the book."

"Then how did she get paired with Samantha?"

"They were friends."

"Seriously? Sam—" I'm about to ask, Samantha has friends, when I remember she and Smythe had a thing once upon a time. No sense angering the beast by reminding him of his poor choice in bed companions. "Huh. Didn't think they'd pair friends."

By his expression, I know my almost slip did not pass unnoticed. But he chooses to not elaborate on the topic.

"They try to pair companionably."

"Then how did you get me?"

"You weren't supposed to have bonded with the *justitia*. I was supposed to return it."

"But you knew when I killed a minion. You appeared in my kitchen." And about scared the holy daylights out of me.

"Since I'd already made contact with you, I was

told to carry it through if need be."

"You make it sound like you didn't want to be my mentor."

"You knew nothing about this life." Sure, it sounds like the training level was just too hard for him, but beneath the surface a volatile mix of anger and self-loathing boils.

He lost a mentee, his friend with benefits. Though he has never told me the details. I wonder how long ago it happened.

Well, I'll be. Another question for my list of things to ask Smythe when he trusts me again.

I definitely need to figure out how to get him to trust me. Too many unanswered questions for my liking.

"Then why did you take the job?"

"Dad ordered me to."

"So without your dad's orders you never would have met me?"

"Pretty much."

"Then who would be my mentor?"

"The next person on the list. We try to rotate. That's why it was such a surprise I was chosen again as a mentor."

"Does that mean Samantha is out of rotation?"

"Possibly."

"Do you regret the order?"

Silence fills the kitchen. I force myself to hold his gaze, to not drop my eyes, to not appear weak. But I cringe inside. I shouldn't have asked. I know the answer. And when he speaks it's no surprise.

"At first. You were…are…troublesome."

"Troublesome?"

"Stop interrupting. You wanted the answer. Let me speak." Anger tints his words red, a warning to keep my mouth shut. I nod, pressing my lips together as proof of obedience. "Then mysterious things started happening around you. And I like a good mystery. But after this morning and that stunt you pulled with a demon. A demon, Gin. I'm not so sure."

I nod. Try to not notice the consuming ache swallowing my stomach. "I'm sorry."

"Well, you still present a good mystery. No *Justitian* has ever sided with a demon before."

"I didn't side with him. I just stabbed an illusion of him."

"Same difference."

Not really, but with his tone full of bitterness, I offer a shrug. "I can't kill him. I don't know why. Yet. I'll try talking to it"—I shake the bracelet—"tonight. Maybe it'll talk back."

"And then what?"

"I'll tell you about the conversation."

"Will you?"

"Of course." Unless the conversation makes me look worse than I already do. "Will you tell me why I have his mark on my neck?"

"A demon should not be able to mark a *Justitian*. Or control her. Or get her to do his wishes. You are a first."

"So you're saying you have no idea."

"I did not say that. I said you are a first. More research is needed."

Translation: he has no idea but refuses to admit failure.

"Okay. You staying for dinner?"

He glances at the kitchen clock and back to me. "That time already, huh? Sure. I'm in the middle of a search."

"Whatcha searching?"

"Trying to discover what the good professor worked on. Top secret. Makes it hard to hack the system."

"Maybe you should hack the government using some other IP address. I don't want the FBI storming my house."

"Gin, Gin, Gin. I'm better than that. Trust me. I don't get caught."

Right. There's a first time for everything.

But he has a point. I pity the agents assigned to bring him in. Smythe the mage, who lobs fireballs and hacks minions with swords versus the FBI with guns. The poor guys don't stand a chance.

Smythe huddles over his computer and stays that way while I cook, his fingers alternating tapping a tune on the keyboard and drumming against the table. He appears oblivious to me sitting across from him during dinner, although he manages to offer a thank-you for the meal.

The thrill of computers over social interaction.

"I'll clean up. Just leave it in the sink." He waves a hand toward the sink, eyes fixated on whatever webpage flashes across the screen.

"Thanks. I'm going to bed."

Dinner and prospective conversation fail to get him to stop staring at the computer, but me hauling ass to my room gets a shocked expression. Go figure.

"It's not even eight."

"Yeah? Well, you drug me all over God's green

earth today, and I have to work another twelve-hour shift tomorrow, so deal with it. Thanks for cleaning up. I'll see you in the morning."

He answers when my hand touches the doorknob to my room. "Good night."

****

Creak! Noise cracks through my dream, eradicating strands of sleep faster than a beeping alarm clock. Echoes of the distinct sound of butt hitting creaky wooden chair cling to the walls as if waiting for the chance to pounce. I am not alone.

My senses strain to hear breathing or movement. My heart pounds a racing rhythm as I still, trying to even the fast, startled breathing of wanting-to-gasp lungs. Shadows dance across the wall in front of me as I lay on my side, but the noise came from behind me, from the door. The urge to remain frozen, to pretend like I heard nothing, battles with adrenaline zipping through my veins.

I can barely make out the sound of air traveling through another's lungs. Barely. But enough to know I'm not alone.

Someone is in my room.

Is it Smythe? Why would he sneak into my room in the middle of the night? No good reason. He, like my twin, would barge in here as if they owned it, slamming the door against the wall, making enough noise to both wake me up and ensure me of a known presence.

If not either of them, then who?

Terror seizes me in its maw and shakes. My hands tremble, my palms sticky with sweat. Not a minion. My *justitia* remains a bracelet.

A bracelet with a tremor. The tremor grows until

the links rattle. A shot of joy chases away the terror, and I realize who sits in my chair.

I take a deep breath, grab hold of the covers, and roll toward the sound.

Light trickles through the blinds, dim, but enough to outline a person sitting in the chair near the door. The pounding of my heart slows as terror recedes, as the outline faces me. My *justitia* vibrates a nice-to-see-you-again tune, making the ID of the intruder a no-brainer.

Zagan.

Now I have a whole other set of chills.

"What the hell are you doing in my room?"

"Enjoying the view."

My hand pauses halfway to the light on my nightstand. No sense in giving the demon-perv a better glimpse. "You know, as much as I like these nighttime visits, you can leave me alone now." I flick my fingers his direction and hope my being a smartass will stop him from noticing my fingers shaking.

Some demon huntress I am.

His chuckle carries hints of darkness and menace. "You know I cannot."

"Sure you can. I'm a *Justitian*. You're a demon. The two don't mix."

"They told you that?" Disbelief shades his tone.

"Pretty much." Not in those exact words, but why be specific? "So what's with following me around? You can't turn me into a servant, and the Agency thinks you're dead so you don't need to be released from your vow or whatever."

After he captured me, he'd told me someone at the Agency had bound him, forced him to promise to capture me and return me to them. Whoever "they" were. Yet another mystery in my life.

"So much talking. Humans enjoy hearing themselves talk. Demons enjoy hearing humans scream."

I'm pretty sure he smiles with those words, but I'm too busy shaking off chills to care. Ignoring my discomfort, he continues.

"It is not a vow. The person from the Agency bound me to them—"

"Who was it?" Interrupting a talking demon might not be the smartest move around, but knowing the identity of the guilty party would cut down the time required to discover who wants me dead. Not to mention outing a traitor.

He snarls. "Part of the vow prohibits me from telling. Or showing. Or in any way disclosing their identity."

Well, damn it. "So you can't tell me who the person was? Not even if it was a man or woman?"

"Did you not hear what I said? No. You must discover this on your own." He waves a hand. "As I was saying before you interrupted. Technically the vow is still in effect since I am not dead. But since they believe I am, they should not bother me again. Thanks to you."

"Hate to tell you, but Smythe saw through your illusion."

Zagan stiffens. "They know I am alive?"

"As far as I know, no one else caught on, and he didn't tell them."

"Why would he do that?"

I pause. Then go with the first thing that pops into my head. "Because it would get me in trouble. And be a black mark on his record." My assumption makes sense, especially the latter. Who wants a warning in their personnel file?

"Ah. He does not want further black marks."

"Further?"

"The whelp did not mention his black marks, eh?"

"No." Not entirely true. Like me, Smythe deals in half-truths and obscurities.

The hypocrite.

"Interesting. Very interesting. Everyone else believed the illusion?"

"As far as I know. No one said otherwise." The adrenaline no longer pounds through my veins, but Zagan's presence twists my emotions into a tangle of confusion. I want him to stay. I want him to go. I want to stop experiencing a split personality. "You might want to leave. I'm gonna have to mention to Smythe you showed up."

"I see." He nods, his head moving a slow up and down. "You wish him to trust you."

I snap my gaping mouth shut. "How did you know that?"

"I am a demon who listens. Not all do, no, not all. Those are stupid creatures. Fear raisers, but stupid." He leans forward, elbows on knees. "You must take precautions against fear. Don't let fear conquer you."

"You've said that before."

"And I'll continue to say it until you have conquered fear."

"Great. Wanna tell me how to conquer fear? Wait. Start by telling me what I fear so badly it needs conquering."

He leans back in the chair, wood squeaking at the

position shift. "If I told you, it would not be challenging."

"Yeah? And why's that a problem?"

He chuckles. "Little *Justitian*, if you are not challenged, you will not learn. You must learn. Train. Conquer. Yes?"

Sounds like the anthem to a superhero movie. Now starring Gin Crawford and her equally odd twin, Tonic. Yeah. Right. As if everyone needs to know our parents named us after their favorite drink.

"Whatever. How did you get into my room?"

"So many questions. You are such a curious creature." With a creak of the chair, he stands, moves toward me. "So curious."

I try to move, to scoot away from him, to activate the *justitia*, but remain frozen, a mouse mesmerized by a snake. His eyes form dark pits of obsidian, shadows dance in waves across his skin. One hand encircles my *justitia*, and a jolt of electricity scorches my skin. The *justitia* answers with its own jolt, a stab of light arcs from the bracelet into the demon, turning his hand and forearm a glowing blue.

Zagan jumps backward, shaking his hand, and the spell he wove around me breaks, snapping me into movement. I'm on the other side of the bed, standing, covers clutched against my chest like a shield before I realize I moved.

"What the hell were you trying to do?"

He stops shaking his hand, his head tilted to the side as if a hawk staring at dinner. "It doesn't matter. It didn't work."

"Doesn't matter?" My voice squeaks into a higher octave and I clear my throat. "Were you trying to fry me or something?"

The second the words leave my lips, the answer comes in a flash of knowledge, the *justitia* showing me images of the distant past, of magic and demons. Of women twisting spells holding them captive into spells freeing them of demonic influence.

A past lost. A past morphed into a myth. A past forgotten until now.

I shake my head, the memories of other *Justitians* who wore my bracelet disorientating in their intensity. Surely not. Surely I saw the wrong pictures, jumped to the wrong conclusions.

"I will not fry you. But I will see you again. Until next time. Heed my warning."

Zagan raises a hand and disappears in a stench of sulfur, leaving me dazed and unbelieving. Perhaps the bracelet took a lesson from the demon and lied.

Yeah, right. The one thing I know, the one thing I trust is the *justitia*. Lying is not in its nature. I might not like what I saw. I might not believe it. But I now understand how my *justitia* knows Zagan.

The demon created the damn thing.

Chapter Thirteen

Bam, bam, bam! My door vibrates from a heavy fist. What do people think my bedroom is tonight? Grand Central Station? I glance at the alarm. Two minutes before it's to go off. Figures.

"What?"

"Get dressed!" Smythe's voice carries none of the sleep noticeable in mine and enough hurry it up for the both of us. "Dr. Sheevers' lab was just broken into."

"Smythe. I have to go to work. What part of that do you not understand?"

"You need to come with me and look for that demon. Now get dressed."

"Work, Smythe. No can do."

"Get dressed, and I'll take you to work afterward."

"Fine. But if I'm late you're explaining what happened to Nurse Hatchet." My boss is a stickler for punctuality. Late is not in her vocabulary.

"Deal. Now hurry it up."

Five minutes later, I yank open the bedroom door, dressed in my scrubs and sneakers, my eyes puffy from lack of sleep courtesy of Zagan. Demon visits tend to keep one awake for the rest of the night. Especially when they come with more revelations than John the Baptist experienced.

When I walk into the kitchen, Smythe grabs my arm as he speaks the portal forming words.

"Wait. I haven't had—" *my coffee* never leaves my lips as he thrusts a mug into my hand, never breaking the rhythm of the spell. Gotta love the man. He might not trust me, but he knows me well enough to know I don't function without a large amount of wake up juice.

The portal swallows us, the freezing cold a breath stealer, but lucky for me the coffee remains steaming hot when we arrive at the medical school.

We're halfway down the hall, striding toward a shield of blue clothed police and security before the caffeine kicks in and my sluggish brain coughs up questions. I grab hold of Smythe's arm and yank him to a stop.

"How did you know about the break-in?"

"You really are slow in the morning."

I shake the coffee mug a little and raise a brow. His lips twitch.

"Police scanner."

"Where do you hide that thing? I've never seen you with it."

The lip twitch becomes a full-on grin. "I hide it in places you haven't seen. Yet."

Attraction slides low in my belly and rolls south. The electricity arcing between us intensifies the longer our gazes lock.

"Oh?" I lean forward, drop my voice to a whisper. "Where is that?"

He taps his ear.

I roll my eyes. "I've seen your ear."

"Yeah, but you haven't seen inside it."

"Nor will I. Whatcha got in there, a wire thingy?"

"In a manner of speaking. Must we go through this now?"

I'm about to say *yeah, we must*, when Nurse Hatchet's face pops into my mind. Can't be late to work. If I continue this conversation then very bad things could happen.

Like a mark in my personnel file.

"Fine. But we will go through it. Later. When I get off work. Along with other things."

"What other things?"

I take a sip of coffee, wink and walk toward the blue coats. Smythe steps beside me, his voice pitched low as he grabs my arm.

"What other things?"

"My favorite demon stopped by for a chat."

"What?" The word echoes against the walls like a hard slap. Every head at the end of the hall turns our direction and one of the cops leaves the pack and strides our way.

I nudge him in the side. "Look sharp. I'll tell you tonight."

"Like hell you will. You'll tell me—"

"Excuse me," the cop's voice booms over Smythe's words. "This is an active crime scene. You can't be here."

After a round of narrowed eyes and a glare strong enough to melt my marrow, Smythe shoves his hand in his back pocket and pulls out his fake badge. A quick open and close, and the cop falls under his spell.

"Agent Smythe, FBI and this is my consultant. We need to look at your crime scene."

"Of course. Right this way."

The cop leads us past the swarm of blue-coated security and through a card-coded door propped open by a stack of books. He stops inside the door, one hand gesturing to the back of the room where several plain clothed detectives talk in a huddle.

"The detective in charge is Zucker." With those words, he leaves us alone.

Smythe strides forward, badge and hand extended. Another introduction, another open and close of the badge, and two more of Dallas's finest fall under his spell.

"Fill me in on what happened."

"This is a locked lab with card access on the hall door. Only the professor and his grad students have access into the lab and only the professor and his doctoral student have access into the biohazard portion." He tilts his head toward the metal door next to him. "The professor was found dead in his home yesterday, probably homicide. The doctoral student went crazy two days ago, stabbed another student before taking his life."

"Yeah, we were called in to that one too." Smythe nods in a false show of camaraderie.

"Because of the deaths and the absence of the professor's access card among his possessions, the hall door was silent alarmed last night. A little less than an hour ago, security noted the alarm going off. When they got here, the hall door was shut, but this door was open a crack. We called in the FBI as soon as we realized what work was being done here, but they said it would be an hour."

"We came immediately, but the main force will be here later."

The detectives nod as if Smythe's explanation makes sense. And it's true. The FBI will show up. Hopefully after we leave.

He might work an awesome spell, but I'd prefer to not take chances.

"And what was in the lab?"

"Didn't dispatch tell you?"

"I want to hear it from you."

"Anthrax. The professor had a contract with the government to work on anthrax."

My brows pop so far up my forehead it gives me a headache. Anthrax? Where's a biohazard shower when you need one?

Suddenly my coffee no longer appeals. Neither does the mug. The news even shocks Smythe into stunned silence.

"Are we safe? Was it contained?" My voice squeaks into action.

"We were told by a grad student that it was contained. This door leads to a chamber and beyond that is where the research took place. We did not look past this door."

"Weaponized anthrax?"

"No idea. The research was secret. That's why we called you guys."

"We'll look around. The rest of the team needs to arrive before we can enter the lab."

This half of the *we* is not entering that lab. This half of the *we* is hauling ass out the door. If Smythe wants to look for a demon, he can activate his own damn demon tactical grid.

I take a step back and he grabs my arm.

Look for the demon signature first.

Are you fucking kidding me? Did you hear him? He said anthrax is behind that door. I'm outta here.

Not until you look around.

I glare at him.

He glares back, determination in his eyes.

I know that look. I'm going nowhere until I do what he wants.

With a sigh I thrust my mug into his hand and close my eyes. After a few deep breaths, along with rationalization that the anthrax was not going to independently hop out of its container and into me, I tap into the entity residing along my nerves. The *justitia* responds with a subtle vibration, its answer to my request. When I open my eyes, nothing happens.

I know the *justitia* activated the minion/demon sensors in my eyes, but no minion strands or demon energy blob exists in the lab. Thank God. Now I can leave, find a biohazard shower, dump my scrubs and coffee mug, and make it to work on time.

Then my bracelet vibrates a different tune, one reminiscent of a child hiding from a murderer. What sounds like a thousand claws raking against metal shakes the room, vibrating goosebumps across my skin. Smythe and I turn toward the noise, the detectives remain huddled in their conversation as if they don't hear the chill-inducing screech. Maybe they don't.

Lucky them.

A red slash appears in the corner, hovering in the air a foot above the meeting of two countertops. Heat pours out as if someone opened a hot oven. Or a passageway to hell.

Black energy seeps from the growing gash, a weeping sore in the air, heralding the arrival of the demon. My *justitia* whines, a whimper for my ears only, as it forms a sword.

"Fuck," Smythe mutters.

My thoughts exactly. Demon in a lab with human witnesses.

And here I thought my nighttime visit from Zagan was the low point of my day.

"Is it hot in here?" One of the detectives asks.

I'm too fascinated with the incoming demon to pay attention to the huddle of brown suits, but Smythe mumbles something to them about it being cooler in the hall. The black blob of demon energy grows into a pulsing tumor of death by the time the detectives leave the lab. My *justitia* longs to join them, which is not exactly confidence inspiring.

Who the hell was this creature to cause a demon-fighting bracelet to tuck tail and hide?

Heat and the stench of sulfur explode into the room as the demon crawls through the red gash in the air, landing on the ground in a crouch. A wave of malice coats the air, inducing a strong urge to flee.

The hair on my arms stands straight. Sweat drops down my back, beading my spinal column in a cylinder of ice. I want to run yet am frozen to the ground, prey caught in the open.

Red eyes peer from a dark face cracked with a thousand lines, a roadmap to a gruesome death. The cracks extend throughout its skin as if Hell's oven burned the creature to a crisp before spitting it out. No hair, no eyebrows, no clothes. Its lips curve into a macabre imitation of glee.

My breath hitches. The *justitia* lies along the back of my hand in sword form, the bite of cold metal an ache of remembered terror. It's crossed this demon before and lost. Badly.

Oh shit. I knew I should've stayed in bed.

I'm two seconds away from taking the *justitia's* advice and hauling ass when the creature speaks, its voice like a cheese grater along my nerves.

"A new *Justitian*. I like new ones." It inhales a deep breath. "They smell good." Its barbed tongue flicks across its cracked lips

I see my death in its eyes.

It takes a step toward me, and I take a step toward the door, trying to control my breathing into something less likely to induce dizziness. On my second step, I hit a solid wall of muscle, otherwise known as Smythe. Something tells me he's about to ix-nay me running away.

My heart pounds a rhythm of escape, and I ram a shoulder into Smythe's chest. He stands as steady as a mountain in a windstorm.

Damn it. What does he have to prove? Running is valid exercise.

Especially when faced with this demon.

My guardian steps to my side, one sweaty hand locked on my wrist. Why won't he run?

"Ah, a guardian." The demon stops by the edge of a lab table flashing me a full frontal view.

I blink several times, a mixture of disgust and relief mingling with the almost overpowering reaction to flee. No reason to be proud of that tiny package.

The parts hide inside until needed. A remembrance of the *justitia's* slams into my mind, releasing a shudder.

Good God, I hope never to see that again.

"Who are you, and what do you want here?" Smythe's tone implies the demon will give a response. He should know better.

The demon barks a laugh. Another round of chills covers my flesh in bumps. "You are not so stupid to expect an answer. I'm not so stupid as to give you one. You will go to your grave never knowing."

A glowing ball of energy appears in its hand. From one blink to the next, the creature releases the ball, aiming for Smythe. My sword moves, deflecting the energy ball into the wall. Plaster explodes, raining debris like hailstones. Small cuts appear along my arm, my hand, blood drips down my face.

Ouch, ouch, ouch. The pain disappears as the *justitia* shuts down nerve receptors. Word to the wise, do not throw energy balls into plaster. Flying plaster shards slice through human flesh like a scalpel, but bounce off cracked demon flesh. And judging by the teeth-baring grin of the creature, exploding plaster feels as good to it as a massage.

My breath catches in my throat. The world turns at a creeping pace, slow enough to see the fine muscles of Smythe's fingers twitch, to watch sweat drip down his cheek. My mentor lobs a fireball of energy at the demon, who allows the glowing thing to smack him in the chest. Flames die, absorbed by the creature's cracked skin like parched dirt.

Ohgodohgodohgod. We're going to die. We should have run while we had the chance.

Gin? T's voice, his presence in my head, penetrates the smothering fear shaking me in its grasp.

Demon. Bad one. I manage to snap the mental doors between us closed, but his intrusion helped. I no longer want to pee my pants.

"That all you got, guardian?" Demon holds its hands in the air, forming two glowing balls of light.

Something shifts inside me, deep inside, as if I possess a never-before-used reservoir, which finally opens wide. A strange energy fills me, leaks from my pores like sweat, fires my nerves with strength.

By the time Cracked Flesh releases its pitch, that strange internal energy covers me with a fine red sheen, the equivalent of a plastic tarp in a rainstorm. And just like rain does on plastic, the demon energy ball drips down me, pooling at my feet, disappearing into the beige linoleum.

Smythe isn't so lucky. His shield, if he even formed one, breaks and he flies backward, slamming against a wall before falling face down on the floor.

The sight of his unmoving body hits me with a jolt of adrenaline. He can't be dead. I scream his name, but he remains nonresponsive. Anger rushes through me, a waterfall of rage washing away the urge to escape.

This damned demon is going down.

I let loose with a cry that would do a karate master proud and swing the *justitia* at the demon's head. The sword whistles through air as the demon leaps to my left, his movements a blur.

What the…

I slam into the side of the table, my stomach a screaming throb of pain. My brain churns, trying to process how I got here. Wasn't I just standing?

The demon grabs my hair, raises my head. I've played the demon form of whack-Gin's-head one too many times not to know the outcome. Putting my free hand on top of its fist, I swing the *justitia* down and back, blade grazing along the cracked demon flesh. The demon loosens its grip.

I kick, connecting with the thing's knee, then twist

my body.

But demons must be impervious to knee kicks because the creature acts like the kick is the equivalent of a tap, tightens its grip and slams my head against the edge of the table.

Fuzzy spots swarm the edge of my vision. My knees weaken. The demon no longer uses my head as a hammer, but its grip on my hair tightens as it drags my unresisting body along the cool, plaster shard covered linoleum floor. A mixture of rage and fear fires my muscles into movement. My feet gain purchase as my free hand slaps against the demon's grip on my hair.

As I rise, I swing the *justitia* into its upper thighs. Yeah, yeah, not a killing shot, but at the moment it's impressive I managed to swing the sword instead of collapse upon it.

The demon yelps and drops its grip on my hair. I scoot backward, using the black lab table to pull myself upright. Fuzzy spots line my periphery, but I draw in a breath and point the *justitia* at the creature.

"Leave me alone."

"Or you'll do what? Scratch me with that thing again?"

Yeah. This fight is definitely not going well. I don't dare glance to Smythe to see if he's moving—please God, let him be alive—as the demon would use that moment to strike.

"Leave me alone, and I'll return the favor."

The *justitia* squeaks, disbelief vibrating along my nerves, its fight instinct overruling the earlier desire to flee. It wants to kill this demon. Wants to rid the world of the creature's malice.

Wants to finish this fight with me intact.

"Favor? You think me leaving you alone a favor?" Its laugh rolls across my skin, dampening my flesh with fright.

The fear sinks deep inside, down, down, down into that previously unknown reservoir of energy. I close my eyes, focus on that reservoir, grab the energy with both hands, and yank. Energy streams out of its hiding place, coating my skin with a red-hot power.

Cracked Flesh's eyes flare. "Impossible."

Yep, definitely impossible. Now that the power has made itself known, I have no idea what to do with it. I try to gather it into a ball to pitch at the demon, but nothing happens.

At least nothing with the energy. Cracked Flesh from Hell busts out a laugh. A marrow chilling cackle. It holds a hand toward me, palm beginning to glow red.

Oh, shit. This is not good.

A slap sounds to my left, a palm smacking the linoleum. I risk taking my gaze off the demon to see Smythe lying on his stomach, one palm flush against the floor, the other held toward the demon. Words flow from his lips like a waterfall of Latin, dripping with age and power. The air pulses with magic, beating against my flesh, thickening into an invisible wall that stretches between me and ole crinkle skin.

Lips pull off yellowed teeth as another laugh booms from its chest. "You think your puny magic can hold me?"

Double shit. Why won't my feet run away instead of freezing to the floor?

Smythe stutters but continues his chant. He's hurt. Blood runs down his face from a slice along his hairline, and the fact he remains prone instead of upright doesn't bode well. But he never wavers in his guardian duties even though the demon's laugh affects him like it does me.

I don't even have to use telepathy to know he wants to escape this creature.

No wonder the *justitia* fears this thing. How do you win against a creature with skin impervious to everything?

I will the power cloaking my skin to form a ball. To do something besides hang out and color me an electric red.

No such luck.

Red demonic eyes focus on me, its yellowed teeth snapping once as the laugh cuts into silence. "Good-bye, *Justitian*."

I feel my eyes pop wide as a bolt of red-hot demon power fires my direction. And then the room goes black.

****

Cotton stroking my cheek wakes me. I'm disoriented. Wasn't I standing? Am I standing? I perform a quick body scan, encountering a lot of pains and about to become bruises, but everything remains intact. Prone, but intact. I'm definitely not standing. Not unless the floor shifted directions and became a wall.

My cheek rests on the cool press of linoleum, my body crumpled in an unnatural—and totally uncomfortable—position. What. The. Hell?

"She's coming around."

I don't recognize the voice, and yet I know who's here. The Agency. We're saved. Thank God.

My once again concussed brain whirls in slow motion, trying to pull up the last minutes before blacking out. Smythe. Smythe cast some spell. Where was he?

Oh God. Did the demon kill him?

My eyes pop open. An Agency medic squats beside me dressed in white with a blue circle over his left breast, a symbol designating his position. Not that I've learned all the symbols, only the medical ones. My sigh of relief turns to anxiety. I don't see Smythe.

"Where's—"

"Here." Smythe answers before the rest of the sentence leaves my lips.

I shove the medic's hands away and push to an elbow. The room spins a whirling dervish. No wonder the medic wanted me to lay still. But I have to know Smythe is okay.

He lays feet from me, on a stretcher, a medic attending to the gash on his head. Pain lines bracket his mouth and eyes, but he manages a grin. "You're okay."

"Mostly." I crawl to him and use the stretcher to pull myself upright. The room swirls a dance as I lean against the side of the stretcher. Good thing the wheels are locked, or I'd shove it sideways. "What was that thing?"

"A demon?"

"Now who's the smartass?" My lips turn as I grab his hand. Alive. Smythe is alive. A sigh of relief travels through me, into him and he starts as if he touched an electrical outlet.

A pulse fires low in my core, growing stronger the longer my skin touches his. I want to ignore the hum singing through my veins, want to deny the pull, but he saved my ass from annihilation, and I need to tell him thanks.

But the words stick in my throat, a lump of regret masquerading as an inability to speak. I drop my gaze to our clasped hands. Swallow. Emotions tumble through me. Relief. Regret. Was he still mad at me?

I raise my eyes. Nope. Not mad. His gaze locks on mine, pulls me into an undertow of longing. Chinks form in his mental walls, allowing me a glimpse into his thoughts, his emotions.

Definitely not mad. At least not at the moment.

"We need to get moving." A mage steps into view, interrupting the silent communion between my mentor and me. "We can't stop time, and time is almost out. We have one minute before the feds and police barge in here. Go, go, go!"

A medic grabs my arm, breaking my grasp on Smythe's hand.

"See you on the other side." Smythe gives me a lopsided grin as two medics grab his stretcher, unlock the wheels, and form a portal. They dash through wormhole, the click of the metal stretcher wheels vanishing into the abyss. The medic holding my arm forms his own portal and a deceptive rush of warm air flows across my skin.

"Ready?"

When we appear in the white landing room of the Agency, the medic hollers for a wheelchair.

Gin? T's voice bursts into my head, his words laced with concern.

Good one, Gin. Forget all about your telepathic twin. *I'm okay. Was attacked by a demon but am okay.*

Goddamn it!

I'm pretty sure it already has been.

Huh? Never mind. You need to get rid of that

fucking bracelet before it kills you.

I close my eyes. Grit my teeth until my jaw aches. *The bracelet is not going to kill me. We've already been through this.*

We're going to go through it again until—

The door swings open, a wheelchair pushed inside by a fast moving medic, giving me the break needed to stop the impending ass chewing. *Gotta run. Am at the Agency, and they're about to take me to the infirmary.*

The infirmary? How bad are you hurt?

Not too bad, but Smythe is a mess. Gotta go, can't talk to you and them. I'll contact you later. I slam the mental doors between us closed, blocking off his curse, but leaving his anger flowing through my veins like a poison.

He hates seeing me hurt. Hates feeling my pain. I understand. The times he's been injured have raked through my soul like claws tearing at tender flesh. But despite my injuries, I like wearing the bracelet.

Provided I never have to see that scary-ass demon again.

A couple of breaths later, I'm shoved into the wheelchair and taken to the infirmary along with Smythe and his stretcher. It dawns on me halfway there that I'm due at work. Like an hour ago. And I'm half a continent away.

This is the first time in my nursing career I haven't shown up for work. Perhaps that history will sway Ruth, my supervisor. Maybe not. We don't call her Nurse Hatchet for nothing.

I reach around and tap the hand of the medic pushing the wheelchair. "I need a phone."

You would've thought I'd asked for a dragon's

head the way everyone looked at me. Smythe wriggles a bit before being stilled by a medic.

"There's one in my back pocket."

"Wait until we get to the infirmary." The medic pushing Smythe's stretcher pats his shoulder, telling him without words to stop squirming. Then he looks over his shoulder at me. "What's the rush?"

"I was supposed to be at work." One hand clutches the other until my fingers blanch. An ache slams into my chest, speeding my breathing, tightening my voice. "They'll fire me if I don't show up."

One of the medics hits the elevator button up. The others stare at me, brows raised.

"Work?"

Right. *Justitians* aren't supposed to hold jobs. Killing minions and demons was enough work without adding mundane toiling to the mix. Their attitude fails to help the sensation of a hand squeezing the beat out of my heart.

"This isn't my main career. I'm supposed to be in the ER now. Think you can take me there?"

The elevator dings, and no one answers me until the doors close and we're moving upward.

"Not until you're checked out. We don't think the demon clawed you, but we need a more thorough exam."

His words turn my marrow to ice. On the plus side, my brain forgets about the panic over losing my job and hops into oh-my-god-I-can't-lose-my-connection-to-the-*justitia* mode. The poison in a demon's claw causes the entity in the *justitia* to separate from its host's nervous system. This happened before when Zagan clawed my neck, leaving behind the mark. The healers had to mix some potion that restored my connection to the *justitia*. I don't want to go through that again. I like the bracelet right where it sits.

On my wrist.

I don't think Cracked Skin clawed me. Slammed my head into a table. Threw energy balls at me. Made me miss my morning caffeine. But I don't recall his claws coming near me.

Which doesn't mean anything. I'm pretty certain I was unconscious for a good deal of his appearance on earth.

But at least I survived. Which is more than can be said of the previous *Justitians* who wore my bracelet.

I perform a quick scan of my nerves, searching for the entity connecting my neural synopses to the *justitia*. A pulse of light purple flows along the connections, and I breathe a sigh of relief. One *justitia*, up and running normally. Thank God, the demon left its claws out of my skin.

The medics wheel me to a bed next to Smythe and help me onto the mattress. As soon as my butt hits the covers, one of the medics hands me a phone.

"Thanks."

He nods and crosses his arms, clearly waiting for me to make the call and give him back the phone. I start to clear my throat, think better of it, and punch in Ruth's direct line. A few rings later and she picks up the phone.

"Ruth?" My voice rasps and I do nothing to clear it. The worse I sound, the better.

"Gin? Where are you?"

"I'm so sorry. I was running a fever when the alarm went off and thought if I slept a bit longer, it might go away. Then I slept too long, but I still have the fever. I'm going to have to call in sick. I'm so sorry."

"You sound horrible. Just get some rest." The concern in her voice morphs into warning. "And if you miss again, you'll need to call before your shift starts. Or I'll have to write you up. Okay?"

"Understand. It won't happen again." I hope. "Thank you."

"Get to feeling better."

That went better than expected. My hands continue to shake as I end the call and hand the phone back to the medic. "Thanks."

"Can't believe you have a job."

"You and everyone else."

A grin traces his lips. More white clothed medics swarm around Smythe like moths to a light. A portable X-Ray machine appears, snaps pictures of him, a couple of me and leaves, pushed away by one of the medics. A couple of them attend to my bruises and cuts, determine I have not been clawed by the demon—thank God, the antivenin ranks among the vilest substances on earth—and leave me alone while they tend to my mentor.

I heal fast, thanks to the *justitia*.

So does Smythe. Provided he hasn't been hurt beyond recovery.

Since no one bothered to tell me to lie flat and stare at the ceiling, I swing my legs off the side of the bed and watch five medics tend to Smythe. How bad is he hurt?

The last time I was in the infirmary was the day I met Zagan, the day he clawed me, the day Micah received her fatal brain injury. After a quick scan, the medics determined she would be better treated in

165

surgery and wheeled her away. I'm assuming, since Smythe remains here, he is not in such bad shape.

I hope.

The only part of my mentor visible through the shield of medics is his black shitkickers. As I watch, his shredded black t-shirt followed by his leather pants drop to the floor, both slashed up the seams for easy removal. A flash of blue light clicks on and off like the rapid fire of a laser.

Except no one wears protective goggles.

Part of me wants to see what's going on and the other part enjoys my ability to see just fine. The part rooting for the ability to see wins. My butt remains firmly planted on the bed, my heart creeping into my throat.

What happens if he doesn't recover? Do I get another mentor?

My breath hitches. What if they give me Samantha?

Nah. That won't happen. Right?

"We've bandaged all the cuts and sent healing energy into the gash on your leg and buttock," one of the medics tells Smythe. "You should be healed in a couple of days. No heavy lifting until then. We'll be back later and give you the results of the X-Ray."

And like a horde of worker ants, the group of medics swarm out of the infirmary, leaving me alone to stare at Smythe. A white bandage twirls around his forehead, his black hair sticking up in clumps above the white gauze. Another white stripe wraps around his chest. Damaged ribs? Or more cuts? A sheet lies from the bottom of his ribs to the top of his thighs, covering the gash the medic mentioned. His eyes meet mine, his gaze reeling me into emotion-filled blue depths. I limp to Smythe's bed and sit on the edge of the mattress, taking his hand in mine.

A sucker punch of pain and anger slam into my mind with the force of straight-line winds, stealing my breath, fluttering my heart into a race of panic. At my gasp and flinch, the emotions vanish as he snaps shut mental barriers.

"Sorry."

"Don't be. You don't normally let me see inside." I crack a grin, trying to ease the pain etched into white lines around his mouth. "I owe you a huge thank you. You saved my life."

He winks. Grimaces. "That's my job."

"Yeah. But I'm pretty sure I get into more trouble than most of the other *Justitians*."

Now it's his turn to crack a grin. "Nah. You just keep me on my toes."

"Ballerina Smythe."

He snorts and twitches his boot-covered foot. No toe dancing for him anytime soon.

I squeeze his hand. "I'm glad to see you alive."

"You and me both. That damn demon knocked me out." His eyes narrow. I almost feel sorry for the demon. Almost.

"That's never happened before?"

"Not like this. Did the thing say who it was?"

"Nuh-uh. But it created a wicked energy ball. I really thought I was going to die." An ache forms behind my ribs at the remembered terror. "Cracked Flesh was scary as hell. No pun intended."

"Cracked Flesh?" His lip twists. "Maybe someone here caught the thing on the monitor and can tell us its name."

Of course. The esteemed demon identification computer program. What will they come up with next?

"What happened to the demon after its energy blast knocked me out?"

He shakes his head. "My containment field kept the full brunt of that blast from us, but did nothing to hold the demon in place."

Hold the demon in place? "Why the hell would you want the demon to stay in that lab? Having the thing disappear was a blessing."

One eyebrow rises. Nice to know Smythe feels good enough to slide into his condescending teacher role. "The field is supposed to hold it until we can banish it back to Hell."

Right. I should've known that. Hadn't he mentioned containment fields during my training?

Note to self: Pay better attention during training.

"How often have you banished demons?"

He swallows. Glances to the ceiling. Great. He's never banished a demon. Not that I'm complaining. He makes up for that lack of skill with his penchant for saving my ass. Which, in my humble opinion, is a far more valuable talent.

The elevator dings an arrival, doors sliding open for David to stride through, his face a mask of worry, concern and anger. His gaze aims at Smythe, and his loafers *click-clack-click* against the polished floor as he heads our way.

"Son! They told me you were here. What happened?"

David stops by the other side of the bed, not noticing me, his gaze focused on his son.

Red tinges Smythe's ears, the top of his cheeks. "The demon was impervious to spells and containment fields."

"Or you were too injured to form a correct one."

That's David for you, always full of encouragement. His crossed arms and down his nose glare give the illusion of anger. Which in man-speak translates to full-blown worry.

I think.

The underlying concern slides past Smythe's notice. A tiny crack in his mental barrier forms, allowing a smidgeon of anger and disappointment mingled with embarrassment to slide into me.

He's just worried about you.

Smythe starts as my telepathic message sinks in. His eyes narrow, and the emotional connection between us slams shut.

"There was nothing wrong with my containment field. The damn creature was stronger than normal. Did you find out who it was?"

"Not yet. The computer didn't capture who it was, only that it appeared. What were you doing at the medical school?"

"Checking on a case." I offer David a half-grin.

"A case? What are you now? A fucking detective?"

"Dad." Smythe's voice slides across my nerves, a low-toned warning.

David runs a hand through his short hair. "Since when do you have a case load? When you see a minion you kill it. You don't open a case to track it."

"Not true." I shake my head. "Sometimes—"

"You know what I mean." His arms cross again, his glare at me full of anger and none of the worry he showed his son. *Why am I not surprised?*

"That demon we just fought is the same demon that appeared a couple of days ago at the med school and killed a grad student of the professor whose lab we were investigating. Happy now?"

"Gin." Smythe's warning flows my way.

Not that I pay it any attention. David prickles my skin worse than a porcupine. Even my *justitia* reacts to him, a subtle vibration of confusion.

"Son, you need to work harder on smoothing over her smartass tendencies. One of these days they'll get her into trouble."

I roll my eyes. *Juvenile, but it made me feel better.*

"She's right though. That's why we went to the lab. The professor was murdered, and the lab was broken into. Then the demon appeared, and you know the rest."

A medic uses that moment to stride into the conversation as if he ruled the place. *Okay, so maybe he does.*

"The X-Ray came back with fractured ribs for Aidan and clear for Gin. No lifting until they heal." He nods to David. "Sir."

David nods back, and the medic slips into the background, vanishing from view, the squeak of his shoes on the linoleum ceasing with the snick of a door closing.

Poor Smythe. Fractured ribs hurt. I pat his forearm.

"They'll heal up but will hurt like a son of a gun until they do. How fast does it take for fractured bones to heal?"

"The pain should be gone in a couple of days. Mages heal fast." David answers before Smythe can open his mouth. "It's part of the magic flowing through their veins."

"Speaking of mages." Smythe grins, the expression not reaching his eyes. "We learned Will Wunderliech is a mage."

Chapter Fourteen

"Will Wunderliech?" David raises a brow. "Is that the doctor who was shot when you first got your *justitia*?"

"One and the same." Smythe nods.

"He wanted me to have it, and that's how it appeared in my pocket."

David scratches his head. "Must've been a soul wish."

"What's that?"

"A wish that consumes your being."

"You mean like I wish for a million bucks? That's a pretty important wish."

David snorts, his twitching lips belying his amusement. "That's not how it works, Gin. Your life and death does not hang on a million dollars."

What a shame he's not altruistic enough to soul wish me a cool million.

"It never hurts to ask." I grin as if I'm teasing. "Will wished me to have the bracelet. A voice inside told him to give it to me." Long live those little internal voices. Without the *justitia* telling Will it needed me I would not be the newest demon huntress.

Which bothers me more than it should. I should wish I'd never seen the bracelet, never fastened it around my wrist, and never had to worry about juggling work with demon hunting. And yet the thought of being without my *justitia* leaves a breath-stealing void in the middle of my chest.

I guess the entity fused to my nerves also bands around my heart.

"We visited him the other day." Smythe continues telling his dad about our meeting with Will. "My research and Will knowing when I started testing him for being a mage suggests Will's father worked for the Agency. Which would explain how he was able to take the *justitia* out of the vault."

"Makes sense." David nods. "Several mages disappeared around the time of the *justitia* vanishing."

"And you never thought to hunt them down?" I shut my gaping mouth.

"I never said we didn't hunt them down. We never found them."

"Why didn't I hear anything about this?" Smythe glares.

"You were too young. It was around thirty years ago. Ancient history. We thought one of them might have taken the *justitia,* but further evidence led us to believe the mages weren't involved."

"What evidence?"

"None of them were strong enough to get past the magical barriers keeping the vault locked."

"What about if they worked together?"

"Even then. Only certain directors had the ability to get into the vault and none of the vanishing mages had that clearance. We never discovered why they disappeared, but we believed them unable to steal the *justitia.*"

"Will said his father had the *justitia* and told his mother to keep it safe. She died protecting it. What if she was a mage, too?" Maybe David can validate my theory.

Or ignore me.

"He heals fast." Smythe states. "He's already out of the hospital and recovering at home a week and a half after being shot multiple times in the chest and abdomen."

Healed physically, that is. Emotionally he was still a wreck over Lara's death. Which might have made more sense if his dead wife had been something other than a bitch of epic proportions.

Men. I'll never understand their taste in women.

"You need to bring him in so we can train him. Doctors are always needed." David raises his wrist, peers at his watch. "Damn. I have a meeting. Glad to see you on the healing road, son." He lays a hand on Smythe's shoulder. A squeeze and a pat later and his loafers snap a loud *click-clack-click* as he strides to the elevator. He gives us an open-handed wave before stepping inside.

The doors slide shut, and my tension eases. Weird how he affects me that way. I swear he wants me dead, and yet he's never mentioned anything other than my smart mouth or my newbie status.

Not conclusive evidence. Unless I'm paranoid.

Tension leaks from Smythe in a slow drip. Guess David's presence gives people and bracelet-dwelling entities alike a dose of nerves.

"You okay?"

He sighs. Closes his eyes in a long blink. "Yeah. Although I'm not sure I can even perform the ritual to boost my energy so I can heal faster."

"Call Eloise." Eloise, one of the Agency healers, a

blind albino with more magic than the average mage, heals with energy instead of medicine and beats popping a pill any day. The woman takes awesome to a whole new level. "Here, give me her number, and I'll call her." I hold out my hand, remembering a second too late that his phone is in the back pocket of the pants lying on the floor.

"Not sure I'm injured enough for her to come."

"Come on, Smythe. She likes you." I slide off the mattress and rummage through his torn pants until I find his phone.

"Put that back." He twists, making a grab for the phone and almost falls off the bed as I scoot backward.

He grunts, white brackets of pain lining his mouth.

I shove his shoulder, trying to stop him from falling, trying to keep a spear of guilt from lancing my chest. "Stay still." I shove until he lays flat. "What's so bad about calling her?"

"I'll heal. I don't need her help."

Right. And a million bucks wouldn't make my life easier.

Smythe and his incessant insistence that if left alone he'll heal up fine. Through a strong application of will-power, I avoid an eye roll.

Time for a redirection. My mentor needs more help than the infirmary provides. And unlike him, I have no qualms about calling Eloise to work her magic. Plus, my care might help rebuild the lost trust in me.

It could happen.

Using the mattress as leverage, I pull myself up to sit on the edge of his bed. "Okay, then. Mind if I use the phone to call T?"

"Fine."

I click the phone on, then hand it to Smythe. "You need to stick in your password first."

He huffs, but takes the phone, unlocks the password and hands it back to me. "Know how to work it?"

This time the eye roll happens before I can stop it. "Nope. Never seen a smart phone before." I hit the contacts button and scroll until Eloise's name appears. A quick punch of the green phone button and the call goes through.

Eloise answers on the second ring, her child-like voice a stroke of pleasure along my spine. "Hello, Aidan."

"It's Gin. Smythe's been hurt. We're in the Agency infirmary. Would you please come heal him?" The words tumble out in a rush as my breath hitches into a high-pitched octave. Smythe glares, reaching for the phone with the speed of a striking snake. I almost fall off the bed but manage to stand as the room spins a dance.

Eloise doesn't say anything. Not a yep, not a no way, nothing. I clear my throat at the dead silence. "Hello?"

A rush of warmth smacks my nape, raising hairs. I yank the phone away from my ear, twisting to see the cause.

Eloise stands on the other side of my former bed, a phone held against her ear.

One hand stretches toward me, and I reach across the bed and grab her palm. No emotional reading, unlike the first time I touched her and caught a glimpse into the landscape of a blind woman. Ever since Smythe informed her of my little touch-and-see problem she

176

forms the same blank mind he does. It's nice.

And equally annoying. I never realized how much I depended upon my despised freakish ability until I met people who hid their emotions behind cement mental barriers. Around these two, I'm no different than anyone else. Correction. Make that no different than any other *Justitian*.

Before I can tell her thank-you for coming, Smythe's voice explodes into irate prickling needles. "What the hell, Gin? I told you not to call."

I shrug, not that Eloise sees it. "You need help."

"I do not."

A grin twists Eloise's lips. "It's nice to see you too, Aidan."

Her head tilts as she tightens her grasp on my hand. "You are also hurt."

"Not as bad as he is. He's—"

"In the bed next to this one. Yes. I know." She drops my hand and I stand there like a fish out of water, all open eyed and gaping mouth. Wasting no time, she marches around the bed to stand by me.

As if her red eyes have no problem seeing.

Maybe she's familiar with the infirmary. Yeah, that's it. She is, after all, a healer.

Eloise glances between the two of us, her sightless eyes seeing more than they should, taking in more than the feel of our injuries. Smythe closes his eyes and smacks his head once, twice against the pillow.

"Do I even want to know how you were able to portal into the infirmary?"

It takes me a couple of seconds to remember that the only way to get into the Agency was through the teenage geek guarded landing room.

Her lips turn up, the wicked grin belying her serene composure. "I'm not one for rules."

According to Smythe, spells cover this building, repelling all attempts to portal anywhere but the landing room. What kind of magic does she possess to break that kind of a spell? Yet another mystery to solve. The case of the rule-breaking healer.

Eloise lays a hand on Smythe's arm, releasing a frisson of his remaining tension. "What happened?"

"Tried to contain a demon."

"This scary assed, cracked flesh demon almost killed me, but Smythe stopped it." I lower myself to the bed as I speak. The longer I stand the more I realize upright is not my friend.

"Cracked flesh?" One pale hand moves to Smythe's forehead and his eyes slide closed. He sighs, the deep release of a man whose anger and pain eased into a relaxing sleep.

"It looked like it'd been burned in an oven and spat out. Cracks all over its skin. No hair. Scarier than the zombie apocalypse. The moment it showed up I was convinced I was going to die."

"Hmm. Sounds like a fear demon to me. Now hush."

I file her demon assessment for later, too engrossed in watching her heal. A wave of bright blue light streams from her hands down Smythe's body, darkening as it flows. Royal blue light splashes against his boots before hovering a few inches above his body.

The times Eloise healed me, I floated in a sea of blue, waves washing against my flesh as if I bobbed on an ocean swell. Peaceful. Relaxing.

Now I can see what a healing looks like from the

other side.

Not as peaceful. Or at least I'm not at peace. And I have to keep quiet and not ask the thousand questions pinging in the back of my mind. Which, oddly enough, is not hard considering I'm fascinated by the little pulses of blue light flickering above his injuries. Bruising lightens, fading into the tan of his skin until it disappears.

Eloise rocks.

She hasn't even healed me, and already tension in my shoulders eases, my breath evening. The longer she works on Smythe, the more relaxed I feel, though I'm still far from peaceful.

I almost lost my life, my mentor, and my job. And worse, I suspect the demon appeared a bit late to catch the anthrax thief.

Or the anthrax.

A chill creeps down my spine like a slow moving spider. I don't need a PhD to realize anthrax plus demon equals a large mess I don't want to be anywhere near.

So who else wants the dead professor's life work?

And can we keep the demon from catching them?

Chapter Fifteen

Eloise removes her hand from Smythe's head, leaving his body coated with the blue healing energy.

"Lie down, and I'll work on you too."

"You don't have to. I'll heal."

Her mouth twitches. Great. I now sound like my mentor. Embarrassing. I swallow and offer her a lopsided grin.

"Guess I sound like Smythe, eh?"

She returns my grin. "Only on that one issue."

"Not on others?"

Her grin widens. "Are you going to lie down or quiz me?"

"Working on it." I swing my feet onto the bed and ease back onto the pillow.

"Sleep."

Her hand comes toward me and the world turns to blue. Blue skies. Blue ocean. Blue waves. A white froth of peace breaks over me, drawing me into its depths, rolling me in unconsciousness.

Disorientation smacks into me, bobbing me out of my peaceful ocean and into the pink hue of a humming florescent light. Where am I? One blink later, and I remember.

The infirmary. Eloise. Smythe.

Smythe.

I turn my head, releasing a breath I didn't realize I

held when I see him lying on the bed next to mine. Where's Eloise? I push up to an elbow, looking around the room. No sign of the healer. Did I imagine her visit?

A quick touch of my face and glance to my arms proves none of my injuries remain. Definitely didn't dream up her visit.

I suppose she returned to wherever it was she lived. Or worked. Or hung out. Was there a bar specifically for albino healers?

Yeah. Right. Even if there was, I can't see Eloise sitting on a bar stool sipping a drink.

And why am I even thinking about her social life, or lack thereof, when my injured mentor lies only feet away?

I swing my legs off the bed and shuffle to his side. A quick peek under the gauze winding around his head shows smooth skin, no sign of the cut. I pull back the sheet, exposing his thigh. No gash.

"Checking out the merchandise?"

At the sound of his deep voice, I drop the sheet and take a step back, heat splashing into my cheeks. Busted.

"Nope. Checking out the vanishing gash."

"You shouldn't have called her."

"You shouldn't be so stubborn."

"Pot. Kettle." His lips twitch, but his eyes glare steel shards.

I cross my arms, swallow, and pretend he's a disobedient patient instead of an irate mage with large fists and strong magic.

Easier thought than done.

I straighten my shoulders, my fingers clenched tight against my palms, and force a smile. "You weren't healing fast enough. I don't like to see you in pain."

Both brows try to meet his hairline. "You don't?"

"What? You think I'm some sort of sick sadist and like to see people hurt?"

"Okay. When put like that."

My fingers uncurl. "Yeah. Besides, you called her on me."

"That was different. You were hurt bad both times."

"And you weren't? That thing threw you across the room. I thought you were dead." My voice cracks, and I clear the damn thing. My breath comes in little hitches like I'm about to cry.

I am not about to cry. Am not. Am not. Am not.

Smythe blinks a couple of times. "I'm okay, Gin." The smooth tone of his milk chocolate voice soothes that twisted center deep inside my chest, straightens the tangles of fear.

See? No reason to be afraid. Smythe would never hurt me. I really need to get over these stupid gut reactions.

I reach out a hand. "I'll help you up."

Electricity zips up my arm from his palm on mine, zips straight to my core, and ignites a fire. Multiple beds. One hot mentor. Nowhere to be any time soon.

What the hell am I thinking? Rules, Gin, rules.

But he feels the zingers of heat too, judging by the way his eyes narrow, the licks of fire hiding in their depths. His grip lingers a little too long, his gaze drops to my lips. My breath quickens, heat builds in my veins, races to my center. The room narrows to him and me, the sounds of our breath, the feel of his skin against mine.

I can almost smell the musky aroma of heat coming

off our flesh. But I know better than to act on it. Having an attraction right after losing a lover is one thing. Acting on it borders on tacky. Not to mention the whole boss thing.

I release Smythe's hand. He clears his throat, his grip tightening on the sheet until his fingers turn white.

Must be a reaction to near death. Yeah, that's it. We both had our asses handed to us and now we want to reaffirm life. Nothing other than biology.

Fake it till you make it.

"Now what?" I sit on my bed facing him.

He blinks. Clears his throat again. "Let's go to my apartment, and we can discuss it. I need to get dressed. Think there's a hospital gown around here somewhere? Not everyone wants to see my ass flapping in the wind."

"First off, it's not flapping. Second, I have no idea where things are kept. Just wrap the sheet around your middle. It's a new fashion statement. Especially with the boots." I waggle my brows.

He shakes his head but stands and wraps the sheet around his middle without allowing me to get a peek. I'm not disappointed. Really.

I'm such a freakin' liar.

I pick up his sliced, discarded clothing, catching up to him at the elevator. "Thought you might want these. They sliced them up the seams. Maybe you can fix 'em."

"Fix them? You mean sew?" His tone implies he'd rather lop off his favorite body part.

"What? Afraid of a little needle?" I offer him a grin as the elevator dings a welcome.

One brow raises, silent talk for *not likely.*

"Afraid?" He steps inside, pushing the button for the third floor. "There're much better things to be afraid of than a sewing needle."

"I see. You can't sew."

He shakes his head but doesn't refute me. I can sew. Maybe I'll exhibit my meager skills and repair his clothes.

The trip to his third floor apartment is uneventful. No one in the elevator. No one in the halls. No one but us. Uneventful and odd. In a high-rise building, shouldn't someone be around?

Smythe punches in a series of numbers, which pop the lock on his door. He steps inside, heads straight for his bedroom, the sheet flapping around his knees.

I shut the door, drop his clothes on the couch and get a drink of water. I want an entire case of beer, but we can't always get what we want. And I've been good for the last nine years. No excessive drinking.

A near-death experience by a demon is no reason to break my winning streak.

Smythe walks in the room as I finish my second glass. I point the empty glass his direction and give it a little shake.

"Sure. Thanks."

I grab a new glass out of the cabinet, fill it with water and hand it to him. "What now?"

"Your place. After you change clothes, we'll go to the med school and track the demon."

"Track the demon?" A shudder rolls through me. The last thing I want to do is get anywhere near that demon. A shiver rattles the bracelet, the *justitia* letting me know it agrees. The less to do with that particular demon, the better.

"Hunting demons is part of your job, Gin. You must set aside your fear."

You must conquer fear.

Isn't that what Zagan kept telling me?

"Which demon was that? Eloise thought it might be a fear demon."

He pauses, brows stitching together for a moment before relaxing. "I've never met a fear demon."

"Well, it was frightening."

"That's why they're called demons."

Zagan's not that scary sits on my tongue, and I swallow the words. Zagan is so scary. Just not in the same way. Zagan threatens something deep inside, calls to a part of me I pretend does not exist, as if I've known him my entire life.

Probably because my *justitia* thinks of him as a friend. Yeah, that's the reason. It's not me who knows him, the feeling stems from the relationship between him and my bracelet.

A month ago I would've checked myself into Blue Shores for that thought. Now? It's par for the day.

"Gin? You with me?"

"Sorry." Head in the game, Gin. Lost in thought in front of Smythe is not a good place to be. He might decide to hop inside my mind and see what's going on. "Was replaying the fight."

"Yeah. That can happen sometimes."

The stare from narrowed eyes bores into me. What feels like feathers brushes against my mind, gentle, soft, a touch to disregard. I slam my mental barriers in place.

Not that my barriers can keep him out.

The feathers vanish. "Good job. Stronger barrier that time. What are you hiding?"

Shit. So much for hoping he didn't notice. Heat smacks my cheeks. "Nothing. Ready to go? I'd like to soak these scrubs before they're ruined."

He continues to stare for a second too long, a reminder that although he respects my mental barrier, he can get in at will. "After you."

I'm out the door and halfway to the elevator before he catches me. I need to stop hiding things if I want to regain his trust. But Zagan is personal. I told Smythe most of it. The what-happened-when parts. The who-said-what parts.

The who-feels-what parts are mine and mine alone.

Smythe pushes the button like he possesses a grudge, a sharp jab, and a glare. As if it realizes a disgruntled mage stands in the corridor, the elevator promptly dings a hello-there, doors sliding open.

A few minutes later we stride into the landing room, the teenage computer geeks—I mean mages-in-training—ignore us as Smythe forms a portal in the corner. Some watch dogs they are. Do they even check who comes in and out? Did they notice Eloise popped into the infirmary instead of coming through this room?

I grab Smythe's arm and follow him into the freezing depths of a swirling kaleidoscope of lights. We arrive in my living room to the sound of a wheezing air conditioner.

I really need to get that thing fixed.

But first, a change of clothes. A girl can't think right with blood—her blood—staining her clothes.

"Give me a sec." Not bothering to see where Smythe heads, since I know the answer—laptop—I dart into my bedroom and shut the door.

Light shines through slits between the blinds. I

might keep them closed during the day, but plenty of light still makes it into my room. So much for trying to keep out the warming sunlight. On the plus side I can see well enough to grab another pair of panties and a bra without flipping on the light.

I'm happy to note the lack of Zagan. Not so happy to note the lack of Blake's ghost.

Why do I expect things I know I can't have? Even if his ghost visits me nightly, I could only see him if I touch my twin. And who wants to touch their brother while having a conversation with their lover?

Not my cup of tea.

Time to accept he's dead and move on. Easier said than done.

Shoving away the maudlin thoughts, I take my underthings into the bathroom, throw them on the closed toilet lid and take a shower. A speedy shower. To appease Smythe's hurry-hurry-hurry attitude.

As if he'd do much more than glare and tap his wrist.

Shower finished and new clothes on, I march into the living room. No surprise to find Smythe feet propped on the coffee table, laptop whirring a happy find-the-information tune.

"Whatcha doing?"

His fingers pause, eyes meeting mine. "Wondering why the demon was in the lab."

"That one's easy. It was after the anthrax."

"The anthrax was missing."

"Maybe he got that memo a little late."

Smythe gestures for me to sit beside him. I take a seat, my arm brushing against his, an unwanted wave of do-me-now crashing through my body. I scoot over an inch, severing contact. Why does the touch of his skin affect me that way? When I touch anyone else, I feel their emotions and occasionally their thoughts. When I touch Smythe, I just want to fuck him.

Maybe I shouldn't complain. The man is a fantasy in the flesh. He cooks, he cleans, he saves my ass on a regular basis, and he can carry on a conversation. Yeah, I definitely shouldn't complain.

Blanking my internal conversation before he dips into my head and sees what I want to do to him, I focus instead on the computer. I'm no longer surprised to see a classified website on the screen.

When we first started working together his hacking scared the shit out of me. What if the police traced it back to my house and locked me away for life? I've learned since then to be chill about the matter. If the man can bespell cops into believing he worked for the FBI, then he can protect himself from being discovered.

I think.

"Are we still going to the med school?" I could've had a longer, more relaxing shower if all we're doing the rest of the day is sitting around staring at a computer.

He runs a hand through his black hair and stares at the screen. "Might as well. I'm having no luck on here. Let's see if we can track the demon."

He closes the laptop and sets it on the coffee table. A few seconds later, we're at the medical school, arriving in a deserted hallway.

"How do you always know no one will see us arrive?"

"Luck." Twinkling eyes are the only clue he's not serious. "First the lab. Then back to where the demon tried to make a minion out of the grad student."

"Lead the way."

My *justitia* tingles where the silver links touch my arm as if it wakes from a long sleep. A comfort knowing it's there. Even if Cracked Flesh scares it half to death.

We stop in front of the lab. Yellow crime scene tape stripes the door like an extra-large bumblebee, a warning to keep out. No one guards the door, probably since the keypad offers a deterrent to most thieves.

Smythe holds his hand over the keypad, his brow furrowed, then he punches in a series of numbers. The lock pops open, and he turns the handle.

"Someone needs to build a better lock." He pushes wide the door, ducking and stepping around the tape.

"Someone needs to follow the law." I step over the tape, ducking to avoid the higher stripe.

"Where's the fun in that?"

He waits until I'm through the tape, then shuts the door, turning the handle so the lock snicks quietly in place. All sealed in.

"Think they have cameras in here?"

"Probably." He strides to where the demon appeared, his hands slamming against his hips as he stops.

I peer into the corners of the ceilings, not finding a camera. Maybe it's hidden as an object in the room. "Shouldn't we check?"

"Why? No one can see us. My spell blacks out the camera view."

"Nice."

I walk to his side. A shudder runs through me, through the *justitia*, a remembrance of the demon appearing right where we now stand. I close my eyes and suck in a deep breath, trying to calm my racing heart. What if the creature reappeared? What would we do?

Stop borrowing trouble, Gin.

My voice? Or the *justitia's*? It's getting hard to tell. Maybe I do need a visit to Blue Shores.

We stand there for some time, me with my eyes closed, fighting to control my breathing and heart-rate, and Smythe, who doesn't seem as panic stricken as me. Jealous much, Gin?

Since he's going to ask me to activate the minion finding sensors in my eyes, I focus on that task, giving up on obtaining calm breaths. Finding the entity living along my nerves, I pull it across my eyes, a small vibration in the bracelet letting me know I succeeded.

Another deep breath in and out, and I open my eyes to a clash of colors, black predominant in the mix. Inches from where we stand floats a pulsing ball of demon energy signature, black ribbons of evil fading into deep red, crimson stains of blood. The crimson ribbons trail into the inner lab, the lab containing the anthrax.

Or where the anthrax used to be stored.

I'm drawn to the inner door, following the lines like a creepy GPS map, Smythe keeping pace behind me. The door has a little window in it, and I peer inside. The room leads to another door, this one metal. A biohazard bunny suit hangs from a hook like a dead rabbit.

The demon trail leads through the door into the lab beyond. And back out to where it portalled in.

"I'm not going in there, and you can't make me."

Smythe looks through the window and shrugs. "Okay. The police went inside earlier. I'll look up their report when we get back. Does it look to you like the demon left the same way it came in?"

"Yep. So, the thing has to use the same portal coming and going?"

"That's what it looks like it did. I wonder if it took any of the anthrax."

"I thought it was all stolen."

"Can't say. I'll look at the report. You notice if it went anywhere else?"

"Nope. You?"

"Same. Let's go to the spot where it first appeared."

We leave the same way we entered, sneaking under the tape, closing the door with a barely audible click. Gin Crawford super-spy.

"Is this what *Justitians* around the globe do every day?" My training—while big on defense moves—lacked most of the day-to-day operations of a *Justitian*. Except for the kill the demon or minion spiel. Which fell into the no-shit-Sherlock category.

"They're more likely to track minions on a daily basis than demons. Minions commit the crimes. *Justitians* track the minions."

"So what you're saying is that I'm part of a crime fighting ring. Like a superhero. A demon huntress superhero."

He shakes his head. "Anyone ever told you you're a goof?"

"Aw, Smythe. You really know what to say to girl." I touch my chest and bat my eyes.

Another head shake forms his answer.

A goof? That's a new one. A freak, sure. Oddball, yep, been there done that. But a goof?

Maybe he has his terminology mixed up.

"Do you know why the Agency's computer didn't record which demon appeared?"

"Not yet."

"Speaking of. If Zagan appeared to me the other night, why didn't someone at the Agency call? Shouldn't they have known?"

Smythe stops so fast I almost give myself whiplash turning to look for him.

"They didn't, did they?"

The squint of his eyes indicates his lack of happy happy.

"Excuse me!" A tall, brown-haired woman in her early twenties carrying a large box stands behind Smythe, who scoots to the side of the hall in order for her to pass.

She toddles off, giving him a brief nod, as she heads in the direction of the original demon appearance. I fail to stop the cascade of shivers tingling my spine.

Jezebeth almost killed me by slamming my head repeatedly against concrete. Zagan kidnapped me, tried to turn me into his servant and popped by for a night visit. But remembering either of them lacks the same visceral sense of wrongness Cracked Flesh inspires.

Just thinking about where he appeared in this hall gives me the willies.

I look back to Smythe in time to see his eyes widen at something over my shoulder. I spin around when a scream and a heavy thud echo down the hall.

The tall, brown-haired woman who passed us carrying a box has both hands held out, the box on the floor the cause of the loud thud. A short blonde woman wielding a knife takes a swing, her aim connecting against the brown-haired woman's arm. Brown-hair's pain-filled scream activates the *justitia*, the sword thrusting out of the bracelet faster than I can say howdy.

Knife wielding blondie is not a woman. She's a minion.

I'm not sure who screams louder, the minion or the woman she's attacking. Don't really care either. I take off running down the hall.

By the time I reach the minion, clusters of people hang out of doorways watching the fight. I shove the injured, brown-haired woman aside as I raise my sword, blocking the knife's downward swing. A couple of phone cameras flash, the light a distraction, a worrisome tingle on the back burner of my thoughts.

The minion's pupils occupy her irises, turning the color a soul searing black. She screams again, but this time no cameras flash, no sounds emerge of terrified observers. A part of me wonders why. Most of me focuses on the minion.

The blonde minion who shoves the knife into her stomach. What the fuck?

She folds forward, sinking to her knees, her gaze rising to meet mine. Black fades to brown, the pupils shrinking as her blood stains the white tiles.

"Possessed." Her whisper shatters my heart.

When I first became a *Justitian* I worried that minions would want to repent, to renounce the demon inside, to be exorcised. Experience coupled with advice proved otherwise.

But this woman's frantic plea seemed like she

wanted to be free of the part of the demon living inside her. And how exactly do I go about doing that?

My arm moves before my brain sends it a reminder, courtesy of the *justitia*. The sword slices across her arm and stays embedded in her flesh. A moan leaves her lips. But the gray mist of the demon escapes the cut, sizzling to death on the *justitia*.

The sword stays imbedded in her arm until the gray mist stops flowing. Running footsteps mean someone comes to help.

Or arrest me. Anytime the *justitia* wants to recall the sword would be good.

Like it heard me, the sword vanishes into the silver links.

The former minion sags forward, falling onto the floor, one hand grasping the knife handle, blood covering her skin. She needs medical attention. Lucky for her, she's on a medical campus.

A quick glimpse shows campus security and white coated professors or doctors rushing our way. I lean forward, my lips against her ear.

"What did the demon want you to do?"

"Office. Dead." Lashes flutter against pale cheeks as I'm shoved out of the way.

Was she referring to Dr. Sheevers's office?

Security kneels on one side of the blonde woman, the white coat on the other. Another white coat attends the brown-haired woman the minion injured.

Scooting like a crab, I give them room to work. I want to run. Did my picture go viral?

Nope. Cameras are easy to erase. Smythe's telepathic voice sounds strained. I turn, left, then right, but he's nowhere to be seen.

Hiding behind a spell. None of the cameras captured you. Act normal.

Normal? No problem. I've been pretending to be normal my entire life.

"Ma'am?" A security guard squats in front of me, sharp blue eyes taking in my blood-spattered appearance. "Wanna tell me what happened?"

I run a shaky hand through my hair, leaving the tremor in place. No faking the shaking. "The injured lady was attacked by this knife-wielding woman"—I gesture to the former minion—"I shoved her out of the way, deflected the knife and then the woman stabbed herself. Why would she do that?"

Maybe the last sentence was a bit too much, but it seemed appropriate. And since my hands trembled, the shake in my voice gave an added touch. The guard's eyes turn sympathetic. Thank God. Sympathetic beat out accusatory any day.

"It'll be okay." He lands an awkward pat on my shoulder after a brief pause, like he wanted a blood-free spot to show support.

Nice. I must look worse than I think.

"Were you hurt?"

"No. The blood's not mine."

"You'll need to stay here until the police come. Okay?"

"Sure. No problem. Can I wash my hands?"

"No. Not yet. Just sit against the wall." He points, and I scoot backward, hands held up, until my back rests against cool tile.

As soon as he turns back to the injured women, Smythe sits beside me.

"Thought you were hiding."

"Can't hold it."

I turn, take in his pale face, sweat beading around his hairline, the sag of his shoulders. I start to holler at someone, stopping myself at the last minute. As if anyone in this hall could help a mage who burned through magic.

"Are you okay?"

"Will be. Had to erase all the cameras. Was drawing attention to myself, everyone was staring, so I had to hide behind a spell. I tried to fuzz everyone's recall about seeing you with a sword, but not sure if I succeeded. Took a lot of magic."

"And you were just injured earlier today. Even with Eloise's healing, I'm sure this didn't help. I'm sorry. I didn't think."

"Don't apologize. You killed part of the demon. Didn't realize you could stab a minion without killing it."

"You learn something new every day."

Smythe leans his head against the cool tile wall, his lashes resting against his cheeks, giving him the appearance of a stone angel. He snorts.

Right. Telepathic mage. Mental barriers, Gin, mental barriers.

I start to pat his hand, decide he doesn't want my blood-stained hands anywhere near his, and focus on the crime scene. By now, several paramedics swarm around both women, while security herds witnesses into the room directly across from where I sit. Even though Smythe tampered with the scene, I can only imagine what the witnesses have to say.

Some chick goes crazy with a knife and another one slices her with a sword.

Maybe security will think everyone too high to give witness.

It could happen.

The police show right when the paramedics lift the former minion onto a stretcher. After a brief chat with security, one of the detectives heads my way, another goes toward the victim. Heat splashes against my cheeks as the detective walks toward me.

He's the same detective who interviewed me about Will's shooting. Right after I killed the minion who shot my doctor friend. Poor Detective Williams had to drive out to my house, which had become a crime scene for my first minion kill, for the interview.

At the time, I was under the impression I'd already recounted my version of events to the police. But Smythe, as I discovered, was not part of the force as he'd led me to believe. Bad mentor. I might have forgiven Smythe for the mix-up, but the good detective kneeling before me clearly remembers my face.

Great.

"Don't I know you?" Piercing brown eyes focus on me, a hawk eyeing its prey. He clearly knows the answer. Must be one of those detective things. Ask a question you know and see if the answer is as truthful.

"Yes." I swallow, risking a glimpse to Smythe. A bead of sweat snakes down his too-pale cheek. His lips move, but no words escape. Was he casting a spell? Why? I focus on the detective, who pays no attention to Smythe. Because of a spell? Or he only cares what I saw?

Detective Williams clears his throat, snapping me out of my thoughts and into the scene. "Sorry. You came to my house to interview me about Dr.

Wonderliech's shooting. He's out of the hospital in case you haven't heard."

Rule number one when dealing with detectives: Don't ramble. A rule I obviously had trouble following.

But the detective only nods. "I heard. Case closed." His eyes narrow and I resist the urge to squirm like a child put on the spot in class. "Interesting that you show up and stop another attempted murder. What were you doing here?"

"I'm considering going back to school and wanted to tour the campus."

He blinks as if surprised I have higher ambitions. Not sure what that says about me, but twin tendrils sprout hurt and anger.

"And do what?"

"Pardon?"

"What kind of degree?"

"Nurse practitioner. Or maybe Physician's Assistant."

"You realize this is a research building, not where the admission offices are."

"It's an unguided tour. Just thought I'd walk around." Learn about a demon. Get a little exercise. Sweat sneaks down my spine. "The victim walked by carrying a box and, the next thing I know, she's screaming. This crazy lady has a knife and is slashing at her and no one is helping so I run down the hall, push the hurt woman aside but before I can knock the knife out of the crazy lady's hand, she stabs herself with it. It was weird."

The detective stops writing and meets my gaze. "You seem to have a knack for finding yourself in these situations."

"Not a knack. A fluke. Trust me, I don't like seeing crime victims."

Uh-oh. Maybe I should have phrased it differently. I can almost see the wheels turning in the detective's mind, deducing I'm some sort of crazy who likes the attention from saving others. I would correct myself, but then he'd think I'm trying to distract him from what I just said.

So I opt for my best innocent smile. As if I threw in a dose of Smythe's compulsion, the detective's eyes glaze, and he nods.

"We need to do some swabs and take pictures and then you can go. I already have your name and address."

What's worse? Being on the police radar? Or having Zagan know where I live?

Hard choice.

CSI buzzes around me, ignoring Smythe who continues to perform his stone angel impersonation, and takes the required samples. A photographer has me stand and snaps bloodstains. Yet another clothing choice bites the dust.

At this rate I'm going to be naked. Or have to shop for a whole new wardrobe.

And why am I complaining about shopping?

When they finish, the detective gestures that I can leave and wash my hands. I look at my hands, then at Smythe, knowing he needs a hand up despite the dried blood coating my palms, but he waves me off.

They can't see me. Go wash your hands then wait for me outside the restroom.

I do as he says, speed walking past the crime scene to the restroom at the end of the hall. After washing the blood off my hands, I push open the door, giving me a direct glimpse of the crime scene. When he sees me, Smythe stands, using the wall as a crutch, both to rise and to walk. My fingers itch to help, but he's right. If he's cast some sort of invisibility spell, then it would look odd for me to act like I'm escorting an invisible man down the hall.

I'm already flirting with the good detective thinking I'm suspect.

So I wait. Smythe staggers beside me, leaning against the wall with a sigh.

"Do I need to call T to pick us up?"

His eyes snap open, his gaze blue glaciers of ire. "I'm not that bad."

Right. I nod so as not to bruise his fragile male ego. He can barely walk, let alone form a portal. "Okay. We can come back after you rest up."

"I don't need to rest up. I just need to sit." He eyes a padded bench around the corner, aiming his lurching body toward the thing like it's a lifejacket, and he's a drowning man. He shakes off my helping hand, relying on the wall for support.

Whatever. That did not hurt my feelings.

"Circle around and see if it's the same black blob of demon energy who turned the woman."

"She said she was possessed. I asked her what the demon wanted and she said, 'office' and 'dead.' I'm assuming she's referring to Dr. Sheevers?"

Smythe collapses onto the bench. "Looks like we need to check out his office too. Isn't it close to where we were?"

"Yeah. I think so. Why does the demon want in his office? Wasn't it bad enough to try to steal his, um, work?"

"Circle around and check out the demon signature. Come back, and we'll go check out the office."

"You sure you don't want to go home? You look like shit warmed over."

"Thanks. You really know how to make a man feel good."

"That's my specialty. Really though. You must've burned through a ton of magic."

"You try erasing over ten cameras while fuzzing out a sword and casting an invisibility spell. See what you look like afterward."

"Thank you. I was afraid I might go viral."

"Not today. Go on. I'll be here when you get back."

One look at his face, and I bit back the are-you-sure comment hanging on my tongue. Shit warmed over only begins to describe him. Maybe it's the florescent lighting, but a pale green tinges his skin like a prelude to the explosion of a certain green comic book character. The faster I check out the demon energy blob, the faster he can return home to recover.

Giving him a jaunty salute, which he counters with a head shake, I circle around until I reach a spot a stone's throw from where the knife attack just occurred. No guesswork on where the demon appeared.

Not far from where I stand, the CSI unit, detectives, security and a spattering of witnesses mills around like overactive bees at a nectar convention. My attention darts from them to the black blob of energy floating at the end of the hall. Dark ribbons encircle the blob, strands of fright woven into the fabric. Like the first time I saw it, I swear the blob mocks me. My *justitia* shivers, silver links rattling an eerie vibration up my arm.

I'm no expert, but I'm going with the theory this is the same demon as before. Ole Cracked Flesh. Shivers cascade along shuddering nerves. I want nothing more than to run.

Since no one tells me otherwise, I give into the urge, darting around corners until I see Smythe. Only then do I slow to a walk.

"Feeling better?"

He nods a lie. The green tinge has faded but dark circles ring his eyes with exhaustion. "Ready for the office?"

"Are you?"

Instead of answering, he pushes to his feet, his strides shorter than normal, his hand avoiding the wall. Nothing like proving he can walk on his own. We avoid the crime scene, heading the opposite direction. When we get to Dr. Sheevers's office, Smythe pulls a lock-pick out of his pocket. The last time I saw him use the tool was when we broke into a warehouse. Where Blake died. Where Jezebeth tried to kill me. Where Zagan kidnapped me and took me to his lair.

My chest aches as if a hand squeezes the beat out of my heart. My breath comes in fits and starts, little punches of air insufficient to send oxygen to my brain. Black spots dot the periphery of my vision. The lock clicks open, and Smythe pushes the door wide.

"What's wrong?" His eyes flare as he takes in my hyperventilating.

"Panic attack."

"Okay. Can you have it inside the office instead of in the hall?"

He grabs my arm, hauling me inside before shutting the door and throwing the lock. For a mage who burned through enough energy to almost pass out, his grasp rivals that of a vise grip.

"What started it? The demon?"

"Your lock-pick."

Smythe looks at the offending tool, one brow rising as if to say what the fuck.

"You used it to pick the lock on the warehouse. Where we found Blake."

"Oh."

One minute I'm focusing on calming my hyperactive breathing, and the next he's slapped the lock-pick into my upturned palm. Warmth floods from the tool and his hand on my wrist, peace vying against panic.

The metal lock-pick looks and feels innocuous. Normal. Not a reason to panic.

I squeeze my eyes shut and haul a deep breath through my nose. There is no reason to fear the thing. It's not my door its picking. Another breath in and out, and my heart slows from marathon fast to a lazy jog. Am I really panicking over a stupid tool? Sure, that tool could get my ass thrown in jail for breaking and entering, but a little jail time is no reason to freak out in front of my mentor. Panic attacks are so irrational.

Using a move Smythe taught me, I twist out of his grasp, slapping the lock-pick against his chest. He steps back as if I punched him, forcing me to grab his arm to keep him from falling.

"Sorry." How bad off was he? Usually he offered a glare instead of a stumble. "You okay?"

"Fine." Sticking the tool in his pocket, he walks

with the speed of an elderly man, stiff-legged and shuffling. Not good. He nails the landing into one of the chairs facing the desk, flopping like a kid off a diving board. "Why are we here?"

"Demon—"

"I mean the office. What did the demon want in this office bad enough to make a minion for?"

"I don't know." I walk around the desk and sit in the professor's chair facing Smythe. "Cracked Flesh isn't acting normal."

"Gin." The growl in his tone rubs bumps along my skin. "It's a demon. They specialize in not normal."

"Duh. I mean, why did it try to convert Mason, the grad student, into a minion? Probably to get into the lab. Then it appeared in the lab. Why not just portal in, grab the anthrax and leave? But no. It waits until the anthrax is stolen before popping in. Same thing today. Why not just portal into this office? Why make a minion?"

"Good point." He rubs the bridge of his nose. "Unless it's not after the anthrax?"

"Okay. Then what's it doing in the lab? I'd bet good money the knife-wielding woman works in Dr. Sheevers' lab."

"She shouldn't have the key to the office."

"Maybe he gave it to her because they were having an affair."

"Watch daytime programming much?"

I shrug. What was the demon up to? If it didn't want the anthrax, then what was it after? My gaze drifts to the pictures huddled on the desk, sticking on the one of a younger professor on his wedding day.

"What happened to his wife?"

Smythe stops rubbing his head. "None of the info I found stated anything about a wife."

I hold up the wedding photo, turn the smiling couple to face him. "See? A younger prof."

"Are you sure that's him?"

"Who else would it be?"

"A brother? A cousin?" Smythe shrugs.

"Maybe she died. Or divorced him. And he still loves her and kept their wedding picture."

"Never pegged you for a romantic."

"Hey, we all have our faults."

He shakes his head. "We still don't know why the demon wanted in this office. Do you see anything out of place?"

"Just us."

Ignoring my smartass response—as if he's used to it—he looks around the room, gaze lingering on the bookshelf behind the desk. I spin my chair around, trying to discover what holds his attention. Microbiology journals line the shelf, clearly demonstrating someone's abhorrence for online reading. A variety of microbiology textbooks sit interspersed among the journals.

Nothing out of the ordinary for a professor's office.

"Notice anything odd?" The gravely tone of his voice causes me to turn.

Screw the demon's quest. Smythe needs medical help. Or whatever mages do when they burn through magic. "Yep. You look like you've been ridden hard and put up wet. We're going home."

He opens his mouth to object, and I hold up a hand, giving him my best nurse's glare. "Not going there. Do I need to call T to pick us up?"

His glare strikes me like a physical blow. "Don't be ridiculous." He shoves to his feet, grasping the desk with one hand while thrusting his other forward, palm facing the wall to my left. A roll of ancient words drips off his lips in an angry rush, opening a slash of light in the fabric of space, a method of travel older than the words used for its construction.

He lowers his hand, his glare speaking for him: *See? I'm not as weak as you think.*

His stumble and near fall belies his I-am-man-hear-me-roar glare.

I raise a brow. *Yeah, right.*

Smythe's eyes narrow as he holds his hand to me. For my support or his? I step around the desk and grasp his forearm. Less chance of him taking a tumble. The deceptive warm air billowing out of the portal greets us like a forbidden lover's caress, spitting us out in my living room chilled and shaken.

And that was before I noticed several cops and a scattering of firemen dressed in hazmat suits milling around my front yard. Crime scene tape rings my yard like a sweat stain on a white shirt.

What the fuck.

Chapter Sixteen

I'm halfway to the front door before Smythe grabs my arm, stopping me from announcing our presence. A fine tremor runs through my mentor, a warning bell signaling an impending collapse.

A bad sign. What does he need to replenish his magic? What should I—

"We need to portal down the street and walk back."

"There's something wrong in my yard. We need to get out there now. And you're too weak to portal anywhere."

His glare frosts my skin, and before I can apologize, he opens a portal and yanks me through it. He stumbles as the portal spits us out along the side of a neighbor's house, and I wrap an arm around his waist to keep him from falling onto a patch of dead grass and paving stones.

"What were you thinking?"

He leans against the house, sucking down air like a man saved from drowning, his face ashen. "They were in the backyard."

"How did you know that? I didn't see anyone." Not that I looked. Seeing emergency responders in my front yard blocked out everything else.

"Standard protocol. We need to find out what happened."

"No problem. It's my house. I'm headed over there

right now. Wait here." I make it two feet before a heavy body lurches into me. "Didn't I—"

"You might need me. I'm fine." His ashen face speaks a different story.

Men.

Smythe manages to walk—or should I say stumble—beside me as I stride two doors down to my house. A shiny red fire truck sits in front of the driveway, fencing in T's car. My brain and feet stutter to a stop in my next-door neighbor's yard, next to my driveway. Oh my God. T was in the house when whatever happened, happened. Is he okay?

As if he hears me, he steps out of the way of a hazmat-covered fireman, gaze sweeping left and right until he spots me. His eyes flare, a smile tinges his lips before vanishing, and he offers me a half-wave.

What the hell happened? Are you okay?

A grim expression sits on his face like a shroud. Did someone die? In my house?

Before he can answer, a cop walks to me. "You can't be here. This area is cordoned off."

"That's my house! My brother! What the hell happened to my house?"

"How did you get here? The street is blocked."

I look over my shoulder. Sure enough the street is barricaded by a police car complete with two sweaty and chatting cops. Good point. I doubt the man would believe I appeared in a flowerbed.

"I, uh, I—"

"She's allowed inside the perimeter." One of Smythe's hands waves an arc in front of his face while he performs his version of a mind trick on the cop.

Who blinks, once, twice, his surprised face

returning to a normal expression as he nods.

My mentor rocks. Now I need to figure out why my yard looks like the training ground for a chemical spill. And help Smythe sit before he falls.

I grab my mentor's waist and lower him to the ground. The cop shoots him a quizzical look, but only for a second. Smythe waves his hand in an arc and the cop's stare fuzzes as if he sees a magic-depleted mage all the time. No biggie.

By the time I straighten, T stands at my side, his skin color giving Smythe's a run on palest face of the year award.

"You're not supposed to be over here." The cop glares and T glances to the ground like a contrite child.

What the heck?

"She's my sister."

"Oh. She's allowed in. But get back to the yard." He points, and T steps back until he stands on my patch of withered lawn.

Again. What. The. Hell.

Leaving Smythe sitting next to my driveway, I follow T to my yard. "What happened?"

T sends me telepathic visuals of what happened, a method faster than speech. On the downside, it leaves me gaping like a student in a dunce hat, which never looks good when faced with a gaggle of cops and white suited firemen. And T has to answer me out loud so as not to cause suspicion.

If they thought my sudden appearance strange, no telling what they'd do when faced with telepathic twins.

"I found an envelope leaking white powder on the front porch."

While he speaks, I run through his memories. T

arriving, planning on pouring salt and iron flakes around all the windows and doors to keep out ghosts and other evil beasties, but instead finds an envelope sitting on the porch, white powder escaping the corners.

Stolen anthrax + demon = unwanted gift for Gin.

I might have flunked math in school, but it doesn't take a genius to add up those facts. Would a demon really bother to leave me an envelope when it could appear for another round of energy ball pitch practice? What were we dealing with?

A demon? T's voice mixes anger with fear.

I return the telepathic favor, slamming my memories of the day into his mind so he gapes like an idiot, too.

Since the cop stares at the two of us as if we sprouted a third eye, I might want to act scared about the possibility of anthrax.

Wait. There. Is. Anthrax. In. My. Yard. Is it in my house too?

Act scared? I don't need to act. A douse of metaphorical cold water freezes my back straight. I go from slightly worried to totally freaked out in under a second.

"What? An envelope? Is it anthrax? Is there anthrax in my freaking house?" My voice lifts into the outer atmosphere, loud enough for the space-station to hear. I can't stop my hands from trembling.

And here I thought drinking coffee close to Dr. Sheevers's lab freaked me out.

T grabs one of my flailing hands, his touch a soothing balm. For a moment. The cop makes soothing noises.

"Gin!" Smythe's voice snaps like a rubber band;

hard and fast and stinging. If he intends to calm me, he succeeds. Huh. "T left it on the porch and called the police from the yard. It's not in your house."

My breath hitches, and I force it into my lungs. On the porch. Not in the house.

"The level one responders are handling it," the cop says, gesturing to a cluster of white-suited firemen on my porch. "But it's now a federal crime scene, and the FBI will be here soon."

My house a federal crime scene? Oh my God.

I glance to Smythe. He still looks mostly dead. Both of his palms are planted on either side of his crossed legs, his eyes are closed as if he's concentrating. While T pales further at the thought of the FBI, Smythe doesn't flinch.

So much for him performing his FBI impersonation.

"The FBI? My house is a federal crime scene?"

"Yep. We also called the CDC. No one except your brother touched the letter. And he dropped it once he saw the powder." All memories now shared with T.

Oh my God. T touched anthrax. One hand covers my mouth as I stare at my twin. What if he gets ill? What if he dies? His pale face mirrors my thoughts.

"He'll be monitored. Don't worry."

Yeah, right, Officer. Not worry? He's my brother, my twin, the other half of my soul. Worry is all I can do.

Worry and kill the bastard who threatened T's life.

"Can I see the envelope? Maybe I'll recognize the writing."

"I don't think that's possible. At least not the real envelope. I'll see if someone took a picture and maybe they'll let you look at it." He heads toward a lone fireman standing by the truck.

T clears his throat. "There's nothing on there but your name."

"No address?"

"Nope. Just your name. And before you ask, I didn't recognize the writing."

The cop gestures me over to the fire truck, interrupting our conversation. When we get to the truck, the fireman holds out a camera, displaying a picture of the envelope. White and legal-sized, the envelope glares like a LED billboard at night. *Gin Crawford* is scrawled across the front in a neat font I usually associate with my mother's generation.

Who the hell left me this?

I shake my head at the picture like it contains a one-way trip to Hell. Which it very well might.

Hell and anthrax. What a combination.

"Recognize the writing?" The fireman asks.

"Nope."

"Don't worry," the cop adds, his platitude not stopping the worry molecules bouncing through my veins. "The FBI will get to the bottom of this."

Not if there's a demon involved, they won't. But what are the chances of that? Demons would rather throw energy balls or turn you into a minion. Sending an envelope full of anthrax powder isn't their modus operandi.

But then again, what do I know about demons? It's not like I passed demonology 101. Maybe anthrax-sending demons are par for the course.

"Thanks." I wave at the camera and head toward Smythe.

"Don't leave this yard!"

Thank you, Mr. Policeman.

T steps beside me as I stop beside my driveway and stare at a closed-eyed Smythe. His coloring looks a bit better but that could just be sun exposure. A Texas summer will do that to you. Step outside, and it's like you've been dunked in an armpit.

"What's wrong with wonder boy?" T crosses his arms and stares at Smythe.

"Burned through too much magic." I turn to face my twin. "Aren't you worried? What if you get sick?" I reach for his hand, his flesh warm under my palm. Peace, clouded with worry, flows between us, the touch not bringing the usual comfort.

For the first time in a long time, a thick clot of fear runs through his veins.

"I shouldn't have picked it up, but I thought it was important."

"How could you have known?"

"You think it's related to what was stolen this morning?"

"I don't know." Why would the thief of Dr. Sheevers' anthrax want me dead?

The sound of an engine interrupts my thought. An unmarked black Tahoe followed by a white van with CDC written on the side drives past the police cars at the end of the street and parks behind the fire truck.

Good thing most of the neighbors are at work.

Two FBI agents—one male and one female— dressed in black suits and sporting the latest style in sunglasses, step out of the car. After a quick glance around my yard, they head toward one of the white-suited firemen. The fireman points to the porch and starts talking, but I can't hear what he says.

Before I can inch closer to eavesdrop, T pulls me out of the way of the two CDC women who wear hooded coveralls and respirators and march up the sidewalk carrying oversized metal briefcases. The FBI and the fireman they talked with meet them halfway. A discussion ensues, none of which I hear.

The CDC women get to work, snapping on gloves and shoe booties. The white-suited firemen retreat and let the women decontaminate the scene.

The women bag the envelope with more care than first time parents buckling a baby into a car seat. After they place the bag in their van, they scrub the porch with some type of solution.

I take this time to inch my way to Smythe, who stands on the other side of T's car. More like uses T's car as a prop to keep him upright. His coloring looks better, but a fine sheen of sweat covers his face. Fever? Or the heat?

"You okay?"

"I've been better."

T sidesteps to us while staring at the CDC women. "I wouldn't want their job."

"Me, either." Even with the hazard suits, cozying up to pathogens creeps me out.

"One brush with anthrax is enough for me."

"Maybe they enjoy the adrenaline rush," Smythe says.

T shrugs. "Maybe."

There is not enough adrenaline in the world to make me enjoy putting my life on the line to be part of a clean-up crew.

A few minutes later, the CDC finishes disinfecting

the concrete. One of them speaks with the FBI and firemen before walking to the van.

"Your front porch is cleaned." The cop we talked to earlier waves at the porch as if I need a reminder where it's located. "They need to decontaminate your brother."

"Decontaminate? How?"

The how turns out to be in a tent set up in my front yard. T's clothes are bagged and he's given a shower and a pair of scrubs to wear. The CDC determine minimal exposure, so his lawn bath is more for caution than actual need. And despite the fact the envelope sat on the porch, they don't decontaminate inside my house.

I would be worried, but Smythe insists the Agency cleaning crew will be around later. Good thing the emergency responders can't hear him speaking in my mind. They might think we've been smoking something funny.

Once T's showered and changed, the CDC and firemen leave. The female FBI agent heads our way, while the male agent talks to the cop.

"Hi. I'm Agent Dean with the FBI. Tell me what happened."

T explains how he found the envelope, leaving out any mention of salt and iron filings or how he planned on using them.

"And you?" Her gaze focuses on me, sharp and piercing. Despite the heat I shiver.

"She came home to this. She doesn't know anything."

Agent Dean's attention snaps to Smythe. Her brow furrows for a second then she nods. Mage mind trick to the rescue.

"Of course. Do you have any reason for someone to threaten your life?"

Besides a demon or Samantha? "No."

"Do you do any political work?"

"Nope. I'm the farthest thing from a politician." What a strange question.

"Any accidents? Run-ins with disgruntled people?"

"No and no. I'm an ER nurse. I go to work and come home. And I get along with my co-workers." We might not be best buds but I can't imagine anyone from work wanting me dead.

"If you think of anything, and I do mean anything, give me a call." She hands me her card. "We'll find out who did this."

She shakes my hand, nods to T and Smythe, and walks to the Tahoe. Her partner shakes hands with the cop, joins her at the car and they leave.

"Finally." T mutters. "I can go inside and get out of these scratchy scrubs. Don't see how you can wear them every day."

I grab his arm as the cop walks over. "You can't leave. You have to be treated at the hospital."

T's eyes widen as the cop confirms my words. "We have to take you to the hospital for antibiotics."

"The hospital?" T pales. No wonder. Ghosts walk at the hospital and flock around my twin like ants on a birthday cake. Used to be he enjoyed their visits.

Right up until our sperm donor died.

Now? He'd rather dance naked in front of a jeering crowd.

"Just the ER." The cop pats him on the arm. "They have to check you out and give antibiotics."

"Which hospital?" Please don't say Blue Forest. I can't show up after calling in sick.

"Dallas County. They're set up to handle these types of cases."

Whew. Saved. Unfortunately Smythe will be left behind if I go with T.

What other choice do I have?

Chapter Seventeen

We're processed through the ER faster than a visiting dignitary. Could be because of the police escort or the call ahead letting them know we were coming. Whatever the reason, the hospital visit only lasts a couple of hours, during which time they run IV antibiotics and check T over for any illness. Three hours later, the cop drops us off in front of my house.

"Nice of him to wait." T watches the taillights grow dimmer as the cruiser drives down the street.

"Yeah. Are you okay?" It's a rhetorical question. Through the bond connecting us, I know he's not. A deep-seated fear rides his emotions, clouding his thoughts. I share the same feeling of powerlessness. Of being controlled by that which frightens me.

"It's like when we were kids. When we never knew what would happen."

A shudder runs through me as I stick the key in the front door and twist. "We took care of it. You'll win this one, too."

"Will I?"

"Never give up hope." What would I do without him? How would I live?

I shove the door open, step into the living room and freeze. Almost literally. For the first time in years, the house is cold during the summer and the A/C sounds normal, none of its usual whining death cadence.

Smythe sits on the couch, head resting on the back of the seat, feet propped on the coffee table. Eloise sits beside him, staring at a closing portal. I can guarantee T's day just took an upturn. The first time they met, after I'd been injured in a minion attack, he couldn't stop staring at her, his attraction a tangible thread in the air. Looks like he still feels the same.

"Hey."

She starts at my voice, turning our direction. T hisses in a breath as he walks into the house, his gaze focused on Eloise, just as I predicted. Fear no longer runs through his veins as the dominant emotion.

Wonder how Jackie would feel about his little crush.

Stay out of my head.

Quit broadcasting to the world.

T snaps shut the barrier between us, walking toward Eloise as if drawn by invisible strings. Smythe speaks without turning.

"The cleaning crew just left. They didn't find any spores inside. Or outside. But they fixed the air conditioner."

"That was nice of them." Beyond nice, actually.

"It was self-preservation." Smythe gestures to the woman beside him. "Eloise offered to check out T." He manages that last sentence with a straight face. He either fails to see the irony or is too tired to care.

I close the front door, locking it with a quick twist. The Agency cleaning crew rocks. I now have cold air blowing out of vents like a normal North Texan.

When I turn, Eloise stands facing our direction, clearly waiting for us to come to her.

T stops at the back of the couch. "Hey. Thanks for

coming."

I walk to Smythe and stand by his side as Eloise motions for T to sit on the couch. Ignoring them, I focus on a pale Smythe. Not as pale as before, but I wouldn't call him healthy either.

"How—"

"Shh." Eloise interrupts me, her hand hovering above T's head.

Heat splashes my cheeks as I kneel by Smythe. *How do you feel?*

Better. Not as tired. I slept some.

Did Eloise help?

She can't heal depleted magic. Only time and rituals.

Should you return to your apartment and do your ritual?

Probably.

I pause, waiting for him to continue. His eyes drift closed.

Then why aren't you?

You're in trouble.

Forget about me! Heal yourself.

Blue orbs snap wide, the heat within firing a response deep within my core. *A burned out mage is better than nothing. A little sleep, and I'll be fine by morning.*

His eyes draw me in, pulling me under, until I swim in the depths of his desire. I'm uncertain if he's spelled me or showed me a glimpse into his inner emotions. The thought no sooner goes through my mind than his gaze shutters, locking the desire behind steel bars of iron will.

What the hell? Smythe finds me hot?

My traitorous hormones tango through my blood. Down girls, down. Not happening.

Not sure the couch is comfortable enough for recharging. Want to share my bed? Wait. Did those words actually transmit to him? Judging by the flare of his eyes and dilated pupils, I violated my own damn rule.

Fidiot.

Too late to take it back. Heat slaps my face as I try to backtrack. *You can sleep on one side, and I'll take the other. No hanky-panky.*

"You are clear." Eloise interrupts Smythe's response. If there even was a response. Maybe he was as embarrassed as I was.

It could happen.

My attention snaps from blue eyes to T and Eloise. Her hand remains on his arm, a touch unnecessary for a healing but pleasing to T all the same. Good thing the couch sits between them. His pole-axed expression masks a roil of tension gathering within, spreading outward to her and back, wrapping them in tendrils of desire.

Gah. While a definite improvement from the Double D Wonder, the thought of Eloise in T's bed creeps me out. I guess when it comes to my twin no one is good enough. Not even the healer.

Not sure what that says about me.

"I'm anthrax free?"

"Yes. Have you considered my request to become a ghost talker?"

T yanks his arm back faster than a striking snake, his expression morphing into narrowed eyes and a stiff spine. "I do not talk to them."

"Why?" Smythe twists around to look at my twin. "You can't have gone this long without trying."

"Bad experience."

"Just leave him alone about it, okay?" I give the offending parties a glare.

But when Smythe peers over his shoulder, I realize I should've kept my mouth shut. His gaze turns speculative. I wonder if he knows. If he guessed our secret. If he realizes his new mentee is a murderer.

The air saturates with a strange tension, a twisting of molecules into small spheres of anger. As if the room holds its breath, waiting, watching.

"They scare me, okay?" With T's words, the tension rolls into the corners, waiting for another chance at an attack. T stalks into the kitchen. Cabinet doors slam, clinks of glass on the counter making me cringe. The tension wrapped around the room slithers behind him, a trailing cape of anger. Anger at himself for admitting a fear. Anger at Eloise for asking. Anger for hoping she wanted him for a different reason.

My poor twin. "Excuse me." I follow him into the kitchen, heated gazes tagging my back like lasers.

T leans against the counter, hands flat, head bent forward. Empty glasses sit before him as if he plays a game of tic-tac-toe in the scratches on the laminate countertop. I reach into the fridge and pull out a beer.

Setting the beer in front of him, I place a hand on his shoulder and wrap him in tendrils of peace. Or try to. Peace is not my state of mind.

The bond between us solidifies, energizes, relaxes. Tension bleeds from his shoulders, releases on a sigh.

"It'll be okay, T. Unless you snap on a bracelet, they can't make you do anything."

He picks up the bottle and chugs it in one fluid motion. "Goddamn ghosts. Why don't they leave me the fuck alone?"

"Maybe you're supposed to see them."

He shoots me a go to hell look. "Yeah. Right." His gaze focuses over my shoulder and his jaw tightens. "Well, shit. Your fucking ghost lover is back."

I spin around so fast I make myself dizzy. Nothing. No Blake. Then I remember. I let go of T's shoulder to turn. In order to see ghosts I have to touch my twin.

Once I put my hand back on T's shoulder, Blake snaps into view.

And my heart feels like it breaks into small pieces. He needs to leave, to pass into the light, not stay on this plane.

Wanting him to remain here is selfish. I need to let him go. No matter how much it hurts.

I swallow the lump lodged in my throat and offer Blake a smile.

Are you okay? Blake's lips move, but his voice echoes in my head.

T points his empty bottle at Blake. "I have iron filings. Say what you have to say because this is your last visit, fucker."

Blake flips him off. Always nice to know relationships continue after death.

Gin wasn't home this afternoon when I tried to warn her. You don't know what you're dealing with.

Understatement of the day. Lately I rarely know what I'm dealing with, so perhaps lack of knowledge is the new norm for me.

"What's going on in there?" Smythe shouts from his resting spot on the couch.

"Nothing." T and I speak simultaneously.

"Why don't I believe you?"

"I don't know. You tell me." I should poke my head into the living room, but I can't let Blake out of my sight.

Talk about issues.

The couch squeaks as he stands. Blake looks to the living room as the sound of shitkickers striking wood floors grows closer.

Why is he always around?

"He's my mentor."

"Are you talking to a ghost?" Smythe crosses his arms and leans against the wall, a pale block of formidable man with a curiosity streak.

Not that I blame him. If I caught him talking to a ghost, I'd want to know what it said too.

Eloise steps behind him as if she wasn't blind. "As much as you want to deny it, T, ghosts always find a ghost talker. You must learn to control your talent before it controls you."

Yeah. Been there. Done that. Experience taught my twin to fear. The less they know about the experience, the better.

T's jaw tightens to a hard ball of muscle, his eyes snapping black fire. He white-knuckles the beer bottle, tension spreading to his shoulders despite my touch.

Intervention needed, stat.

"Blake's back." I gesture to his ghost while mouthing 'sorry.' Blake shrugs, a silent whatever.

"Ask him who we're dealing with."

"I told you what you're dealing with." Eloise answers Smythe, her eyes narrowing, aggravation coloring her tone.

"I said who, not what."

Okaaaay. Wonder what happened between those two to set off the stare and glare game?

Gin, Blake's voice snaps my attention away from the wonder factor back to reality. *I can only tell you that who you're looking for is not who he appeared to be.*

"Appeared?"

You've already met him.

"Then who is it?"

I've said all I can say.

"What do you mean by that?"

Blake shakes his head. *It's all I was told. Please don't let T pour iron filings. I won't be able to see you.*

"Okay."

"Bullshit." T crosses his arms, almost dislodging my grasp. "You are outta here."

"It's my house."

Tonight must be stare and glare game night. Someone forgot to send me the memo.

No.

Is so.

What if he pops in like some fuckin' peeping Tom?

T, he was my lover. What hasn't he seen?

T draws in slow breaths until the anger disappears from his gaze. *Fine.*

Thanks.

I turn to Blake, but he's gone. And just like that my chest aches, a soul deep pain turning my insides into mush. I stare for a moment where he stood, using the time to collect myself. I refuse to fall apart in front of Smythe.

"He's gone." Yay, me. Strong voice without a

hitch.

"What did he say? Did he tell you anything regarding the demon?"

"It's a fear demon, Aidan."

"I know that, Eloise." Gritted teeth warp his voice.

What the hell happened between them? They seemed happy when we first walked into the kitchen.

"Will they leave me alone if I do what you want?" T leans back against the counter, eyes narrow, the muscle in his jaw twitching.

"Say what?" Was he really considering using his ability?

Eloise smiles a devious smile worse than any expression David ever wore. What the hell? "They are more likely to leave you alone if you attend to their needs."

T pauses, the muscle twitch beating in time with his heart. "Fine. I'll think on it. I'm going to bed."

He takes the hall route, bypassing Eloise and an about to fall down Smythe, the weight of their stares a physical punch.

Eloise recovers first, her lips turning with a secret glee. "I bid you good-night, Gin. I will return tomorrow. Aidan." Her hand waves a circle in front of her face. A second later, a portal swallows her head first, leaving Smythe leaning against the wall and me wondering what the fuck went on with T.

I try to hop into his head, but he's formed mental barriers thicker than ten feet of stone. Not getting through those things.

Smythe takes a step toward me, stumbles, and grabs the wall. Thoughts of T vanish as I rush to my mentor, throw an arm around his waist, and head him toward my bedroom. He lets me without saying a word. Not a good sign. Normally he'd insist upon walking himself. That nothing was wrong. That he was fine.

Instead, he leans into me, allowing me to absorb his weight like a human support stick. After a stumble he doesn't seem to notice, I manage to help him into my bedroom, where I deposit him on the bed. He falls onto the pillows, legs hanging off the edge, as if unable to decide upon standing or lying.

Or maybe he's being polite and refuses to put his boots on my bed.

More likely, he used what little energy he regained to stand like a tough guy and grill us about Blake's ghost.

Since he lies still as a sleeping lion, I check his pulse—slow but steady—remove his boots and lift his legs onto the bed. Even with the working A/C it's too warm for covers, so I flip on the lamp on the nightstand, before walking into the bathroom.

I shut the door and lean against it. Smythe is in my bed.

A thrill lights a fire inside, invisible flames rushing through my veins straight to my core. I'm a sad case. Sad, sad, sad. I see my dead lover and promptly lust after another man.

Freud would have a field day with me.

A round of Blake-is-dead-you-can-find-another-man battles with Blake-is-dead-you-should-be-mourning-him. I sink to the cool tile and let the voices in my head duke it out. Guilt warring with lust.

Not like lust is going to win. Not tonight anyway. Smythe can't even open his mouth to say, 'thanks.' Little chance of his dick hopping up and waving do-me.

Guilt assuaged—but in no way vanquished—I do my business in the bathroom, change into a loose pair of shorts and an oversized t-shirt and return to the bedroom. Smythe snores like a battery-operated car, quiet and with little noise. Just enough to let me know someone else sleeps in my bed.

As if I could forget.

He looks peaceful sleeping. Pale, but peaceful. As if a demon didn't attack him. As if he didn't have to expend all his magic to protect me. As if an anthrax filled envelope didn't find its way to my front porch.

That thought punches me in the chest with the force of a Mac truck. Someone tried to kill me. Who? Samantha? No, not her style. Why use anthrax when she could call up a regiment of minions to do her dirty work?

Speaking of, Smythe still hadn't linked her to that attack. David refused to believe me, taking little miss bleached blonde at her word. Damn bitch.

Yeah, she hated me. But she wouldn't leave me anthrax. Which circles me around to who did it.

The butler in the pantry?

I wish.

I click off the lamp, crawl on top of the covers, and stare at the ceiling.

Who tried to kill me? Who wants me dead? Who stole the anthrax?

Gah. I need a drink.

Cranking my fingers into fists and holding them as they shake helps center me. I really don't need a drink. Or T's stash of weed. Or anything stronger. I need to solve the mystery of who wants me dead. Mind-altering pharmaceuticals won't help me there.

My nails press into my palms, the bite of pain a reminder of how far I've come. How I've turned my life around. How I've made more of myself than I thought possible.

I'm good. Now. I won't slip into destructive patterns. Again.

Nope. I won't. Really. I think.

To take my mind off my internal monster scratching for release, I replay the day's events. Missing anthrax. Scary-ass demon. Blonde minion woman. Saved that one. File away how I saved her for more thinking. Exhausted Smythe. Letter containing anthrax.

Not a stretch of the imagination to connect the dots from the missing anthrax to the stuff showing up on my porch. But why? And who?

A little niggling thought jostles the back of my mind. I reach for it, but it dissipates like steam rising from a lake in winter. What was it? Will Blake come back?

I see his smile, the look in his eyes as we make love. The slash on his neck from Jezebeth's claws.

I turn onto my side. Squeeze my eyes shut. A wave of emotional exhaustion drags me under, drowning me in a riptide of sleep.

Chapter Eighteen

Blake kisses me, his lips hot on mine, his hand slipping under my shirt. Why am I wearing a shirt? I break the kiss to yank off the offending item, then press against him, chest to chest, skin to skin, his heat warming mine. His kiss feels different, less loving and more demanding as if he brands me a possession.

I don't mind.

His hands slide up my ribs, over my breasts, his mouth drawing my nipple into its moist depths. Sparks explode through my veins, a cataclysm of fire he swallows as if water to a dying man.

Red-hot energy wells from a spring deep inside me, searing flesh, branding me a beast of desire.

I've never felt like this with Blake.

Blake. My lover. My dead lover.

Dead. Stiff. Blood staining his shirt, his skin, from the gash in his neck.

What the fuck?

"Mmm, Jennifer," he moans. "You taste good."

My eyes snap open. Smythe lays on top of me, eyes shut, his jean-clad package pressing against my core, hips rocking against mine.

It feels…good.

What the hell is wrong with me? I shove his shoulder. "Smythe. Smythe."

He pauses, lips against my neck. But only for a

second and then he's back to playing vampire on my neck. Except instead of blood, he's draining my energy. I pop him upside his head. "Wake the fuck up!"

Smythe raises his head, brows stitched together in clear confusion. I give him another smack. "Wake up."

When his eyes flare, mouth forming an O, I shove his shoulder. He scrambles off me so fast he lands ass first on the floor. Part of me wants to help him. The other part tingles with an unholy fire, an orgasm three licks away from rocking my world.

I shove my head into the pillow and stare at the ceiling, my heart pounding a racing rhythm, exhaustion coupled with desire riding my bones. What the hell did he do to me?

Besides the obvious. And damn me for a hypocrite, but when can I invite him back to my bed for real? Or was it all a dream?

"I'm so sorry, Gin." Smythe sits on the floor next to me. "I was dreaming. No excuse though. I'm so sorry. I'll go sleep on the couch."

"You called me Jennifer." Okay, Gin, jealous much?

"I'm sorry."

"She was your mentee before me, right?"

A long pause. "Yeah."

"She was to you like Blake was to me."

He scrubs a hand down his face. "It was wrong."

"Yeah. Messing work with pleasure never ends well."

"It wasn't that. She…" he trails off. Enough light creeps through the blinds to show his jaw clenched. So much for learning why the relationship was wrong.

Or why I'm jealous of a dead woman.

I roll on my side, facing him. "And what was with the energy thing? Was I dreaming, or were you really being an energy vamp?"

"Oh shit." He reaches out a hand, draws it back. I grab his palm, watch as his eyes widen. "I'm sorry."

"I get that. Energy, Smythe, energy. What the hell were you doing?"

His fingers tighten on mine, his eyes dropping to the floor. Bitterness creeps into my skin, a rare read into his emotions.

"A ritual with herbal tea isn't the only way to replenish a mage's energy when they've burned through magic."

"Oh." Disappointment kills the zipping tingles. I'm a means to an end, not the cherry topping.

Really, I shouldn't be so disappointed. Really. I should not.

"I'm sorry. I—"

"I know. You were dreaming, and you needed more help than a good night's sleep. I understand." Understanding did not make me feel better.

Gah. Hormones are stupid things designed to make a reasonable woman crazy.

"I'm sorry."

"I get it. Now what?"

"I go sleep on the couch."

I sigh. Sleeping on the couch did not make for a restful night. Waking in the morning to a grouchy Smythe was in no one's benefit. And keeping him in bed with me was the right thing to do.

"You can finish the night in here with me. Just stay on your side of the bed." I give his hand a squeeze as his gaze snaps to mine.

232

"I don't know what to say."

"Thank you?"

"Yeah." One side of his mouth turns up. "Thank you." He stands, pitches me my shirt, grabs his t-shirt off the floor and yanks it on.

I pull on my shirt while he slides back into bed. The A/C vent crackles like a static-y radio, but blows cool air. Thank goodness. I'm already hot and bothered. Cool air might help.

Smythe touches my shoulder. A simple touch, not sexual, and yet my core fires heat, tingling with anticipation. Down, hormones, down.

"Thanks, Gin. I owe you."

"Sure, whatever. Good night." I take his promise as a sign he trusts me again.

I really should stop fooling myself.

*****

The gentle touch of morning light wakes me, stroking my cheek with the softness of a lover's touch. I want to slap it silly. Instead, I crack a lid and leap out of bed. I'm late for work. Adrenaline pounds a race and I'm halfway to the bathroom before I remember that today is my scheduled day off.

I hate it when I do this. But since I'm awake, I might as well get going.

Smythe lays curled on his side, facing away from me. I leave him alone, letting him recharge his batteries before he tries to drain mine again.

I don't feel drained. I feel energized. Which should not be the case after yesterday. Clearly I have issues.

None of which can be solved without a dose of coffee. Or several doses. After a quick run through the shower, I face the already steaming coffeepot, pour myself a cup, and think.

T either overslept or already left. Mug in hand, I walk to his room and open the door. No T. Already left then. His window sits cracked open a couple of inches, hot, humid air circling his room like a miasma of pollution. I pause, staring at the open window, while a mixture of emotions twist a jagged path inside my chest. Then I sigh and close it.

T, you okay?

Ouch! A sharp pain whacks the top of my head as T bumps his head on the underside of a car hood. Oops.

Sorry. Just wanted to know how you were.

I was fine. I can almost see him rubbing his head, easing the pain in mine.

You still feel okay?

Yeah. Someone from the health department is supposed to call but this is the best I've felt in awhile. I'll have to tell Eloise thanks personally.

You already did.

It never hurts to be nice.

Or to flirt with a woman he finds attractive.

I heard that.

Oops. *Just admit the attraction and move on.*

Whatever. Work needs my full attention. See you later? I'll be home early.

Sure.

He snaps our mental connection closed, leaving me chuckling. Him and Eloise? That's funnier than imagining Jackie as a genius in disguise.

Instead of completing my morning ritual of coffee and newspaper, I walk my mug into the living room and open Smythe's laptop. For a man who clutches the thing like it's about to be stolen, you'd think he would bother to password protect it.

A couple of button pushes later and a sharp sting bites my fingers. Ouch, ouch, ouch. What was that?

I touch the mousepad, intending to open a browser, and get a shock that blows my fingers off the keyboard and numbs my arm. A high-pitched squeak passes my lips, unrecognizable as my voice, a clear result of an almost electrocution.

No wonder the laptop wasn't password protected. A spelled keyboard protects better than any password in existence. And hurts like a son of a bitch too.

Footsteps pound a rhythm toward me, a barefoot Smythe stops feet away, his gaze roaming between me and the laptop. A shit-eating grin spreads across his face.

"I see you've met the spell."

"Yeah, thanks for telling me about it." I set the computer on the coffee table and pick up my mug with tingling fingers.

"It's funnier to watch you try."

"Glad you find humor in my tingling fingers."

His mouth opens like he's going to make a smartass remark, when his face clouds, all traces of his smile vanishing. "Are you okay? I feel unusually good this morning. You must be drained."

"I'm fine." As his brows snap together, I amend the sentence. "Really. Fine. Woke with a ton of energy, which is strange." I almost didn't need the second cup of coffee, but not drinking another meant throwing out a whole pot and that's a waste of good coffee.

And money.

He runs a hand through his hair and takes a step back. Away from me. As if he's afraid. Or ashamed.

"Don't take this the wrong way, but your energy tasted different than anything I've had."

"Good thing you're not a vamp. I vant to suck your blood." I use my best Dracula voice as I stand to get more coffee.

"Seriously, Gin. Why?"

"How the hell am I supposed to know? Maybe because I'm an empath?"

His expression speaks his doubt. I leave him alone with his thoughts and go pour myself another cup.

"It's something else."

Coffee splashes over the edge of the mug as I jump. Smythe stands behind me. Not where I expect him to be since I didn't hear him follow me.

"Sorry."

"You've said that enough to last a lifetime." I grab a paper towel and clean up the spilled mess. "Why don't we figure out this demon instead of discussing last night? It happened. It's over. We can forget about it."

He blinks. Right. Not over for him. But I can see the gears switching to another mode as he considers what I said. I pitch the paper towel into the trash and walk back into the living room. Smythe can heat his own drink of English breakfast tea. He's been staying here so often I no longer need to play the gracious hostess.

But this morning he follows me sans tea. "It's not the demon." He beats me to the couch and grabs his laptop. One side of his lip kicks up as he winks at me while opening a browser. "The anthrax is more worrisome than the demon."

"Especially since it showed up at my place. Who

the hell wants me dead?"

"The real question is why."

I take a swallow of coffee and let its heat wend through my frozen veins. Why does someone want me dead? Besides Samantha? That bitch might have thrown a party if I'd breathed in anthrax spores, but that didn't mean she left the envelope. Not her style.

I flop on the couch and peer at the laptop. The Department of Defense flashes across the screen from their internal website. I have no idea what he's looking for. Names and numbers scroll across the screen in an eye twitching, nausea inducing dance.

"Ah-ha." He plops the laptop on the coffee table and stands. "I'll be right back."

A couple of seconds later the bathroom door shuts. I pick up the laptop, but avoid touching the keys. I'm a quick study.

The page is open to a bio on Dr. Sheevers. No mention of a wife. Maybe he was divorced?

Smythe walks back into the room. "Thought you learned not to touch it."

"I learned not to touch the keyboard. I can pick the thing up just fine."

He takes the computer from me, sets it in his lap as he sits. "There's nothing about a wife."

"Just what I was thinking. Maybe he's divorced."

"Or has never been married."

"Then who's the woman in the wedding picture on his office desk?"

Smythe shrugs and opens another browser. A few clicks later and Dallas county records scroll across the screen. He pauses the cursor over a name.

"Huh. Look at that. A Dr. Stan Sheevers sues the

Dallas City Council for seizing his property under imminent domain. He lost."

"Stan? I thought Dr. Sheevers first name was Dan."

He clicks back onto the DOD page. "Yep. Dan. Maybe a brother?"

"See if you can find a picture of this Stan."

The words no sooner leave my lips than Stan's picture appears on the screen. We both lean forward as if our eyes stopped working.

"Stan looks enough like Dan to be his twin."

A few more clicks and Smythe nods. "Stan is his twin."

"What happened to him?"

He flips to the other browser window. "Says Stan's wife died of a heart attack after their home was seized. Then the lawsuit. Then nothing. That was almost a year ago."

A thought niggles at the back of mind, just like it did last night. "When was Dan Sheevers killed?"

"A couple of days—"

"No. I mean the time of death. What does the police report say?"

"Oh. Let's see." Hacking skills rule. The Dallas Police Department flashes across the screen. He pulls up the case file and starts reading. "Looks like the time of death was in the morning." His brows furrow. "The morning of Blake's funeral."

"Oh my God. Remember how I touched Dr. Sheevers and thought I saw a vision of him dying? It wasn't a vision. It was me being an empath and seeing his thoughts. That was Stan at the funeral. Why the hell would he show up to a funeral after murdering his brother?"

"Who said anything about him killing his brother? He might have walked in after the murder."

"And let him lay there without calling the police and then masquerading as his twin at a funeral for someone he probably didn't know? Trust me, as a twin, that would not happen."

"You're close to T. Maybe he wasn't close to his brother."

"Clearly, if he killed him. I know not all twins are close, but still. Even if you didn't get along, that's some bizarre-ass behavior. I think we're looking at Dr. Dan Sheevers' murderer."

Smythe pokes a few more buttons before leaning back. "Okay, let's say you're right. Why would Stan kill his brother? Why would he pretend to be his brother? What would he gain?"

"Money? Aren't most crimes for passion or money?"

"I guess. If you were to commit a murder, why would you do it?"

And just like that I go from inquisitive to wanting to hide. He knows. Panic slides into my chest, hitching my breathing, racing my heart. What will he do? Will he turn us in? Blackmail? The coffee mug hangs frozen in my hand, halfway to my mouth. Frozen, like my body, like my mouth. My mind though, that traitorous mind, replays years ago events like they happened yesterday.

A breath full of liquor mingled with the stench of unwashed body. Pain flaring along bruised flesh. The knowledge death stood a step away. The feel of cold iron in my palm. The sound of metal meeting flesh. The rush of blood dropping against my skin.

"Gin?" Smythe touches my arm, his hand hot against my chilled flesh.

I swallow. "Sorry. Just thinking. I'm a nurse, not a killer so I have to think on it." Liar, liar.

"You don't look so good."

"I'm fine. The question just caught me off guard. What about you? Why would you commit a murder?"

"If someone tried to kill me or the ones I loved."

"Good answer." Does that mean he thinks those reasons are okay?

I shake my head, stare at my mug, and make my eyes flare. "Look at that. I'm out of coffee. Would you like some?"

He shakes his head but eyes me as if my trembling limbs might fall off.

"Okay, then. Be right back." What were the chances he'd forget about my reaction while I poured another cup of coffee? Slim? Or none?

I lean against the counter. Draw in a breath. And another. Pour the coffee into my mug. Maybe he'll chalk my tremor to too much coffee. It could happen.

"You were right." Smythe hollers from the other room. Right about what? Oh. The murdering twin remark. At least I hope that's what he's referring to.

Perhaps my luck will hold after all, and he won't question me about things best left buried. I grab the mug and head back to the couch.

"I told you Stan killed his twin."

"Looks like there are fingerprints for Stan in Dan Sheevers's house. According to the police report, the brothers hadn't seen each other in years. Stan is under investigation, but they haven't been able to find him."

"We've seen him, though, right? That would've

been him we talked to at the med school." A realization slams into my mind, hitching my breath. "What if he's the one who stole the anthrax?"

Smythe clicks more keys, nodding at the result. "The police suspect him. Still doesn't explain why you got it, or why the demon appeared. Or where the demon is."

"Or what it is." And please, oh, please, don't let me see the thing again.

So much for being a demon huntress.

"Eloise thinks it's a fear demon. One of the worst kinds."

"A fear demon is one of the worst demons? Or this particular one is badder than most?" I need a demonology textbook to keep all these demons straight.

"Yes."

"Which one?"

"Both. Either. Instead of discovering the mystery of the Sheevers twins, we should be working on a plan to stop the demon."

"Stop him from what? Returning? Because hopping a portal to Hell is not on my to-do list for the day."

He shakes his head. "*Justitians* do not jump portals to Hell. We wait until the demon appears. If it appears. This one isn't following the normal parameters."

"It doesn't make minions from bad people." That's one demon lesson I learned early. "The students it's hopped into had souls too good to allow the possession. A waste of the demon. Why bother?"

"Yep. That's the question of the day." He sets the laptop on the coffee table and stands. "I'm hungry. We can discuss the game plan over breakfast."

Having a man around who can cook, rocks. I hate fixing breakfast. If it's not cereal, coffee and the obligatory piece of fruit, then it doesn't get made.

But Smythe loves his bacon and eggs. Being the gracious host, I hand him a skillet and let him go to town. Another cup of coffee and the paper, coming up.

I pull the protective sleeve off the paper, pitch it in the trash and plant my butt in my chair. Only to choke on a mouthful of coffee.

"You okay?"

I point to the paper. "We know where the anthrax went."

Chapter Nineteen

Smythe abandons his skillet to lean over my shoulder. He lets loose a low whistle as he reads the headline: *Anthrax found in City Councilmembers' Mail.* "Damn. How many city council members found an envelope in their mailbox?"

I scan the article, flipping pages to the continuation. "All of them in their home mail. Looks like the letters contained a false postmark. Stan Sheevers has been a busy man."

"Provided he's the perp." Smythe squeezes my shoulder and returns to the stove.

"We've been through this. Of course he is."

"Innocent until proven guilty. Not the other way around. And since now it's a police matter, we can concentrate on the demon. Maybe we should look at other anthrax labs and see if it appears."

"Why? Anthrax can be found in nature."

"Not the purified kind."

"Any kind is not a good thing."

He snorts, his concentration taken by the bacon sizzling in the skillet.

I return to the paper. I'm right about Stan being the perpetrator. I know I am. I know I have the name of the person responsible for almost killing my twin with an anthrax-laced letter.

Unfortunately, he's not a minion and I'm not a

repeat murderer. I sigh. As much as I don't want to admit it, Smythe is right. The police need to handle Stan. We have to concentrate on the demon.

For once my *justitia* fails to get excited about a potential demon hunt. And what does that tell me? Right. Maybe I should stay home and concentrate on something I can handle. Like cooking dinner.

Chances are good T and Jackie will show up and expect a meal. Either I cook, or Jackie will try her hand at not burning the kitchen again. Do I really want to tempt fate twice?

I grab my mug and head to the cabinet containing the cookbooks.

"Whatcha doing?"

"Trying to come up with something to cook tonight."

"Preplanning meals now?"

"I don't mind fixing dinner. It's breakfast I hate to cook."

"Lucky for you I made breakfast." He gestures to a skillet of scrambled eggs and a plate of bacon on the stove.

"I knew I kept you around for a reason."

A half-grin kicks one side of his lips. Does that mean he trusts me again? Asking would make me seem insecure. No sense in clueing him in.

I grab a plate, load it with bacon and eggs, pick up my mug, and carry everything to the table. Smythe follows, shoves the paper out of the way before sitting.

"I want to know why the demon wants the anthrax." He amends the sentence as I shoot him a for-real stare. "I know the demon wants to wreak havoc with it, I'm not stupid. But why this anthrax? Why not another batch?"

"Why do demons normally appear on earth?"

"What does that have to do with anthrax?"

"Nothing. Everything. Why do they?"

His brow raise accents his disgusted tone. "I taught you that your first week."

"Maybe I need a refresher course."

"Your first week was a week and a half ago. You do not need a refresher course."

"Are you going to lecture me or answer the question?"

His glare offers an icy one-way trip to hell. "Remember this—"

"Yes, O Master."

"Mentor." One side of his lip twitches. "Demons prefer not to appear on earth. When they do, they usually try to make minions to do their dirty work for them. When they appear, it's brief."

"And captured by the Agency's computers, right?"

"Yes. As long as they are on earth for at least thirty seconds."

Zagan pops into my mind. Did the Agency know he paid me a visit the other night? "Always?"

"Demons disrupt the space-continuum. The computer program picks up that rupture. At least it's supposed to. It picked up the fear demon as a flock of birds." He shakes his head.

"Yep, that was a bad mistake. A flock of birds? Really?" I'm pretty sure if I made a mistake like that in my job, Nurse Hatchet would fire me.

"The programmers will fix the bug. It works most of the time, or we wouldn't use it. The computers picked up this recent demon. But the program doesn't track where the demon goes, only when it appears from hell."

"So it can appear, blend in, and the Agency would lose it?"

"Demons don't blend in. But in theory, I suppose. Why?"

"No reason." Zagan was safe. I refuse to give attention to why that matters. Even my *justitia* sighs in relief at the thought.

Smythe stuffs his last piece of bacon into his mouth and talks around it. "Do you think the demon is loose in the world hunting biological weapons?"

"Not really. I'm trying to understand why the thing wastes energy on making minions it can't keep. It doesn't make sense."

"It's a demon. That's all the sense you need."

I shove back my chair and grab my plate. "Okay then. Enough about demons. I'm going to prep dinner."

"I'll take a shower while you do that."

Now why did he have to go and mention showering? My mind hops from cooking dinner to cooking of a whole other kind. Why can I not keep my mind out of his pants? What the hell is wrong with me?

One oversexed empath coming up.

Smythe leaves me alone with the dishes, a cookbook, and the hormone levels of a bitch in heat.

Damn it.

Instead of focusing on a naked, buff Smythe with water rushing over his rippling muscles, I turn my attention to dinner. A flip through the cookbook and shuffle of pantry items, and I place the ingredients for Virginia chicken casserole on the counter. By the time Smythe's footsteps stride to the living room, I have the ingredients assembled, the oven heated, and the dish ready to cook.

A heavy squeak of the couch springs indicates my mentor relaxes with his laptop. I poke my head around the doorframe into the living room. Always nice to know my ears heard things correctly.

I put the dish in the oven, set the timer, and head to the bedroom.

And come to a complete stop. The bedcovers hang in a haphazard mess, the result of Smythe falling out of bed to come to the rescue of his laptop. I straighten the covers, plump the pillows. My hand lingers on his pillow, the same pillow Blake used. If I close my eyes, I can see Blake lying here, waiting for me, his smile a caress of love.

My fingers tighten on the pillowcase, skin blanching, memories of our time together playing through my mind. I grab the pillow, bring it up to my nose, and inhale. But it's not Blake I smell, it's Smythe. Like a dog, covering the scent of another, erasing memories from my heart.

Instead of smelling the pillow, I need to use it to whack some sense into my head. A couple of hits later, I return the pillow to its place. No sense damaging the thing on my thick skull.

Blake is dead. Smelling his scent, remembering his expression as he looked at me as if I was something precious, only leads to sadness. Remembering him for who he was, my friend, my lover, one of the few who understood me, then letting him go was the only way for me to survive his death.

Easier thought than done. I want him in the flesh. I have him as a ghost as long as T's around. Where's the fun in that? And shouldn't he be doing something in the afterlife? Like twirling around on a cloud with a harp and a hot angel?

I giggle at the mental picture of Blake dancing on a cloud. Then slap both hands over my face and draw in a shaky breath. When my hands drop, I wish I'd left my eyes closed.

Zagan leans against the wall, his six-foot tall muscular frame looking good in a skin-tight white t-shirt and black jeans. Black hair pulled back in a tie at his nape and olive-toned skin gives my heart palpitations.

Where's a defibrillator when I need one?

My *justitia* explodes into its happy-happy, joy-joy dance, its excitement a vibration of energy along my nerves. It wants me to draw closer, to touch, to…

Oh, hell no. I am not walking that road again. The bracelet can calm itself down.

Zagan raises a brow as if he sees inside me, as if he hears my internal conversation with the *justitia*.

Embarrassment mixed with wariness turns my knees to rubber and heats my face. "What are you doing here?"

"You did not listen to me last time. Do not let fear conquer you."

Understanding dawns like rays of morning sun hidden by clouds. Fear. The demon. "That's its name."

"No. Fear is the type. There are many fear demons, but this one is the leader of them all. Agramon is his name. And you will kill him."

"And how do you propose I do that? In case you weren't watching we"—I hold up my wrist with the bracelet and shake it—"were almost annihilated by your fear friend."

Zagan's lips twist, his nose wrinkling in disgust. "He is no friend. You will conquer him. You will destroy fear the only way fear can be destroyed. I have given you what you need."

Apparently Zagan takes lessons from Smythe in how to flap one's lips and still be evasive.

Before I can ask what the heck he's talking about, Smythe yells, "What?" loud enough to wake a hibernating yeti. I turn, take a step toward the hall, in case he needs my help. Two thuds follow his yell, his feet smacking against the wooden floor.

"Gin! Get out here! There's been a demon appearance."

My head snaps around so fast I give myself whiplash. But Zagan is gone. Vanished. Not even a trace of his portal remains. Part of me thinks I imagined him. It's a little part and quickly squashed by remnants of the *justitia's* happy dance through my system.

Loud thumps of bare feet against the floor precede Smythe down the hall. "What are you doing? Get ready. Where are those leather pants I loaned you? Don't just stand there, move!"

Captain drill sergeant to the rescue.

"What demon?" Please don't say the one in my bedroom.

"Not sure, but it's at the city courthouse. The Agency's bringing in other mages to help contain it."

"Any *Justitians*?"

"Just you."

Do they have confidence in me? Or is this a mass conspiracy to kill me?

"Is Samantha coming?"

"No."

Confidence, then. Or a hope I'll fail even when set up to succeed.

I'm a conspiracy theorist at heart.

"Good."

"Get dressed."

He stalks to the living presumably to put on his shoes. Hard to fight a demon barefooted. Now to find those leather pants.

Not in the closet.

I dash into the bathroom and dig through the dirty clothes hamper. Crap. Guess I have to wear dirty pants. Good thing black leather hides minion blood.

I'm pulling on my thick-soled ankle-high leather boots—an inappropriate shoe choice for summertime in Texas—when Smythe pokes his head into the room. Little sparks of anxiety pop around his head as if he's a firecracker. I blink and they disappear.

What the hell?

No time to think on it. He vibrates with enough energy to give a rocket a boost into outer space. His gaze rakes over me, professionalism morphing into heat. Which he banks as he holds out his hand.

"Ready?"

Halfway to his hand I realize the oven's on. "Just a sec."

He follows me into the kitchen, his boots thudding an impatient beat against the floor. By the time I turn off the oven, he has a portal open, warmth spreading through the kitchen like I left the back door open.

I grasp his outstretched palm and step into the icy depths of the in-between.

Chapter Twenty

Loud voices raised in fear and anger assail my ears as the portal spits us into a deserted hallway. Dallas City Hall, I'm assuming. At least that's where we're supposed to go. Smythe hits the ground running, but I take a couple of breaths before following, my shoes thudding a hesitant echo.

He darts around the corner, and I almost run into him when he stops.

"What the—"

"Fuck." A strong hand grabs my wrist and yanks me to stand beside him.

No wonder he stopped. Chaos reigns in the atrium.

Stan Sheevers stands by one of the front doors, holding some object—I can't tell what—above his head, a gun grasped in his other hand. Security surrounds him, guns pointed, fear written in the lines on their faces. People hover in the background, unable to escape, or too curious for their own good.

Smythe curses as Stan's gaze lands on us.

"You!" Stan points the gun at me, causing the guards to turn our way. Smythe waves a hand and the guards return their focus to Stan. Unfortunately, his spell fails to stop Stan from continuing to yell at me.

"You should be dead! I left you a gift for poking your nose in where it didn't belong. Just like Dan. Trying to stop me from doing what needed to be done.

Refusing to give me a sample of his anthrax. I showed him, didn't I? I did. So why aren't you dead?"

"Hey, buddy," one of the guards asks. "Who you talking to?"

Stan's attention snaps back to the crowd of security surrounding him. "Her." He waves his gun my direction at the same time Smythe mutters a spell.

This time the spell works to hide us from view, judging by the furrow between Stan's brows.

I unclench my fists. Knowing I was right about Stan leaving me the envelope failed to bring happiness. The fucker almost killed my brother. And unless he turns into a minion, I can't do one damn thing about it.

"Do you see the demon?"

Smythe's words snap me out of my impotent rage. I can't do a thing about Stan, but I can find the demon. I close my eyes, tap into the *justitia*, and activate the minion sensors in my eyes. An action which no longer seems odd.

When I open my eyes, I see nothing but a ton of concrete. Concrete walls rise stories above us, an architect's delight of balance and modern art. Maybe one of these days I'll return and gawk.

Now I need to find a demon in this concrete monstrosity before Stan does something stupid. Like take a potshot at me.

I turn a three-sixty, unease prickling my skin into bumps, looking for the black blob of demon energy. I know the thing is here. Not only did the Agency computer say so, but my *justitia* vibrates a deep hum, acknowledging a demonic presence without forming a sword.

Guess it needs a visual.

"Stay back, or I'll drop it! I mean it!" Stan yells, shaking the unknown object in his hand.

A couple of security personnel step back. One wipes his forehead on the back of his arm. Haven't they seen a crazy guy in here before? After all, this is where the city council meets.

"Shit!" Smythe's eyes flare.

Did he see the demon? My gaze follows where he looks, but he stares at Stan. Not a demon to be found. And as much as I want to hurt Stan for hurting T, he remains human, not a minion. Unless I want a trip to jail, I need to let the police handle the crazy killer. Being locked behind bars is about as appealing as thinking of my last demon fight.

If no demon or minion, what is Smythe upset about? The answer hits me like a speeding truck, hard and fast and life changing. It's not the gun Stan waves with more flash than aim. It's the object in his hand. The object I now see clearly. A vial. A vial like those in Dr. Sheevers' lab. Tubes of weaponized anthrax.

Oh shit barely scratches the surface.

Dizziness spins my vision as I struggle to draw in a breath. I grab Smythe's arm. Give it a shake. "Form a portal. Now. Get me out of here."

He shakes off my hand like waving off an annoying fly. "Once the team arrives, we'll contain it."

"Are you kidding?"

One raised brow informs me I've insulted him. Deal, buddy.

"We train for situations like this."

"With anthrax?" I clear my high-pitched voice. "Mages train for bioweapons?"

He swallows, his gaze bouncing from Stan to a

point by my ear. "We can handle it."

"Handle this. I'm leav—" The words die in my mouth as my backward step runs me into someone. Strong hands grab my arms, keeping me upright. Images flash through my mind, energy bolts, demons, dead minions, all laced with a glee bordering on the maniacal.

"Aidan." The hands release me before I determine whether they belong to a psycho killer or someone who's really into their job. Let's hope it's the latter and not the former.

"Chris."

I turn while Smythe answers the greeting to see Team Agency en masse behind us. Six men, no women.

Someone needs to speak with HR about gender equality.

"Where's the demon?" A tall, dark-skinned mage with a voice like James Earl Jones and a body like the statue of David, asks.

Smythe shrugs. "We've got a problem. That man," he points to Stan, "probably has anthrax in that vial he's holding. We need to be ready with a containment field in case he drops it."

Judging from the f-bombs, not a team member is happy about the potential for mass casualties. Or they aren't as confident in their containment abilities as Smythe claims. Sweat beads on their foreheads as if they spent too much time outside in the Texas heat. A couple lick their lips as they check out the Stan show. Despite knowing a bioweapon might drop and kill us all, not a one of them forms a portal, grabs me and escapes. Damn men and their sense of priority.

Although I'm a fine one to be talking. Just because

my heart pounds a run-away-run-away beat, and I really need a potty doesn't mean I can leave. The silver links fastened around my wrist guaran-damn-tees my ass stays in direct line of the bioweapon.

And I wanted to be a *Justitian*? What was I thinking?

After a brief discussion on the best way to handle containment—to my relief it appears Smythe wasn't blowing smoke with his 'we can handle it' claim—Team Agency spreads out, two mages slithering along the wall to stand on either side of the guards circled around Stan. Two take positions between Stan and us, palms held outward but close to their bodies. The remaining mages, including the James Earl Jones echo—whose name is actually James—stay with us. And give me dirty looks. As if I should be risking my life to stop Stan from dropping the vial. Or maybe they think I should be doing a better job of hunting for the demon.

Okay, fine. Maybe they have a point. But hunting a demon when I really want to flee takes more willpower than I possess. And it doesn't help that my *justitia* would rather join me in the run-and-hide move instead of fighting and killing.

"Gin?" Smythe's blue eyes grab my gaze. "We're in position. Where's the demon?"

I cross my arms, rub my hands up and down goosebump covered flesh. "I don't see it. Have you looked?"

"What do you think I've been doing?"

"I don't know. Trying to form a containment field?"

Smythe's eyes narrow. *Focus and stop smarting*

off.

"I'll try again." I blow out a puff of air, uncross my arms, and focus my gaze on the shadows thickening in the corners.

My *justitia* shivers as if it senses the demon. A quick glance around the atrium shows no demon. At least not a visible one. I step around Smythe as he talks to James and Chris about containment spells, my gaze drifting to the corners. Enough light shines through the several stories tall windows to obliterate shadows, yet behind a potted tree a shadow shimmers a malevolent hue.

The demon? Or trick of the light?

"I will do anything to pay those assholes back!" Stan screams. "Anything! They stole my land! They killed my wife!"

The shadow moves into the light, solidifying into Cracked Flesh, aka Agramon. Jagged red lines streak across his charred black body. Bright red eyes focus on Stan. The room shrinks, walls growing closer, a threat of impending doom hanging in the air like a visible mist.

The demon takes a step, the sound a shotgun blast of pure terror across my nerves. My pulse throbs in my ears as a sword explodes out of the *justitia*, the metal cool against the back of my hand.

"Anything?" The demon's voice slides across my skin, into my bones, a cold needle invading my marrow.

Time slows. Stan, Smythe, and Team Agency are the only ones who glance at the demon. No one else seems to hear it.

Lucky them.

I need to kill the thing, to stop whatever nefarious

plan it has, but my knees freeze, the *justitia's* fear reaction turning my nerves into long shards of ice. I can't do this. I can't fight this demon. I can't win.

Stan nods, his wide eyes focused on the demon as if the thing holds a winning lottery ticket and believes in sharing. A deep rumble comes from the creature's chest, a laugh, a roar, the malevolence slamming into me with the force of an eighteen-wheeler.

I want to run, but I'm frozen in place, in time, eyes wide like I'm caught in a horror movie. Worse than a horror movie. This is real. This demon wants me dead. I can't stop it from killing me. Ohgodohgodohgod, what do I do? Why can't I run? I'm going to die. Why won't anyone help me?

Frozen, I can do nothing but watch as the demon exhales a visible puff of air that floats to Stan, engulfing him in a coat of evil.

Stan stiffens as the pulsing demon's essence sinks through his skin, turning his eyes black and his aura the throbbing red of a minion.

Shit. Looks like I can kill him after all. Knowing Stan's a minion and on the top of my kill list fails to chase away the fright riding my bones. Why did I ever call myself a demon huntress? I can't kill a minion, let alone go after a demon.

You must conquer fear. Zagan's voice drifts through my mind.

He's right. But how? How do I conquer a demon when my body remains frozen with fright? Despite my *justitia* forming a sword, the entity along my nerves would rather shrivel into an invisible, quivering heap. Which doesn't bode well for the upcoming fight.

Stan throws his head back, his maniacal laugh

swallowed by the concrete walls. A full body shiver shakes through my skin, settles into my bones. I draw in a breath. I am a *Justitian*. I am. It's my job to kill these things.

Really. I can kill the demon. I must kill the demon. No other choice exists.

No other good choice, that is. Worst case scenario. The demon could kill me. Or Team Agency. Or Smythe. I can't allow that to happen.

My *justitia* twists along my nerves, sensing my determination, fueling my frozen muscles into movement. The sword tip dips, shakes. I draw in another breath. Take a step toward the demon. Stan might be the easier target in the sense he's a new minion. In theory new minions are weaker, not as powerful as older ones.

But he holds a container of anthrax. When faced with those killing spores, I'll take my chances with Cracked Flesh. Team Agency can handle the bioweapon.

Another breath and I sneak closer to the demon. Why do the regular humans not notice it? Do demons possess cloaking devices the average human can't see? Why do random thoughts bounce through my mind when I should be planning an attack?

Another step, my limbs trembling a dance of terror. Agramon turns its head, its gaze like obsidian pools splashing with anguish. Its lips part, edges turning with an unholy glee.

"Little *Justitian*. You live. For now."

My heart pounds hard enough to shake my shirt. My mouth turns into the dry sands of the Sahara. Did I really think I could fight this thing?

You can. You will. I know how. The *justitia's* thoughts or am I hearing voices?

I vote for the *justitia.*

How?

Silence.

Great.

Agramon's hand draws back. Before my mind processes the movement, I'm flying through the air, limbs outstretched, a flying monkey toy complete with high-pitched screeching. No more internal conversations for me.

A male scream fills the air right before I hit the ground, my fall broken by an invisible mat, a clear courtesy of Smythe. Thank God for mentors.

Fear washes away under a good dose of pissed off. I roll to my feet, facing Cracked Flesh. One of its hands drops, a fading glow of an energy bolt giving a reason to my sudden flight. It got in the first hit. Now it's my turn.

Stan screams a threat, a curse, but I tune him out, my focus riveted on the demon. Smoke encircles its hands, a prelude to another energy bolt or some other demon trick. No matter. The thing is mine.

But I can't defeat it. I can't. A cold wave of fear crashes into me, freezing me solid. Inside the *justitia* roars. Or maybe that's a sob. The two of us want to fight, want to defeat the demon, but how can we when my feet refuse to move?

There is nothing to fear but fear itself.

Zagan's voice? Or my own remembrance? Either way it's a lie. There's a lot to fear. Stan and the anthrax. Smythe never trusting me again.

The demon throwing another energy bolt.

This time I fly into the wall sans invisi-mat. Ouch, ouch, ouch.

Getting all up in my head when I should be paying attention to the demon who wants to use my body as its bowling ball is not a good idea.

Smythe, James, and Chris throw a flash of energy at the demon, their bolts striking Agramon in the chest, none doing damage. Unless you count the crazed cackle the beast releases. Yeah, that one releases a round of whole body goosebumps.

Fear. How do I conquer Fear?

Together. Trust me. My *justitia* whispers along my nerves, giving me a glimpse into its thoughts, its memories. It still fears the demon. The only demon to scare it.

A memory long buried surfaces, floats beneath the water of time, sinks beneath the surface, out of my grasp. But the *justitia* remembers. The *justitia* knows.

And the *justitia* shuts down all my pain receptors, forces my legs to stand, to hold my weight instead of collapsing.

The demon throws a bolt at Smythe. Light flares around my mentor as he forms a shield. Then he flies backward, smacking into James, both mages hitting the ground hard. Before Chris can toss his energy ball, the demon smacks him with a bolt, knocking him onto the James and Smythe pile.

Rage fills my soul, blots red dots across my vision. Anger more akin to T than me boils out my pores, drives away the fear, replacing it with a healthy dose of you-hurt-my-mentor-and-you-must-die.

I let loose with a loud cry and run toward Agramon. Who turns right before I nail it in the back with my sword. The *justitia* screeches as the blade scraps along its arm, fingernails across the chalkboard of its skin.

The demon roars, its lip pulling into a snarl as one hand reaches for me. "You will regret that, little *Justitian.*"

Its words stroke along my body, igniting a fire of fright. A fire easily doused with a dose of anger. I want this demon dead. Dead, dead, dead, dead, dead. The spell its words try to wrap around me falls to the ground, a failed attempt at control.

Take that Fear. Up yours.

Pain shatters along my jaw, snapping my head to the side, windmilling my body. What the hell just happened?

I reach a hand out to catch myself before I face plant on the concrete. Claws grip the back of my shirt, the waistband of my leather pants.

And I'm airborne, sailing toward the mass of security guards paying my fight no attention. Right before I smack into a guard, an invisible wall of foam breaks my flight. I sink to the ground, shaken and dizzy.

Huddled on the concrete floor, I listen to the click of claws growing closer. And they grow closer.

Cracked Flesh squats before me, yellow stubby teeth appearing as his lips turn back in a macabre grin. "You are more fun than the other *Justitians* I've killed. All these memories. All these secrets. All this pain. I could gorge on you for days. Unfortunately, I do not have time." It reaches for me, claws extended, then pauses, its lips pulling wider, exposing more teeth. "But I know how to finish you. Watch as I kill the one you care for. Watch, for you will be next."

It stands to face Smythe, its palm turned face up. Energy boils, hovering above its outstretched hand. My gaze focuses on Smythe, who struggles to stand, his face pale and sweating.

Like hell it's going to kill my mentor. Not while I'm still standing. Or shivering in a huddle as the case may be.

I leap forward a second before the demon releases the energy bolt, twisting, extending the *justitia* to catch the bolt of light. My sword explodes in flashing red light as if it turned into a disco ball. Meant as a killing blast, the red energy knocks me off my feet. Once again I perform my best falling with style routine, arms and legs windmilling as if that will help me catch my balance while airborne.

The red light travels up the *justitia* until it sinks beneath my skin. I should be dead even with a magical entity attached to my nerves. Instead, I bounce off another invisi-mat, landing in a crouch halfway between the approaching demon and Smythe.

Red fire licks my skin, tries to sink inside. Death. What should be my death stops skin deep. As if some internal force holds it in place.

Trust. The *justitia* sounds in my head.

Trust what? The entity living alongside my nerves? And then pain cuts through my center, and all thoughts disappear into a screaming void. Sounds rip through my ears. Sounds I make. Sounds of a wounded, enraged animal.

Me.

And I'm pissed off.

A healthy dose of anger rips off the band-aid of

fear and pain surrounding me. Red saturates my vision, colors the scene in a crimson shade of death. This time the anger taps into the strange well of power deep inside, entwines the two together and yanks. Power streams through my being, my veins, my limbs, a red-hot power like an endless well of energy at my disposal.

The power stops the advance of Agramon's energy against my skin, turning that power around, shoving it out my skin and up the length of the *justitia*. My sword gleams with a pulsing red light, a deadly combination of that strange internal power and the demon's energy.

Cracked Flesh's eyes widen. "Impossible! It cannot be done!"

I can't help the smile spreading across my face. The expression feels wicked, evil. Like it belongs to another.

"I'm no longer afraid of you. You hear that? No. Longer. Afraid." Why should I fear? Whatever power races around my veins lends me strength. Cunning. Power.

I am invincible. And the demon is not.

The thing stands stunned, even as I race toward it, sword pulled back for a killing blow. It gathers energy in its palm a second too late, for I'm upon it, *justitia* infused with the red power.

It hisses, the 's' drawn out until I'm no longer sure if it's trying to say a word that starts with an 's' or one that starts with a 'z'. Not that its last word matters. My *justitia* slices through its neck like a scalpel through fat. Its severed head bounces once and rolls to a stop against the wall.

And that's when Stan drops the glass vial of anthrax.

Chapter Twenty-One

Right before the glass shatters on the concrete, the mages on either side of Stan wave their hands and the vial clinks against the floor as if laid there by a careful hand.

My breath explodes out my mouth as Stan drops to the ground, arms around his middle. Black mist streams out of him, races to the headless demon, a sprint to return to its host. Without thinking, I step between the mist and the demon, *justitia* raised. The mist smacks into the metal, popping, and sizzling before dissipating as gray smoke, dead and defeated.

With a flash of light, the demon's body and head turn to a fine, black ash.

I grin, an expression done often throughout a normal day, and yet the movement feels different, sinister. Not that I stop to analyze the reason. I want to jump around, pumping my fist in the air like a touchdown scoring football player. I killed it. I killed Fear. I defeated an enemy of my *justitia*. I really am invincible. The *justitia* leaps along my nerves, its version of the happy dance. We won. We can do anything.

A strong hand grabs my arm. I turn to a frantic Smythe. A small frisson of guilt lances my chest. I should've checked on him sooner.

"Your eyes."

I blink. Raise a brow. What does that have to do with the dead demon? "My eyes? That's all you can say? Are you okay?"

"Your eyes were red." He returns my puzzled look, gaze searching for specks of crimson.

"Must've been a trick of the light. Did you see? The *justitia* caught the demon bolt."

"And your eyes turned red."

His grip tightens. Hurts. "Smythe, stop it. Are you okay?" I try to yank my arm from his grip but only manage to put a twinge in my shoulder. "Let. Me. Go."

He releases me. "Sorry. You look fine now. I thought...never mind."

Noise from the Stan show draws our attention. One of the guards yanks Stan to his feet. No longer a minion, Stan flinches when handcuffs snap onto his wrists. Looks like he won't meet the sharp end of my *justitia* today. My vengeance will come in the form of the courts. Stan better get a good look around, for this is the last daylight he'll see in a long while.

Team Agency regroups around the pile of demon ash.

"Doesn't look like anyone noticed your fight," James says as another team member waves a hand at the ash, disappearing the silt. "Good job. That was one scary-ass demon."

"Thanks." This time my grin feels normal, not a sinister thing about it. The earlier sensation must've been a fluke. A leftover feeling from fighting Agramon.

Smythe grabs my arm as if he fears I might run. A shock of lust rockets through my veins, centers in my core. He startles as if he feels it too. As if he wants me.

Definitely an after effect of the fight. We lived. We

want to fuck. No biggie.

And not gonna happen either.

"We should report this to the Agency. Looks like the police have the crazy guy under control." Chris waves at Stan. Good thing no one stands close enough to overhear our conversation. I'm pretty sure calling a suspect 'the crazy guy' would not look good in a court of law.

Even if it was true.

"See you there." Smythe grabs my arm and escorts me around the corner, out of sight.

"Aren't they coming?"

"Yep. But they need to clean the scene first. Shouldn't take them long." Ancient words flow over his tongue as he holds out his hand. When the portal opens, he slides his hand down my arm, grasping my palm. "Come on. Let's get this over with."

He tugs, and we step into the in-between for one breath-stealing moment until the portal spits us out into the bright white landing room of the Agency. The line of computer geek teenagers raise their eyes, a brief once-over to make sure we aren't the boogie man, I mean, a demon.

I'm still not convinced the mages-in-training can do anything but scream or pop a zit on a demon if one did decide to appear. But whatever. I'm not in charge of security.

David stands from where he sat in an overstuffed white chair as soon as the portal closes. Great. More fun with the big boss.

At least he shows concern for Smythe. That's one point in his favor.

"Where's the rest of the team?" The tone of his

voice hints at Smythe being the cause for Team Agency's tardiness.

Maybe I should subtract that point for starting the wrap-up with an accusation.

"Cleaning the scene. In case you're wondering, I'm fine. Thank you for your concern."

David's eyes narrow. "Good. Don't like to see you hurt." He clears his throat. "Tell me what happened. The demon blipped off the radar. Don't tell me it escaped."

"I—"

"The demon is dead." Smythe rolls right over my words, giving my hand a squeeze, a silent command to keep my mouth shut.

Since when do I obey? My *justitia* fires a warning, a subtle vibration as if it senses a demon. The same reaction it always has at the Agency. A reaction that cements my mouth closed. Not obedience, per se. More like a quiet assessment of the situation.

Smythe launches into a blow-by-blow of how Agramon went down. I tune him out, focusing on the puzzled warning emitted by my *justitia*. Why does it think demons roam the Agency hallways? The fancy row of computers and their demon finding programs nix that idea.

Maybe all the white noise? A hidden machine generates static, white noise prohibiting conversations from being overheard. Static gives me the jitters, why not my bracelet?

The *justitia* hums a negative note. It senses demon where no demon is. Or has been.

A brush of warm air snaps my attention to the present, to Team Agency arriving. Chilled bodies fill the room with an excitement only a win can bestow.

I caused that excitement. I won the fight.

The smile no sooner turns my lips than David pulls his attention from the arriving team to me. A ridge forms between his eyes, then he shakes his head, blanking his face.

"Any problem?" His crossed arms and widened stance obliterate the concern in his voice.

"Nope." James shakes his head. "The demon's dead. The scene's been wiped clean. The crazy guy with the anthrax has been arrested. All is right with the world."

"I wouldn't go that far." Was that a grin making an appearance on David's lips? Stranger things have happened. I think.

"I'm assuming Aidan told you about the fight?"

"Of course." Smythe's voice bristles like porcupine needles.

"Do we need to debrief?"

"You just did. Nothing more to say." David uncrosses his arms and starts the male back slapping routine. "Good job. Until next time."

The men file out, shaking David's hand, performing some more back thumps. I want to go home too, get out of these clothes. Crash on the couch. Let T know I'm okay.

One of those I can do now.

But before I can contact my twin, David interrupts the attempt.

"There's something different about you." He points a finger, as if there's any doubt to which 'you' he refers.

I shrug. "I won."

"It's called confidence, Dad. She's more secure in her abilities."

David nods. "Good job, son. Guess you can teach well after all."

"Was there ever any doubt?" I impale David with my best nurse's glare.

Smythe squeezes my hand. *Shut it, Gin.*

"Of his teaching or your ability to absorb it?"

Yeah, I should've known he'd turn this back around to me. Samantha isn't the only one at the Agency not happy with my status as a *Justitian*.

"Dad."

"Just sayin' son. She's new. Didn't know a damn thing about us. It's hard to train someone like that."

"I'm a quick study."

"I'm sure you are. Run along now. Get home and enjoy knowing you won." He sticks out his hand then withdraws it right before my fingers grasp his. "Sorry. Forgot you were an empath."

"No problem. Wouldn't want to see inside your head." Actually I would, maybe he can explain why my *justitia* thinks this place crawls with a demonic presence.

He ignores me, turning to Smythe. A back slap and half hug later, we step into the portal and out in my kitchen.

A sweating T clutches a beer bottle by the kitchen sink, staring at the table. No one sits at the table, but a row of beer bottles march across the countertop like a drunken army.

"T?"

"Damn fuckin' ghosts." He points his bottle at the table. "Why can't they just stay dead?"

Chapter Twenty-Two

A chill slides down my spine as I stare at the table. Is Blake there? I grasp T's arm and light coalesces into a transparent figure. Blake leans against the wall behind the table, arms crossed, staring down T in a way he never did in life.

"What?" Smythe steps behind me, close enough for me his body heat to warm my back.

"Blake is over there." I wave at the wall.

Blake smiles, his arms dropping, his pose relaxing. *You won.*

"You know that already?"

News spreads fast. Blake steps closer. T steps back, my grip on his arm the only thing stopping his retreat. My twin gulps the rest of his beer, smacks the bottle on the countertop, and reaches for another one.

"And you? How are you?"

I am free. You are safe.

"What does that mean?" I know, though. I don't want it to mean what I know it does.

You know. You've always known. This plane is not mine to inhabit.

"But you're doing a good job of it. Why can't you stay?"

A smile curves his lips. He reaches for my cheek, the touch of his transparent fingertips against my skin a brush of cold. *I only stayed for you. And now that you are safe, I must go.*

"Will you come back?"

He shakes his head. *Good-bye, Gin. I always loved you.* His lips stroke mine, once, twice and then he's gone, vanished as if he never existed.

"Blake? Blake? Blake!" My wail knocks the men back a step.

But only for a moment. And then T's arms surround me, the peace of his touch flowing over me, through me. Or trying to.

Blake is gone. Gone. Gone. Gone. I know this. I do. But seeing him again made me wish he could stay. It wouldn't work. I know it. How would I talk to him without T around? What kind of private conversation would that be? It wouldn't.

But the heart wants what the heart wants, no rhyme or reason to logic. Which leaves me sobbing on T's shoulder, Smythe patting my back in those small circles men do when confronted with a hysterical woman.

What seems like hours pass as my grief subsides, switching into acute embarrassment. Smythe heard my one-sided conversation; T heard both sides, and both heard my whiny plea for a ghost to stay on earth. Geesh, could I get any more embarrassed?

I shove T's chest until he releases me. He swipes fingers across my wet cheeks, his gaze catching mine.

Are you okay?

"It'll be okay, Gin." Smythe gives me a pat on the back as I nod and answer T.

I will be. I guess I, well, it's silly.

Yeah. He wasn't good enough for you.

Doesn't matter now.

Stick to the living. The dead will only get you in

trouble. His eyes grow haunted, his memories mine. I swallow and drop his gaze. Any more private talk and Smythe might grow suspicious and butt in.

Which would be more awkward than him overhearing my chat with Blake. Guess there is something more embarrassing after all.

"I'm gonna go change. Be right back." Without looking Smythe in the eye, I dart into my room, shut, and lock the door.

As if that will keep out my mentor. Or T for that matter. Locks are not an impediment to either of them.

I rest my forehead against the door, lean on the wood as if it gives moral support. Blake is gone. I won't see him again. And the knowledge twists a knife in my heart almost as bad as seeing him dead.

Grief settles like a heavy blanket on my chest, the weight pressing tears out of my eyes. The door offers a support of sorts, a way of avoiding reality. If I turn, if I face my room, the pictures of Blake and me, the memories, I'll have to face reality.

I'll have to stop crying.

The air vent above the door rattles a tune, that and a blast of cold air lets me know the A/C still works. I sniffle one last time. Remove my head from its resting place against the door. I can't stay here forever, hiding behind a door, wallowing in grief.

If my life has taught me one thing, it's that I have to be strong. I have to go on. Face the future, not the past.

Easier said than done, but I have to do it. I draw in a deep breath, wipe the tears off my cheeks, and turn around.

The instant I turn, my blood freezes, the beat of my

heart a loud throb in my ears. My breath hitches. I swallow but nothing happens.

What an ending to an otherwise good day.

Zagan stands by my bed, arms crossed, stance wide, looking hot in his standard outfit of a pair of jeans and a white t-shirt. And judging by the wide grin he sports, he's happy to see me.

Can't say I feel the same about him. Although I no longer want to cry. Fleeing takes priority.

"You did well." Zagan's smile extends to his black eyes, igniting them with a red hue of Hellfire.

A tingle starts low in my gut, spreads through my limbs, igniting a dose of confusion. Scared with a chaser of attraction. I clearly have bigger problems than I thought.

Zagan's smile grows wider as if he reads my mind. Which he can't. I hope.

"Yeah. Thanks, I mean." No use in telling the big baddie about the freaky red light when my *justitia* absorbed Agramon's energy bolt, dealing the demon a dose of his own medicine.

"I like you. It is odd. But no matter." He waves a hand in dismissal. "You and I can do great things together. Even without you as my servant."

"Um, yeah, about that. I don't think so."

He chuckles, the sound like silk sheets against my skin. A shiver lodges deep, spreads a prickling foreboding.

"Little *Justitian.* One day I will learn how you avoid my spell. Then you will be my servant. Until then, I enjoy our arrangement."

"What arrangement? You sneaking into my room? Why are you here anyway?"

"You invited me in."

"I did no such thing. A closed door means keep out."

"Ah, yes. Humans."

I wait for him to finish his thought, but apparently I'm to take a wild guess at his meaning. Good luck understanding a demon. "What about humans?"

"They think a closed door keeps out a demon." He winks. Steps closer. I try to step back, but the door stops me. I opt for a deep breath and slam my hands against my hips. Fake it until you make it.

"Stop right there, buddy."

"Buddy? I do not believe I have ever been called *buddy* before. I find I like it. You will call me buddy again." He waggles his brows. Teasing? Or serious?

"Yeah, Zagan," I draw out his name, watching as his eyes flare. "Not happening. On all counts."

"You are injured. I only mean to help."

"Huh?" His topic changes spin my mind.

"Your head. It hurts."

Okay, so it does. Not that I'm admitting it. The headache probably stems from my crying jag. Along with the red blotchy cheeks.

I reach a hand to the back of my head, to the spot I cracked my skull against the wall when Agramon bolted me across the atrium. A knot the size of a golf ball causes me to jump when I touch it. Ouch. Guess I am injured. Either adrenaline, the *justitia,* or seeing Blake numbed the pain.

"And you want to be nice and heal me?"

"Just heal you. If you'll let me?"

I've been around the block a few times since the last time Zagan healed me. His gaze locks with mine, a plea to let him help, to let him heal. My head nods as if not connected to my brain. I'm pretty certain my brain knows better.

But before I can stop him, Zagan stands beside me, one hand over the lump, the other gripping my shirt-covered shoulder, holding me in place. Red hot heat pours out his palm, spreads down my body, igniting the *justitia* into a raging fire of glee. The entity leaps with excitement, as if seeing home after many years gone, but despite its shaking a happy dance, I sink into a wave of bliss.

Healings rock, whether given by Eloise or a demon, a drug as addictive as the ones I used to use. The blue skies of a Caribbean ocean beckons and I float on gentle waves. A wave crashes over me, drawing me down, spitting me out into reality.

An expanse of off-white floats into my vision. I blink. And again, before it dawns on me I stare at my ceiling. Specifically the ceiling over my bed.

So much for the feeling of bliss. Knowing Zagan carried me to my bed creeps me out. At least he left on my clothes.

"Do you feel better, Little *Justitian*?" His hand on my shoulder avoids contact with my skin. Lucky me. Seeing into his mind shorts out mine. Something I learned. Something my *justitia* compensated for by blocking my empathic abilities. It was either that or let my brain explode in pain. Not an experience I want to relive.

"You picked me up?"

"Consider it part of the healing. How is your head?"

"Much better. Thank you." Southern manners insist

I thank him. Some things are too deeply engrained to rip away.

"You are depleted and need a replacement."

"Wha—" I can't get the word out.

His finger touches the mark behind my ear, his mark, his brand and with his touch tangles of evil course through my mind.

My body arches, but the *justitia* blocks his connection, allowing me to draw in a breath, allowing my brain to not hemorrhage. All that happens in one breath. His gaze locks mine, as a wave of red power, like the power flowing out of me during the fight with Agramon, flows into me. The same reservoir deep inside swells, absorbing the power he gives me, filling me until I buzz with an unholy energy. My girly parts tingle, my nipples harden in anticipation. I'm three seconds away from an orgasm, and his fingers are nowhere near my core.

Right when I reach for him, to place his hand where it's needed, right when my body overrules my common sense, he removes his finger, his lips curling into a satisfied grin.

I lay panting, my body prickling in all the right places for all the wrong reasons. Did I actually consider fucking Zagan?

I need a mind transplant.

"Get away from me."

"Humans. You always say what you do not mean."

I shove upright, avoiding his hands, his talented fingers. Damn me for a fool. "What did you just do?"

"What needed to be done."

"You loaded me with power. Why?"

He shakes his head. "One day you will understand.

I am helping. In return, you will be mine."

"Never." My words stand in contrast to what races through the back of my mind, what tries to gain footage, what I refuse to release from my subconscious.

"You are mine, *Justitian*. Never forget it." He waves a hand and an obsidian portal swallows him into its depths.

I unclench my hands. Rub them along my leather pants. My insides shake like I've been stuck in the Arctic. While disturbing, my do-me-now reaction to Zagan is not what I fear. I fear what I know. What I don't want to be true.

The demon of deceit speaks the truth on occasion.

A word about the author...

Karilyn Bentley's love of reading stories and preference of sitting in front of a computer at home instead of in a cube, drove her to pen her own works, blending fantasy and romance mixed with a touch of funny.

Her paranormal romance novella, *Werewolves in London*, placed in the Got Wolf contest and started her writing career as an author of sexy heroes and lush fantasy worlds.

Karilyn lives in North Texas with her own hunky hero, a crazy dog nicknamed The Kraken, and a handful of colorful saltwater fish. Find out more about Karilyn at www.karilynbentley.com

Join her newsletter at: http://eepurl.com/ba_0Rf